SOUL REAPER SERIES
BOOK II:

Soul Reaper

CRYMSYN HART

PURPLE SWORD PUBLICATIONS, LLC

This is a work of fiction. Names, places, characters, and events are fictitious in every regard. Any similarities to actual events and persons, living or dead, is purely coincidental. Any trademarks, service marks, product names, or named features are assumed to be the property of their respective owners, and are used only for reference. There is no implied endorsement if any of these terms are used.

SOUL REAPER SERIES BOOK I: MASQUERADE
Copyright © 2012 CRYMSYN HART. All rights reserved worldwide.
ISBN: 978-1-61292-038-2
Cover Art Designed by Anastasia Rabiyah
Edited by Brieanna Robertson and Traci Markou

Published by Purple Sword Publications, LLC
Tucson, Arizona, USA
www.PurpleSword.com

PROLOGUE

France, 1749

Marie searched the faces of the men at the bar. All were the normal drunkards who wandered into the tavern night after night, looking to submerge their miserable lives in a tankard of stale beer. Some were shopkeepers, some were thieves, and the others were homeless and begging for a scrap of food. The other girls, her sisters of the night, filled the bar as well. Like the thieves, they kept their eyes open for loose coins that might be dropped their way. Marie dismissed them without a second thought. The innkeeper had already picked the customers she would entice. Besides, most members of the sour lot were more interested in the watered-down brew than the services she provided.

Tables near the entrance to The Boar's Tooth held nothing more than gamblers. These men were so engrossed in their games that even if Marie shoved her tits in their faces, they would still only be interested in Lady Luck. The other girls pawed over them to get business. Marie never lowered herself to the dirty louts who got a quick touch, thinking her body was something to relieve their daily tensions on.

Since Marie was Xavier's favorite, he always made a point to check on her at the end of the night. She wondered how much the innkeeper really cared for her. He'd never bedded her as he had the other girls. For some reason, he'd taken her word that she'd worked in taverns before. That had been ten years ago.

Now, as the years had progressed, she'd noticed an increased affection from him. He pitched out any customer who raised a hand to her and tended her wounds if he could not get to her fast enough. He even let her discipline the other girls. She'd become a den mother and something of a legend, as she had been there for ten years and had not been tossed aside. Many of the prostitutes hated her, thinking she somehow manipulated the owner so that she got all the rich clients.

Xavier's brown eyes lit up as he handed a mug of ale to one of the braggarts at the bar. He smiled as Marie floated onto the floor, and she couldn't help but smile back. Xavier was big and burly, but despite his size, he rarely got angry, keeping a quiet tone whenever he hauled out a peasant who couldn't pay. She'd seen him angry only once. His outrage had been enough to clear out the entire brothel.

Marie leaned on the bar, taking in her boss. His hair was brown with a smattering of gray appearing around his temples and a few wrinkles around his wolf gray eyes. She knew he was strong. By the way he lifted the kegs of ale, she also knew he wasn't feeling the signs of his age.

She was, though. Marie was only twenty-four. Her bones ached with cold; her flawless complexion was now marred with tiny lines around the corners of her mouth. Her green eyes had lost some of their dewdrop sparkle, and her dark blonde hair seemed lank. The one thing that always stayed the same was her bosom. Her breasts popped out over the top of her corset, which made them appear more plentiful than they really were.

As she bent over the bar, she felt the stares of all those around her. That was one thing she'd never gotten used to. She might spread her legs for money, but she always felt naked when she made her entrance for the night.

"Anyone good tonight?" she asked Xavier. She counted on him to direct her to the richest men in the tavern. That was another thing she liked. He enabled her to make a living, and she had a feeling that when she couldn't earn her keep, he would still allow her to stay.

She remembered the day he'd taken her in. Water had exploded out of the gray clouds above, soaking anyone who stepped outside. Marie was fourteen at the time and had been thrown out of the house where she worked in Paris. The Madam had accused her of stowing away her money, and not paying her fair share. Marie had lived there since she was eleven, after her mother had abandoned her to Madam Lorraine.

Marie understood why her mother had done so, but had no clear memory of her. In her mind, the Madam had taken on her mother's role, teaching her the tricks of the trade until she was thrown out with only a few francs sewn secretly inside the hem of her skirt.

She'd walked for days, rejected by all the inn-keepers, until she came to The Boar's Tooth, starving and with no money. Men had propositioned her, but she'd fought them off until, when she was nearly falling asleep, another man had approached and smiled. He'd told her to go upstairs, that there was an empty room if she wanted it. She'd said nothing, trusting his warm eyes.

Now, as Xavier served ale, she was still in awe of how his eyes melted her and made her heart throb.

"No, just the normal scum," Xavier responded to Marie's question. "Henry's been asking for you for an hour. I told him you were booked. Joshua started earlier than usual. I've already thrown him out twice." Xavier ran his hand over hers.

He contemplated whether to tell her about the stranger who'd spurned all the other girls. An unsettling feeling about the foreigner had fallen over Xavier. There was something off about this stranger, but the thought of losing business overpowered his sensibility, so he let the other girls entice the traveler. All were rebuffed, but he knew Marie could loosen anyone's purse strings. "A gentleman came in at the beginning of the night. He's been sitting by himself. All the girls have gone over, but he doesn't seem interested. I thought maybe you could give him a try, *cherie*, since all the others have failed."

"Maybe the *monsieur* wants a woman instead." Marie chuckled.

The innkeeper smiled. "Maybe. If so, you're the one for it, but be careful. Something about him doesn't set right."

"I'm always careful. If not, you'll rescue me." Marie giggled, grabbed Xavier's chin and kissed him lightly on the lips.

"Go get him," he whispered in her ear, and then nibbled the end of it.

Marie held in a squeal and sauntered over to a darkened corner of the tavern, trying to glimpse the foreigner. It seemed he and the shadows were one, merging, making him invisible. Still, she wasn't deterred. She pushed through the thickening crowd, ignoring the stares and little pinches she received along the way.

Marie sized up her potential client as she arrived at his table. His worn leather boots rested on the table, and he wore a powder-blue vest embroidered with leaves and flowers over a white shirt. The hint of golden thread, along with highly polished silver buttons, glinted in the candlelight. Marie smiled. This man was not the normal customer—not even the regular ones Xavier put aside for her were this wealthy. This traveler could fund her living for a month.

On top of everything, he was handsome with a face that reminded her of an angel, with chalk-white skin and the darkest eyes she'd ever seen. His lips were almost like a woman's with faint pink lines etched into them. Marie had never seen such beauty in a man. By the looks of him, she thought he might want some young boy to satisfy his desires.

"I don't want any more ale. I just wish to sit in peace," he said without looking up.

"I didn't come to see if you wanted more to drink, *monsieur*," she said softly, running her hands over her corset.

"Ahh. You've come to see if I want to fuck. The others girls have tried, but none interested me. What makes you think you're more enticing?" he asked, meeting her eyes for the first time.

When his gaze met hers, Marie bit down on her lip, tasting blood. She felt like a bear caught in a trap as she tried to free herself from his eyes. Marie tried clearing her throat, but felt as if she'd swallowed too much honey. Her breathing became labored. Her head started to spin. The stranger's eyes absorbed everything about her. Her entire body ached, as if fine threads of her soul were being unwoven from the tapestry of her skin. Her heart raced a marathon in a few seconds as pain exploded through her like a cannon discharge. The sensation made her stumble. She yearned to call to Xavier, but when she blinked, the anguish stopped. Air flowed into her lungs freely. Her heart resumed its normal speed, and the stranger's eyes were no longer snares to be wary of.

As Marie broke his hold, the stranger's expressionless face came alive in the darkened corner. Whatever spell had hidden him in the dimness fell away as he leaned over, caressing her thigh. Her moment of distress disappeared from her mind.

"Maybe I've changed my mind," he cooed. "How much?"

"We'll discuss that upstairs," she said, seductively taking his hand. She noticed his skin felt cold, like uncooked sausage. Marie ignored it, winding him through the labyrinth of people up the wooden stairs.

A worried look moved over the innkeeper's face, but Marie disregarded it, knowing Xavier was only concerned. So she crossed the threshold of her room, and her patron shut the door.

Her customer scanned the space, taking in the sparse surroundings. There was a bed, a clothes chest, and a small vanity.

"You're different from the other humans I've come across."

Marie laughed as she unlaced her corset. "I've always been different. And very good at what I do. I'm sure you'll be quite satisfied by the time I'm done with you." She crossed the room, deliberately swaying to accentuate the curve of her hips and the subtle bounce of her breasts now that they were free.

Hunger burned in the stranger's dark eyes. They flared red. Marie assumed the odd color came from the candlelight. Slowly, he brushed a piece of stray hair from her neck, taking in the line of it rather than the rest of her. His caress quivered her insides as his fingers elicited a pleasure no man had ever given her, awakening hidden desires she'd never dreamed she had. Her customer looked at her as if she were a buried treasure.

"So how much?" he asked, tracing the expanse of her cheek.

"Five francs for the hour. Fifty for the night," she said, sucking on the inside of her lip. She was growing uneasy as she stood half-naked in front of him. Being unsure of herself was not something she was accustomed to. Marie was always in control, but now her palms were sweaty. Her knees were weak. Not even Xavier had this effect on her.

Her customer chuckled. "You think highly of yourself, especially considering where you live." He ran his hand over the crude wooden bed frame. Marie scowled. Then, he kissed her. Marie folded in his embrace, but he pulled away too quickly, leaving her wishing for another caress.

"But," he whispered as he licked her lips. "You're worth it. And I'll give you more than you've ever dreamed."

His hand wrapped around her waist and rested on top of her ass. The other brushed her breast so the nipple hardened instantly. Marie smiled. All her nervousness drained away. Bedding a man was usually nothing, but still, this one caught her off guard. Different or not, she was still going to give him the ride of his life.

She slid off his vest, opening the collar of his shirt to expose a hairless chest that was perfection in itself with hard muscles and no scars. This was no fancy boy who sipped tea and fucked boys all day. Marie felt herself pulled to him like she was drawn to Xavier. Something about him made her want to give him the best fuck of his life. She couldn't put her finger on it, but she knew this man could have any woman he wanted. Now that she was alone with him, his energy screamed that he liked it rough.

He squeezed her ass as she pressed against him. His dick was hard through his breeches, waiting for her to take it into her skilled hands. His fingers tickled her spine, feeling every little crevasse between her vertebrae, down her back and then up again, wrapping around her neck. Every small movement he made melted her professional exterior. His nails dug into the back of her neck. His lips pushed against her throat. His other hand found her clit, and she was already moist. For once, she gave in to the pleasure of this skilled magician. She found herself falling, trying not to lose herself in the thrilling experience, and somehow, she found the strength to pull away.

A look of annoyance crossed her customer's face. She smiled seductively, moving her hand into his pants, sliding it up and down his cock. Marie watched her patron. His eyes were half-closed at the pleasure of her caress. Her lips found the hollow of his throat as she nipped, tasting the tang of grit and dirt on his skin. Marie didn't mind. She'd sampled much worse.

Moving her tongue along his neck, she heard him suck in a breath through his teeth. His dick grew even fatter and he moaned. Marie bit harder above the vein. His fingers squeezed her ass severely enough to leave bruises, but she was used to rough treatment. His breath quickened as she sucked, drawing the skin between her teeth. He pushed her onto the straw mattress.

Marie held out her arms, inviting him to her. His fingers settled on her nipples while he buried his face in the crevice of her sumptuous breasts. She held him there, enjoying the sharp sensations that enraptured her each time his tongue flicked over her flesh. But, for some reason, she suddenly wished her client were Xavier. It had always been his face in her mind as she rode her clients. Now, she longed for his warm eyes instead of her new fare.

As his tongue replaced his fingers on her breasts, all thoughts of Xavier disappeared from her mind. Marie barely noticed the change in his touches as he pinned her between his legs. His mouth became insistent as teeth tore into her, and she felt twin piercings of pain. But not until he began sucking did she realize something was off. When he stopped and looked down at her with red-tinged eyes, she knew the color was no effect of candlelight.

Marie screamed.

He covered her mouth with his hand. Blood dribbled down his chin. She watched in terror as the skin danced over the bones of his face. Marie tried to worm herself out from under his knees, but knew she wasn't going anywhere. Her eyes darted back and forth, looking, praying for someone to rescue her. She tried screaming again, but he wouldn't allow another sound to escape her lips.

"Shut up. I'm not going to hurt you," he whispered. "I'm going to give you the best gift of all."

Marie quieted. She trembled, petrified of what he would do to her. Her death loomed in his cold, obsidian eyes. He leaned back, leaving her mouth free. Marie went limp, waiting forever as he decided her fate.

"Good," he muttered, smoothing a piece of hair from her cheek. "I know you're scared and you think I'm a monster, but soon all your pain and doubt will fade away. Pain lasts a few fleeting moments in our lives. What I can give you lasts for eternity."

She stared wide-eyed and nodded, knowing that, somehow, he spoke the truth. His eyes told her so as they held her in thrall. Without another word, he descended. Agony sliced through her soul. As he predicted, the anguish only lasted an instant. As the pain receded, she felt a tugging on her neck, reaching down to her heart as its beat accelerated, striving to keep up with his sucking. Marie lost part of herself with each mouthful, giving herself to him in a blissful haze until he stopped.

When he gazed at her again with faint green eyes, she wasn't afraid anymore. On the contrary, Marie was intrigued. She felt like they were now kin, and he could hand her the universe.

Slowly, he bit down into his wrist, holding the open wound over her lips. The blood dripped into her mouth. With the first taste, she tried to turn away, but her attacker forced the blood down so she had to swallow. The liquid was sour like bad milk, but the more she took in, the sweeter it became. Marie needed to sate the newly awakened desire burning within her. Her hands wrapped around the stranger's wrist. Ecstasy filled her soul for a few blissful seconds until his wrist was yanked away.

Marie's eyes flew open as she saw her customer on the floor. A blazing need to help the man overtook her, but a wave of dizziness overwhelmed her before she could act. Marie glanced at the commotion on the floor through tunneled vision. Xavier was on top of her savior. Part of her understood that the innkeeper was trying to rescue her, but she didn't need him now. Her fear was left behind. All she desired was the one who had awakened her.

Her Master.

Something stirred in her consciousness. It urged her to find the strength to rise and help the Master, but she couldn't. She was still too weak, looking out through newborn eyes. The otherness within her screamed to help, but she could do nothing as her

Master lay dead on the floor, and she floated into oblivion.

1

CHAPTER ONE

Boston, Present Day

My name is Brenna.

"Good afternoon, Boston Tearoom," I said for the fifteenth time. All the weirdoes kept calling, asking if we removed curses, performed exorcisms, or even knew how to raise the dead. As usual, I was the only one answering the fucking phone.

The woman on the other end babbled on about booking a tea party for her daughter's wedding. Every time I tried interrupting, she talked over me in a high-pitched know-it-all voice. As she rambled, I glanced at the calendar and saw it was the first of the three days of the full moon.

"Great," I sighed.

"What?" asked the woman.

I realized I'd spoken aloud. At least I'd gotten her to shut up.

"Ma'am, I'm sorry. We don't do tea parties. This is a psychic salon. We read tea leaves. You know. Divine the future. Is there anything—" The bitch cut me off again.

"Well...then why were you in the phone book under Tearoom?"

"I didn't... It was—Look, it doesn't matter. Have a nice day!" I slammed the phone down and fought the urge to rip the cord out of the wall. Sometimes it was hard to deal with humans. They were petty, jealous, and never knew when to shut up. Then again, my emotions had become difficult to control since my transformation. I took a breath, tasting the heaviness of sage, vanilla incense, and cigarette smoke as the particles stuck to my lungs. Breathing was a throwback to my mortality that I did out of habit, but I didn't have to. I fluffed my dark brown hair, contemplating pulling it out.

One thing I actually liked about being a vampire was that I'd never age. I remained twenty-seven, frozen in eternity like an unchanging statue. I shrugged off my thoughts of self-mutilation. They really wouldn't do me any good.

I sighed, wondering what other nut jobs would be calling or coming in. Many had ventured to the Tearoom over the past eight months since Edmund died. The public seemed to know the place was under new ownership. The universe was testing me, making me put up with all the crazies. Now that I had taken over, the Tearoom was probably realigning with my energy. Edmund had left the business to me, and that was something I'd never truly expected.

My old friend might be dead, but I hadn't stopped sensing him. He still hung around even though I wasn't able to talk to him yet. All of my psychic abilities were intact since becoming undead, something unusual among my kind. Then again, I was an oddity in the first place.

My old boss was someone I'd worked with through college. I'd told people their fortunes and discovered I had the ability to see and speak with the dead. After school, I moved to New Orleans. There, I started my own business, which allowed me to live in a world I'd created for myself.

I was Goth. The night was my home. I had fallen under my own spell, believing I was a creature who hunted the hazy streets of New Orleans looking for victims to bed. My relationships never lasted more than a few months. I didn't want my paramours discovering the secret that I wasn't truly a creature of darkness. Many had assumed I was something more than a normal mortal. My fake acrylic teeth and emerald green contacts had helped complete my disguise. Now, the contacts were left behind in another lifetime. I didn't need them since I'd been made into a more perfect creature. Then again, I had to drink blood to sustain my existence. All life had its price. As a human, I'd had everything backward, but that was before Veronica bumped into me.

To save me from death, she'd given me her blood after her former lover, Devon, left me hanging in limbo. Edmund had convinced her it was my destiny to be as I was. I believed he was right. All vampires were demons at the core, and even I had some of their aspects ingrained in my personality, though I didn't share their bestial side. Their alter ego was the demonic beast that entwined around the human personality, normally infusing itself into it, although some vampires, like Veronica, lived like humans with split personalities. I had nothing of this bestiality, just the demonic instinct, and even that was something I held in check most of the time.

When fully transformed, the undead have wings like old leather. Their maws of sharpened teeth are surrounded by thin, black lips with a black, forked tongue. Their eyes are bottomless obsidian one could fall into forever. Their bodies are covered with brown or black fur, with fingers and toes that turn into six-inch, bone-hard talons. All the creatures care about is fucking with humans to amuse themselves during their long, drawn-out existences. Their vampiric seed sprouts from the blood of the Master vampire. When they are turned, the blood races through the human system and settles into the mortal soul. As the demon awakens, it overtakes the host body. Most of the newborns end up like the others— monsters toying with their food.

Vampire games are all about domination and who is strongest in the pack. Undead children are loyal to their Masters, except for the random few who maintain their humanity, fighting the invasion in their souls. Like Veronica.

My lover survived for over two hundred years with a psycho who forced her to be a vicious killer, trying to mold her into a soulless, cold thing that thrived on bloodshed. She wasn't like the asshole who'd fashioned her. Devon—I first knew him as Cain.

Vampires can shape-shift. Devon had changed his appearance into a blonde beefcake manipulating me into loving him, planting the suggestion in my brain. Veronica took it upon herself to protect me from Devon, but since he couldn't influence her into returning to him, I became his pet project. To befriend me, he sent Aria.

In her human days, Aria had been a Delphic Oracle. She'd gouged out her eyes after seeing her own future as a vampire, but they grew back once she was turned.

Aria predicted the future for Devon, telling him that, one day, a different type of creature would be born, and if he possessed it, then he could use its powers for himself. Of course, the creature was me.

Using everything Aria told her Master about me, Devon ensnared me. He used me, talking to the remnants of the vampire in my soul, the part of me that only wanted to be fucked and used. But he stirred something else inside me, as well, and in the instant that something arose, I destroyed Devon.

Now I was a creature apart from vampires, yet within their bloodline. My transformation left me with some aspects of the undead, but when I changed, I was nothing like a demon. My wings were raven's wings, black and feathered, with my face distending just a little. As for my teeth, I only had a double set of canines, and I also possessed talons. All the powers of the vampire, I inherited; the one thing that set me apart from the undead was that I didn't have to kill to survive. However, the instinct to kill was still in me because the blood that fashioned me was demonic. The lust for blood was hard to ignore, and I was trying to control it.

Now, as I sat back on the smoking couch, my Goth identity melted away, I tried to act as mortal as I could. It was hard to function within humanity when I no longer belonged to their race. Veronica was much better at that than I was. Then again, she'd been pretending for over two centuries. I sighed as I thought of her, hoping she'd be back tonight.

The door was in my view, as I was the only staff member available for customers. Peter was buying stamps for our monthly mailings, and Fredryck was in the middle of a reading. Both of them had worked at the Tearoom forever.

My senses tuned to Fredryck's reading. He spoke in a sustained whisper that was hard even for me to hear. He related the circumstances of her husband's death to his client. The customer's grief came off her in waves that slammed into my psyche, allowing me to glimpse her pain. She was overwhelmed because Fredryck knew the intimate details of her husband's passing. He stopped occasionally to laugh, and his chuckle reminded me of a teddy bear that squealed if you pressed its stomach.

Fredryck never seemed to age. His head was littered with white hair, and his wire-rimmed glasses accented his gray eyes. A neatly kept mustache sat on his upper lip, and his left pinky had a nail an inch long. He was the most social human being I'd ever met. He was a blueblood by birth, but his title wasn't recognized. That was all I knew about him. It'd be easy to peek into his mind, stealing his secrets. I wouldn't, though, because he was my friend and I had respect for those close to me and for humanity in general.

As the psychic's laugh ended, the elevator thumped to a stop, sounding like a bomb going off next to my head. My senses turned off for a second, leaving me deaf and blind while my body adjusted to normal human levels. As quickly as everything had gone dark and silent, it all switched on once more.

The elevator door yawned open. Two women stepped out. One was tall, dressed in a tan business suit that accentuated her slim legs. Her blonde hair was caught up in a French twist, and her sharp cheekbones were accented with a light maroon blush that matched her eye shadow and lipstick. Her energy played against mine and seemed to be all tied up. Irritation played against my mind; I sensed that this woman was being dragged along and didn't have one iota of respect for the woman with her.

Her companion was just the opposite. She wore jeans and a black windbreaker, and her brown pixie haircut didn't go with her round face. Her energy was relaxed and laid-back, as if she could get along with anyone, and I suspected she knew nothing of how her companion felt about her. Their energy vibrated like bumblebees against mine, piquing my interest. The bitch's energy was agitated, like a hornet, while the other's buzzed around me like a drone. I wanted to swat them away, but my ears perked to their conversation.

"What'd you hear about Haley?" the short one asked.

An air of uneasy silence hung around the suit as she leaned against the sky blue wall of the hallway. "The police haven't said much, except there wasn't much left to bury."

Her companion hugged her. The blonde hesitated before accepting the embrace, not wanting her hardened exterior to crack. Stuffed-down pain washed over me like tidal waves, crashing into my brain and then my soul. This woman might be a bitch at heart, but her anguish broke mine and made me want to know more.

"They think she was slaughtered by a pack of wild dogs or something."

Wild dogs? Like hell! I thought, thinking about the packs in the city wreaking havoc on the local dog-catcher. The back of my skull tingled. This girl's death had to be the work of a vampire, probably one too insane to hide its kill. I despised the undead in general, but the ones who slaughtered mortals for the hell of it irritated me even more. The crazy ones left their remains out in the open, but this killer could have been a sloppy newborn, as well.

Whichever one it was, I wanted to hunt and destroy it. This demon had torn apart a family. I wanted to jump into their conversation and learn more of the details, but their conversation was lost even to my ears as the elevator slammed to a stop again. My fangs vibrated at the thought of the beast that had killed the girl.

I threw my mind into the suit's, casting aside my moral policy of not invading human's thoughts. The victim had been the blonde's sister, Haley. Haley had been walking on Commonwealth Avenue, heading toward Kenmore Square to meet a friend at a local bar, but she'd never arrived. The friend had grown worried and called the cops. At first, the police did nothing except tell him to file a missing person's report. Hours later, a jogger found the corpse under an overpass amidst piles of pigeon shit.

Before I realized it, I was in the main room chasing after the two, who'd recognized they were on the wrong floor and decided to take the steps back down. I stopped. The itching in the back of my brain became more insistent. There was an even pressure on my skull, as my guides wanted to appear and give me their advice in person. But I wasn't up for their vanishing act and cryptic messages. Their presence annoyed me so much that I pulled out of the suit's mind and came back to myself. My premonitions could turn into my guides speaking to me directly, as words running through my mind or just as pictures. Even if the inklings were wrong, I would listen. In this business, you had to learn to trust your instincts, even if they were wrong at times. If you didn't, the client would never be satisfied.

My mind was on fire as Zach sauntered into the Tearoom. My guides were probably forewarning me about something to do with the seer. If the message had to do with Zach, it was bad news anyway. I moved the suggestions out of my mind and focused on what he wanted. I only employed him as a favor to Edmund.

I collapsed on the couch in the center of the main room. The elevator was summoned down again, shaking on its cables. Zach sat next to me wearing an old Megadeth T-shirt and faded black jeans. His short, bleached hair showed brown roots underneath. His eyes were bloodshot, and the aroma of old booze and stale cigarettes clung to him like leeches. It was a shame he had a drinking problem. He really was a good psychic, but his addictions got the better of him. I cringed at the scent of the burning filter of Zach's cigarette as he sucked on it, trying to down the last of the nicotine.

Thank the gods my only vice is red and tastes like pennies, I thought.

"How ya doin', Rav'n?" Zach asked, using the name I did readings under.

"Fine, Zach. What brings you here on your day off?" I knew what he sought, but I wanted to hear it from him.

He shrugged his shoulders as he snuffed out his cigarette butt in a bottle cap on the coffee table. I watched as he rearranged a few of the magazines, almost knocking over a vase full of yellow roses. Then, he lit up again and pulled the smoke into his lungs before answering.

"I was headin' down to the pub and wondered if Peter wanted ta join me."

I smiled slowly. He knew I wasn't going to give up one of my psychics when there were only three of us working. I eyed him, taking in his wrinkled shirt, wondering what women saw in him. He fucked most anything with legs. Maybe it was his boyish, rugged looks. Worn in was probably the best description for him. One could tell he had many secrets, as there was something mysterious and sinister about him. In my mortal days, I'd been drawn to him from time to time, but now all I saw was another human wasting his life.

"What do you really want, Zach?" I asked as Peter limped in carrying a bag and a shoebox under his arm.

Zach ran a hand through his greasy hair and put out his cigarette in the bottle cap again. I glanced over at it, making a mental note to throw it away. It wouldn't be good to have the Board of Health seeing the butts. We were supposed to be a non-smoking establishment, but I allowed the employees to smoke, as it made for a much better work environment.

"I was hopin' ya could spot me some money. Edmund used ta once and a while, ya know, and—"

"I'm not going to give you money so you can get plastered." I got up and began pacing the room, wondering what gave him the gall to ask me. He knew I wasn't going to say yes. I wouldn't let the Tearoom revert to what it had been before I'd acquired it. Edmund hadn't been the best at paying his bills. It had taken me eight months to start making a profit and catch up on the back rent. The likes of Zach weren't going to drag the Tearoom back down again.

"Edmund would've—"

I growled, losing the composure I struggled so hard to keep. He watched me disappear and then reappear centimeters from his face. "I'm not Edmund. Get used to it."

Fear inked into his eyes as the blood drained from his face. His heart jumped into his throat, racing like a scared jackrabbit. Through his stupor, he saw something of what I'd become.

"Shit. Fuck. What the hell happened ta ya?" he asked, halfway sober now. "Where's the quiet girl I used ta know ages ago?"

"She died," I breathed. "I took her place. Now get out."

Zach blinked as Peter cleared his throat to get my attention. I stepped back, realizing I was shaking, holding back from lashing out as Zach scampered out of the room.

"Sorry to bother you, Raven, but I wanted to let you know I was back."

I smiled wearily and wrapped my arms around myself to stop quivering and regain some of the human façade I'd lost. Peter knew I'd seen him walk in off the elevator with his new shoes just minutes before. Good thing, too, or Zach's head would have been on the floor. With Fredryck and his client just feet from us, that wouldn't have been good. "Time for a new pair?"

"Yeah," he said, walking back to the smoking couch. His limp was less noticeable now that he had the new shoes. When he was a teenager in Germany, his left leg had been crushed by a train. He bought new shoes once a month to ease the pain.

I sank down next to him, thinking he was the only true friend I had at the Tearoom. He was a tall, thin black man with shots of gray in his hair and mustache. He wore glasses that only had one arm. No matter how much I pestered him about it, he wouldn't buy a new pair. At fifty, he was very stubborn, and he'd taken me under his wing when I was human, treating me like his long-forgotten daughter.

He hadn't seemed surprised when he'd learned Edmund had left me the place. Peter had only said that the Tearoom and I were meant for each other. Peter used to be a teacher, and somehow, he'd gotten sucked into the psychic vortex of the Tearoom over a dozen years ago. Whenever I needed advice or a shoulder to cry on, he was there. He always understood what was on my mind before I did, and nothing about me turned him away.

"Vhat did Zach vant?" he asked, a bit of his German accent slipping in.

I chuckled. "Just the usual. 'Hey, how ya doing? Can I have some money?' What else is new?"

Peter sighed. "Zach'll never change. He expects everyone else to help him, instead of doing for himself. I thought you were going to fire him?"

I glanced at Peter, unable to hide my shock. He always knew what was on my mind. "I was—I am—I don't know. I think I keep him around as a favor. But Edmund—"

"Isn't here. You miss him, but this is your place now. You've done vonders to brighten it up. Ve've never been busier. I think the Tearoom likes you, or the Universe is giving us a break. You remember the vay it vas before and how ve never got paid on time?

Look at it now. I think you must have some vonderful guardian angel looking out for us."

I chuckled. The only angel looking out for this place was the Angel of Death.

I'D BEEN WORKING late one night, only three months after I'd inherited the Tearoom. I listened to the music filtering in from Charlie's below, and to the phantom hammering coming from a small back room. The pounding came from the spirit of a shoemaker who'd died in the Tearoom years before. On occasion I saw him. We had an understanding. He didn't trouble me, and I didn't bother him. I may be a vampire who sees ghosts, but it was still unnerving to find translucent beings wandering around when you thought you were alone. In my mind, the shoemaker appeared just as any normal human would, only he was two-dimensional. The times we'd bumped into each other had been around eleven or so, exactly this time of night.

I'd been balancing the books, trying to catch some of the mistakes Edmund had made. At the time, Veronica was still in New Orleans learning to deal with her other half. The elevator stopped, but I didn't bother to look up, figuring it was some drunken folk pressing the wrong buttons. But after a few minutes, I realized I hadn't heard any voices in the elevator, and an overwhelming calm and chill descended on me. A dark shadow loomed over the Tearoom. The air seemed thicker. Even I found it hard to breathe. The candlelight dimmed until, I looked up to see why it was going dark.

In front of me was a man, a being I'd never met before. I sent a quick question to my guides for assistance, but they were silent. So I faced him alone, hoping he didn't want to kill me because, whatever he was, I knew I was in way over my head. I examined him and realized he was an angel. He had a blazing white-yellow aura with the outline of his wings standing out against his energy signature. His wings were bigger than mine and just as black, but they were not located in the same dimension as either his body or mine. I thought that strange. But, hell, he was an angel and could do whatever the fuck he wanted. He was almost seven feet tall. Dark hair fell in waves below his shoulders. His black, piercing eyes held the mysteries of the universe; peering deep within my soul. He knew all my secrets without having to enter my mind. To top it off, he was dressed in a black trench coat, and underneath that I glimpsed a charcoal suit.

Hello, Brenna, he said, without having to speak aloud.

His voice was soft with a melody like harps blowing on the wind, falling directly into my mind and ears. I almost expected him to pull a harp out and start plucking, but that was silly. I couldn't help but stare. I'd seen angels before, but I'd never had the courage to speak with one. Honestly, I didn't know what they'd do to me. I was on the opposite end of the spectrum from them. I had an inkling that these Higher Beings held the answer to what I was, and now my chance stood in front of me.

"Hello," I whispered back.

He smiled. His sculpted features reminded me of some ancient bust that should have been in a museum. To say that all angels were androgynous was ridiculous, but he was beautiful, rapturous. As he grinned, I saw his teeth, all straight and perfect, but his canines were longer than they should've been, brushing the top of his bottom lip. They reminded me a bit of mine, as did the paleness of his skin. He was more magnificent than I could ever have imagined.

He extended his hand. His nails were long, scratching the inner side of my wrist, leaving faint pink marks akin to cat scratches—but the marks faded instantly. As my hand connected with his, warmth filled me, easing the apprehension I'd sensed about his entrance. Then, a deep chill replaced the warmth, as if I'd been plunged into a solar eclipse. I tried not to shiver, but my self-control wasn't that good. Little goose bumps rose all over my body. He took his hand from mine and sat on the couch.

This is a lovely place. Business has been getting better for you. That is wonderful.

"Thank you."

Why not come and sit next to me?

I did what he asked. So many questions burned through my mind. Could he help me? Was I really part of the demon race, or something else? Were my speculations correct? Was I a new type of creature? These were only parts of the things I yearned to ask him, but the most obvious question came out first.

"What are doing here?"

He smiled again. *Do you know who I am?*

"You're an angel," I said. *Duh!* I felt like an idiot, or a schoolgirl asking out her first boyfriend.

Idiot, idiot, idiot, played over in my head.

He laughed. The sound reminded me of a hundred birds' wings beating together. *I am not just any angel. I am Azrael, the Angel of Death. And you are far from an idiot.*

The Angel of Death. My eyes widened. This is just what I need.

My guides hadn't signaled anything out of the ordinary. Usually, they were pretty good about preparing me for tragic events. I'd assumed, when it came to my own life, they would at least give me a hint. That was the only thing that sucked about being a psychic. It wasn't very easy to divine my own future. The path of my life was predestined to a certain extent, though I could still make some choices. Free fucking will and all, but my road had been chosen before I'd been born into this incarnation. That was the theory. If not, then I wouldn't be a vampire. If the Angel of Death was here and my guides hadn't forewarned me, I would have to have a serious talk with them, if I survived.

I am not here to harvest your soul, he answered, reading my mind. *I just wanted to introduce myself.*

"Ummm…okay. Thanks." What else was I supposed to say? He was an angel.

He glanced around the room and then up at the ceiling. I followed his gaze and saw that the mural of Saturn wasn't stationary, as it should have been. The planet rotated as the comets grazed across the sky and the stars twinkled. A feeling of awe came over me as the painting came to life. When I glanced back at the spot where Azrael had been, he was gone.

NOW, AS I SPOKE with Peter, my eyes found the collage of pictures on the wall opposite the restrooms. Many were of Edmund, of past events, and psychics who used to work here. My former boss' death hadn't been a shock. He'd been sick for years, but no one had known when he would expire. It seemed fated that he'd died the same night Devon had taken me. The coincidence might have been Destiny's design.

I wasn't around for my friend's funeral because I was interring Devon, but I mourned Edmund on my own. At times, I felt Edmund's presence in the Tearoom, but I wasn't able to talk with him. Not enough time had passed since he'd moved on to wherever it was that spirits went after life. After a year and a day, a medium could communicate with the dead. It would be good to speak with Edmund, just to say thanks for all he'd done for me.

The man had taught me that, even though I heard voices in my head, that didn't make me insane. He showed me how to control my abilities, as well as how to keep grounded while power flooded through me. Even now, when I did readings, I made sure I focused my energy out of the soles of my feet to connect to the earth, channeling the power along my spine to align myself with the universe. My endowments didn't come from me alone. They flowed through me, given to me by my guides.

I was also grateful that Edmund had convinced Veronica it was my destiny to be as I was. As a human, I'd been infatuated with vampires. I'd become so hung up on the idea of being a vampire; I'd been able to literally change others' perceptions. I'd learned to manipulate the frequency of my aura and morph it into that of the undead. The ruse worked while I attended college and frequented the Black Rose, the local Goth club in Cambridge. My disguise worked so well that the vampires never bothered me, and my masquerade almost fooled Veronica. She mistook me for a vampire because she desired a kindred spirit. For years, she'd been running from Devon. But she'd fallen back under her Master's spell; it was the bestial side of her, Ronnie, who answered its Master's call. Then, Ronnie got the sense Devon was using her as a fuck toy. She hated him then.

I, too, had fallen under Devon's charms. But at the last moment, before I fell completely under his control, my true nature had awoken. Now, I was something the undead race had never seen.

"Raven." Peter rattled me out of my thoughts.

"Yeah." I'd been so lost in my own mind that I hadn't even felt him get up from the couch or heard the elevator door open.

"Your appointment is here."

Appointment? I'd forgotten all about it. Forcing a smile, I thought of my next victim. *Client,* I corrected myself.

My short temper with Zach and my lost train of thought were some of the beginning signs of my hunger, along with the faint numbness I felt in my big toe. I would have to feed soon. I loved the taste of blood, and the thrill of it coursing through me was like nothing else I'd ever experienced. But, for now, I pushed the bloodlust aside and focused on the human waiting for me.

Stretching my senses, I tapped into his thoughts. He was in his mid-forties. A bit overweight and scared as hell to be here. He kept wondering what had made him come. Why had he ended up at a psychic's office? Was his life so bad that he needed help from the crackpot his cousin Irene saw? His relative was nuts, practicing Voodoo or whatever shit she did. He surmised she sacrificed chickens and goats at the stroke of midnight in New Orleans.

I smiled.

He'd been given my name by one of my New Orleans clients. When I moved, I kept about sixty percent of my old clientele by doing phone readings.

Fresh meat. I ran my tongue over my teeth. My canines were a little sharper than they should have been, but he wouldn't notice. If he did, I would see to it he wouldn't remember. I motioned for my client to follow me. He began to sit in my leather desk chair, but I gave him a dirty look. He glanced down, cringed like a frightened dog, and sat in the chair opposite me.

I settled down and extended my hand. My nails had grown just a bit and brushed along the bottom of his palm. My gentle touch aroused him, and whatever crazy thoughts he'd had before vanished. He didn't care what I said to him. All he wanted to do was stare at my breasts. I smirked as fleeting thoughts of him fucking me on the table passed through his mind and into mine as I riffled through his memories, gathering information to do his reading.

I didn't like to invade my clients' minds to do readings, but when I was hungry, my reason usually seemed to get lost between my hunger and my vague desire to dominate everything I saw. Even as my control slipped, I knew I had to be careful and not reduce my client's mind to mush. Desire replaced the fear he'd had before as he stared at me. His brown eyes widened as he took in my smile and eased out of my grip.

"I'm Raven. How can I help you?"

2

CHAPTER TWO

My name is Miranda.

The clanging of spoons against porcelain coffee cups and the whirring cappuccino machines were all I heard. Customers were getting impatient. A long line was already curling around the coffee bar while the staff hurried to get the orders. The bell above the door hadn't ceased as more patrons entered and went downstairs to find a place to sit in the subterranean rooms. All the tables upstairs were full. We were busy, although it wouldn't do me any good to go behind the counter to help. I would just get in the way.

Claire and Gina were waiting on clientele. Linda and Stephanie were making drinks and sandwiches. I smiled, knowing Gina could do the work of ten people. Gina did the books, working more shifts than I did. My best friend was a workaholic, but between the both of us, we always knew what was going on. Claire was worse. She was the manager. She'd put in over sixty hours this week. She'd started when Crimson Liquids opened, and after a year, we promoted her. She'd become a good friend of Gina's, but she and I had never really sat down and clicked. Then again, business had tripled since we first opened. Whenever I worked with Claire, we were too busy to get chummy.

Crimson Liquids had been my idea. Gina and I had pooled our resources and opened the café. We lived together, as well. Many predicted that, with us in such close quarters, we would hate each other after a year. We fooled everyone and stayed together. Our schedules were so different, we hardly ever saw one another. When we did, she worked and I read.

The one thing I loved about the café was that I'd decorated it. Most people who entered were shocked by the decor. Horror and vampire movie posters adorned the walls, along with strange knick-knacks I'd picked up over the years. There were other special touches as well: bats and spiders suspended from the ceiling, fake hands coming out of the wall, and even a few props peeking out behind corners, making the customers look twice. Gina thought it all silly. But after living with me and knowing my obsession for horror and vampire movies, she let it slide.

The customers thought the furnishings a bit spooky, but they loved the coffee and kept coming back. That was the most important thing.

I stared over the table, observing the pedestrian traffic on Beacon and Park Streets through the huge glass windows. My cafe was in a great location— kitty corner to Boston Common and across from the State House. Everyone from senators to the homeless stopped in. It was a great place to meet people. I squinted against the glare of the sun as it poured through the windows. The rays caught the faint cracks imbedded in the glass, sending rainbow threads onto the walls.

I reclined in the wrought-iron chair, sipping away at my tea. Looking at the passersby, I wondered where they were rushing to. From my vantage point, a group of kids protested on the steps of the State House. I laughed a little. There was always something going on. The protestors would probably come in later, adding to the confusion. My gaze drifted back to the counter. The crowd had died down to only a few stragglers.

"Even on your days off, you can't get away from this place, can you?"

Gina sat across from me, taking a minute to catch her breath. Her short platinum hair contrasted with her bronze skin. Black, horned-rimmed glasses hung from a chain around her neck. She wore a white blouse, a denim skirt, and red knee-high leather boots. Many thought she was a college student, but she was twenty-nine, a year older than me.

"Yeah. Well, I have to make sure you don't run the place into the ground." I laughed.

She picked up my newest book and read the back. Her eyes darted back and forth over the book jacket, and she shook her head.

"You really have to stop reading these things. They'll fill your head with too many ideas. Besides, maybe these are the real cause of your dreams. Not your imagination."

"You know I read them to take the edge off my dreams. We've been over this a hundred times." I slammed my teacup down hard enough to make its contents slosh over the edges and onto the table. I sopped up the mess with a few napkins I grabbed from the counter. "I'm sorry, Gina. I didn't sleep well last night."

My friend signaled for Linda to bring over another cup of tea. She took it from the counter and sat back down. "Another dream?"

I nodded slowly. The dream she referred to was a recurring nightmare I'd had since I was four. It was of a man standing inside a darkened doorway, observing me. At first, I saw nothing except his outline.

"Answer me one question and I'll leave." His voice was smooth as cream, with an air of power. I felt like somewhere, deep inside, I should have known his voice.

I tried answering his question, but before I could, he materialized in the light. He had blond hair, a pointed chin, and two rows of sharpened teeth. His tongue was forked like a snake's, but long and all black. It was his eyes that frightened me the most. The longer I gazed into them, the more I fell into forever blackness. His hands reached for me with sharpened claws like those of a tiger, but before they touched my skin, I woke up.

Growing up, I'd had the dream infrequently. But as a teenager, I'd barely gotten any sleep because the nightmare haunted me three times a night. Even when I didn't dream, I was so afraid I'd see the demon that I forced myself to stay awake. In the end, I resorted to burning myself with matches to stay conscious. Scars dotted my arms, but most of them had faded to small puckers. When I was sixteen, my father put me in a hospital so the doctors could figure out what was wrong with me.

After three months in the hospital, I had started sleeping, but something else happened that affected me even more. Ruth, my roommate, tried finding ways to kill herself at least once a week. She had numerous marks on her wrists and arms from slicing. I didn't understand why I was placed with her, since her condition was far worse than mine. I kept to myself and didn't argue with the doctors. All of them liked me because I listened, but my psychiatrist tried to tell me my dreams were some repressed shit about my father. That was bull.

Then one night, everything changed.

Ruth had gotten hold of something sharp. I'd drifted off for a moment. When I woke up, I thought I was still dreaming. My roommate was lying on the bed. One hand hung over the mattress while the other lay on top of her chest. Both were bleeding. The one on her chest formed a pool over her heart, and the other dripped onto the floor. A small puddle spread on the pink-and-brown-tiled linoleum. The sound of it plopping transfixed me.

I'd wanted to get up and run for the nurse, but a small voice whispered for me not to. The voice wanted me to catch the remaining droplets. Longing for Ruth's blood had blossomed deep inside me. My body was no longer under my control as I walked the few steps to her. The voice inside my head grew louder, more like static coming in over a bad radio station. Everything inside me tingled. The blood had filled my senses, and when I was inches from taking her slashed wrist and drinking from the wound, light overtook me. The voice inside my thoughts had retreated to the nightmares of my mind. Nurses pulled me up and took me out of the room. Only then did I realize I was shaking. Doctors tried to console me, saying it wasn't my fault. They called it a terrible accident and said I shouldn't dwell on it. The strange thing was, I never had a nightmare about Ruth.

After the incident, my father took me out of the institution and decided to try alternative therapy. Over the next couple of years, I underwent hypno-therapy, meditation, and drugs. I tried just about anything my father could think of to keep the night-mares away. I never blamed him for what he'd done. He was just doing what was best for me. I went to college, and strangely, my dreams stopped troubling me. My nightmares were the least of my worries as I tried not to flunk my classes. The best thing was that I got a decent night's sleep. Even though my night-mares didn't plague me in school, the presence that they'd awakened inside my brain lingered. Whenev-er I got anxious, I craved blood. I concocted, but never acted on, strange fantasies. I just ended up biting large chunks out of my inner cheeks. Gnawing my lips helped as I took in my own blood, but some-thing always seemed to be missing.

Lately, my hunger hadn't been bothering me. It was my dreams that had been haunting me for the past month. My nightmare had begun recurring two or three times every night. I tried to stay awake, and if I did fall asleep, I did so only because my body shut down. My supply of tea had dwindled and I'd redoubled my reading, plowing through my collection of vampire novels and buying new ones just to stay awake. Ironically, the vampire books actually helped ease my imagination. They fulfilled some weird urge, placating the thing deep inside the recesses of my mind.

I knew I was crazy, but not wanting to spend my life in a padded cell, I lived with my demons. The coffee shop took my mind off my problems. Gina knew how to distract me, but lately, her efforts weren't working either. I didn't understand why my nightmare came so often. The stress of life was minimal. The café brought in tons of business. I had no worries.

"Earth to Miranda. Miranda!" Gina pulled me out of my thoughts. "Did you hear me?"

I shook my head. The heaviness of sleep weighed on my lids. The night before, I'd survived on tea while I finished two new books. This was the third one I'd ordered online, because now I'd bought out the local bookstore. I could have fallen asleep at the table if Gina hadn't brought me out of my daze.

"Sorry." I yawned.

The lack of sleep was really catching up to me, but I was too afraid to close my eyes. I laughed internally. After all these years, I was still frightened of a dream.

"I said there's that hunk who's been coming here the past few weeks. I think he wants you." She nodded over at the counter.

I glanced over and saw the tall blond she spoke of. He seemed handsome enough, with blue eyes and a little bit of scruff on his face. His skin was pale, but with a tinge of red, as if he'd just gotten a slight sunburn. His gaze caught mine, and he smiled. Blood rushed to my face as I stared back. Something about him kept my eyes glued to his frame as he got his coffee cup and walked downstairs. Before he disappeared, he glanced over at me again, raising his glass.

"Ooo, I think he wants you. Every time he comes in here, he keeps his eyes on you. Go down and talk to him," Gina urged.

I laughed. Gina had been trying to set me up ever since my two-year drought began after I broke up with Gary. My ex hadn't understood my dreams and had wanted me to go see another shrink. I'd explained that I'd done all that, and there really wasn't anything doctors could do. I even told him about Ruth and how she'd killed herself. I never mentioned the blood thing. It would have creeped him out. He knew about the burns. I'd stopped doing that when I went to the hospital, but I refused to see another head doctor. That was one of the reasons we'd broken up, but not the main one.

As appealing and handsome as the guy who went downstairs was, I wasn't interested. I didn't want to start a relationship with the way my dreams were.

"I feel like someone scraped me off a sidewalk. I doubt this is the best moment for me to go scoping out guys. He probably wants you. Besides, if he's been coming in here for weeks, then there's no point. He probably has a girlfriend, or he's gay."

"Well, flirting's better than sitting here, chasing off bad dreams. If you don't want him, I'll give him a try."

"What about Jeremy?" I asked. Jeremy was her off-and-on-again boyfriend. Their relationship was all about sex. Jeremy was a nice guy, but I didn't understand how Gina could go through so many men. I guess that was why she kept trying to fix me up. She figured I just needed to get laid.

"What about him?" she called back.

"Whatever," I said, and stuck my nose back in my book. I'd just come to a juicy part where the main character was about to learn the man she loved was a vampire. I loved movies and books where vampires won in the end. I guess I always rooted for the evil guys.

Go get him!

Taking a sip of my cooled tea, I got lost in my novel. I licked my lips subconsciously, anticipating when the vampire would bite into his girlfriend. The thought of blood stirred the thing inside of me, but I shook it off and let my consciousness drift away in the fictional pages in my hand.

3

CHAPTER THREE

My name is Brenna..

The clock read 7:30 PM, and I had no more appointments. It was close to closing time, and the elevator thumped to a stop for the thousandth time that day. A prickly sensation encroached on the back of my neck as a crowd of laughing girls got off the lift. At first, I assumed the sensation came from my guides, trying to give me some sort of message, but this feeling was different. It felt like someone was watching me, but there was no one there. The tingling intensified as I glanced over. A growl rose in my throat.

Before I could inspect the intruder, the flock of girls entered the Tearoom. I wrapped my aura around myself and went invisible to the human eye.

The girls came in and looked around, wondering where everyone was. Their peppy glee was irritating as I waited to see what this unseen presence was going to do. It hovered on the outside of the Tearoom, but it wouldn't come in. It didn't feel like a ghost. Ghosts felt hollow. This being was more substantial, as if I could reach out and touch it. It almost seemed like the shadows had come alive, but there was no one there.

Peter appeared from the back with a strange look on his face. I should have been there. Since I wasn't, he waited on the four girls as they perused the menu of our services. I tuned out the conversation and mentally searched for the interloper, but whatever creature had caused my hackles to rise had now retreated.

I glanced at the painted ceiling. Saturn was the center of the universe instead of the Sun. The ringed planet was the guardian of the Tearoom. Around it were drainpipe covers, some turned into planets while others were meteors. Shooting stars streamed across the painted sky, leaving trails of fire against the midnight blue backdrop. The borders of the mural were made to look like the ceiling had fallen away to reveal the galaxy.

I left my table and went into the Fire Room so Peter would think I was hiding from the crowd. He knew I wouldn't do readings anyway, since I read by appointment only. As I strolled into the other room, I took in some of the other murals in the place. On the left, a golden dragon flew in a black, star-studded sky. A goddess stood in a glade among several standing stones. I smiled. The goddess had a life of her own, as did most of the paintings. In another, a Pegasus and a gryphon were locked in an eternal battle. My favorite mural was on the wall next to my table. This wall was decorated to resemble a castle with a window on either side—one stained glass, and at the other, a gypsy woman enticing people into her lair with a wink.

The girls stormed out as Peter told them to come back tomorrow. Their agitation blasted through the plaster walls, touching upon my mind. Once they entered the elevator, I unraveled my aura and walked out of the Fire Room, surprising Peter.

"Raven, I didn't see you. I just told them we were closed."

I smiled. "That's fine. I have to meet Veronica anyway. See you tomorrow."

The sun was still low in the sky as I left. I covered my eyes against the glare, but it really didn't bother me. I could spend hours in the sun without suffering any damage, as I was something more than a vampire. Veronica, on the other hand, only lingered three hours in direct sunlight. After that, the sun ate away at her flesh like acid. This was part of her curse. It didn't matter, though. She'd brought me into the world, and I owed her everything. My life and my love.

I smiled when I thought of her. My Master. Things between us had been a little strained after I'd killed Devon. Veronica had stayed in New Orleans for six months in my old apartment, coming to terms with how she felt about me and with her newfound freedom. Only in these past two months had she become more comfortable around me. Still, at times, Veronica's anger would surface and Ronnie would emerge. Skin would dance on her face and her violet eyes would swirl to total blackness. Hatred would burn in its aura and hit me hard. But then, as time passed, Veronica took over and everything changed.

Now, I looked on my loved one and saw that she was the same as ever as the wind touched her black hair. Her eyes were alluringly purple in the half-light, and her jeans and charcoal T-shirt accentuated her slender form. Our energies merged like two rain-storms.

She smiled when she saw me, reaching out to take me into her embrace. The subtle scent of violets wafted from her as I kissed her. The softness of her mouth was a sweet surprise, even as her tongue parted my lips and caressed my teeth. She pressed the tip of her tongue against the points of my teeth, and my fangs lengthened in response. A drop of her blood rolled into my mouth. It was much stronger than human blood and had an oily texture. In the one drop, I discerned the remnants of the last human she'd fed on, but they were faint. She'd need to feed soon, but I'd choose her blood over the mortal liquid that kept me going.

My heart picked up speed, as did my breathing. Veronica's nipples went hard against mine as I placed my hands on her ass. Her hand settled onto the curve of my hip as we just enjoyed each other's embrace for a second, not caring what the public thought as we held one another.

"It's good to see you too." She smiled and slung her arm through mine.

A breeze blew up and rushed down Winter Street. The molecules caressed my skin and thrust hair into my face. The wind held the dingy, hot smell of the subways, along with the faint taint of urine from the homeless man relieving himself somewhere in the vicinity. There were numerous aromas of pizza and burnt coffee, along with the mingling perfume of humans strolling around us. On any other day, I could trace all of the scents if I wanted to, but now only one thing held my interest.

We moved through the gust and made our way to a small, quaint café up the street called Crimson Liquids. At first, I'd assumed the place was another vampire hangout, but it was just a coffee shop, unlike the Black Rose. Veronica and I had started frequenting the café because it offered chai tea and was one of the best places in town to get it.

We strolled in the front door, pushing through the hopeless humans who crowded around it, making it near impossible to open. We ignored them and went downstairs to find a seat. The poster at the bottom of the landing was from the original Dracula movie. Bela Lugosi stood with his arms outstretched with his small fangs striking fear into all those who passed. That was another reason I enjoyed this place—the owner had great taste. The whole café had a dark theme and was filled with horror movie props and posters. The room on the left had a throne at the far end. Two Victorian couches lined the wall with several small glass coffee tables in front of them. On the wall, to my left, was a big screen television that played snippets from random horror movies.

We chose to sit in the room off to our right. Tables and chairs were strewn around the room, many large enough for six to eight people. Then there were the tables for two, but the big attractions were the three ovenlike apertures to sit in. We chose one that was open. I plopped down in the cushy chair as Veronica put her coat on the chair opposite me.

"I'm going up to order. You want the usual?"

I nodded, remembering the first time Veronica and I had met in New Orleans. Our worlds had collided when she thought I was a vampire, and I assumed she was human. How simple life had been then.

Veronica walked off as I settled back in the chair. Stretching my senses, I felt the minds of the humans pressing against mine. Their thoughts filtered through my head like radio stations changing too quickly. Losing myself in the noise, I caught glimpses here and there of their lives. As I did, I sensed something familiar. It was the same presence I'd felt earlier in the Tearoom. It only lasted a moment, then it retreated like it had been caught. Maybe it was some errant ghost following me, and now it would leave me alone. I pushed the presence from my thoughts and got lost once again in the distraction of the human minds until Veronica returned. As I let myself go, I didn't hear my lover sit down. It wasn't until the table hit my knee that I opened my eyes.

"Hey, how was—"

Veronica wasn't the one sitting across from me. A man dressed in a black trench coat, black shirt and pants stared at me. His skin was white, almost as pale as mine was. Dark hair fell in waves to his shoulders while his eyes held the knowledge of endless time. His clear, pointed nails caressed the ends of the chair. His face was expressionless, passionless, as always, and his two pointed teeth rested on lips the color of bleached roses. This creature was no vampire, but the Angel of Death.

I sighed, wondering what he wanted. His appearances were always full of puzzling conversation, as he popped up at the most inconvenient times. Something about him irritated me, but I could never pinpoint what it was.

Hello, Brenna. It's nice to see you too, Azrael said. His voice was flat but melodic as it burrowed into my mind.

"What are you doing here, Azrael?" I asked impatiently.

I assumed you might desire my company. You seemed lonely just a moment ago as you sought solace in the minds of the humans at this establishment.

My temper flared as he sat before me. It didn't matter if he was an angel. There was just something about him. Like other angels, his energy was bright, fluttering across my skin like warm sunlight. There was also a slight chill that sank down to my bones, but that was his own special signature, since he was the Angel of Death.

He was the first angel I'd actually had a conversation with. However, I never got a straight answer from Azrael, so I'd stopped asking questions. Whenever I glimpsed other angels, they smiled, but were gone in a rush. Angels existed in a different dimension than humans, and normally weren't perceived unless they wanted to be. Fairies were the same way. Humans saw the beings for something other than what they truly were. Since I'd become a vampire, I'd been able to see all these different creatures, but I'd kept this ability to myself and never told Veronica. I assumed she didn't have the power.

Your intuition seems to be flourishing. Your companion is as beautiful as ever.

"What do you want, Azrael?" I asked again.

He smiled, showing more of his teeth. His canines made me wonder if he was something of a vampire himself, maybe living off the souls he collected.

Dead roses are the ultimate flora to adorn the remains of the deceased. In the end, it is in darkened dungeons that Destiny makes herself known.

"Is that all you came to say?" I growled. "What the hell is that supposed to mean? Can't you just once appear, or go poof, or whatever you do, and—"

He leaned over the table, placing his hand on mine. A chill entered my heart, circulating throughout my body. It became hard to breathe as he held me in his thrall. His eyes burned with a blue fire that imprinted itself in my mind. It seemed like a star had detonated in his eyes, and the cold of space filled me. Liquid ice replaced my blood as the shards ripped my veins to shreds. My heart stopped in mid-beat as

I froze from the inside, but it was so frigid it burned away my rage. That was his point. He'd never touched me before, never done anything except give me cryptic advice. But crypts were his territory.

Those close to you are only elements in your own destiny. You are the key. Think before I descend on your doorstep again.

The chair was empty.

Veronica walked toward me, holding two cups of steaming liquid.

"Brenna, are you all right?"

I looked up as she sat down and handed me my tea. I couldn't feel the cup as it went into my hands. Nor did I notice as the beverage splashed on my fingers. It scalded my flesh. I acknowledged the burn a few seconds later as my heart started beating again and the pain dissipated. Life returned to my limbs as the affects of Azrael's magic wore off. I would never forget the image I'd glimpsed in his eyes, like a starburst exploding in the cosmos.

"Brenna, what happened?" Veronica asked as she settled into her chair.

"Nothing," I muttered.

My Master knew nothing of Azrael and the strange visits he paid me. She wouldn't understand my relationship with the angel. Besides, I didn't want her worried that I had an angel on my tail. Who knew if angels and vampires were enemies? I didn't think we were. Veronica had to deal with the undead she encountered in the city. The only other supernatural beings she encountered were ghosts. She'd mentioned glimpsing the cobbler a few times at night in the Tearoom. Not many vampires truly saw the natures of the other entities that shared our space.

"It's just been a long day." I paused, searching her violet eyes. The conversation I'd overheard earlier popped into my head. It had been gnawing on my consciousness more than I realized. I had a soft spot in my heart for helpless victims. That was how I'd gotten involved with Veronica. Still, I didn't know how she'd react to this new murder. If there was an insane vampire roaming the city, then I had to destroy it before it killed more innocent humans.

But Veronica thought I should leave the other undead be. As long as we left them alone, she reasoned, they'd do the same for us. She'd tried avoiding them, but I'd had a few run-ins with some fledglings. I'd growled and showed them a hint of my power and they'd left me alone, but I hadn't encountered any Old Ones. I wondered if the elders were smarter, or simply not interested in matters outside their own broods. Sometimes I wondered if Devon's demise had been felt among other vampires, or if they were all connected somehow. They must have sprung from somewhere. They had to be all webbed together somehow.

"I overheard something today. A woman lost her sister. The body was mutilated. The police think it was a pack of wild dogs. I think it was one of you— one of us that did it."

Veronica sipped her coffee. Worry lines creased around the corners of her mouth and eyes. "It could have been a pack of rabid animals or even a mortal. Humans are just as capable of horrendous acts as we are. Remember, we used to be like them. Why do you readily assume it was one of us?"

"Just a hunch." I sighed and crossed my arms over my chest, feeling very weary, as if Azrael's touch had sapped everything out of me.

"And what if it's a vampire? Are you going to destroy it? Would you kill it for taking a human life so it can survive?" she growled. Her voice deepened as the beast came to the surface. "Damn, Brenna, you're a hypocrite! You continue your existence, but hate vampires, yet you're involved with me. If you hate our kind so much, why don't you kill me?"

I sighed. People were starting to stare. I quickly reached over the table and grabbed Veronica's arms. This was the same argument we'd had on and off for months, always initiated by her other half. Ronnie had caused enough problems in our relationship. It didn't understand how I could hate other undead, but still love her.

"Enough, Ronnie." I almost choked on the nickname Devon had given her, but it was the only thing her other half responded to. "We've had this conversation before. Now, can I please speak to Veronica?" Tension drained from her face, and her humanity settled back into her features.

Veronica was different from Devon. He'd made Veronica torment and then kill her victims, which went against her very core. When she'd been turned, her mortality had survived. She'd constantly fought with the beast inside, whereas Devon had embraced it. Her Master had loved to hunt and play with mortals until the fear in their blood was ripe. That was the way of most vampires. Some, like Veronica, killed because it was an instinct to survive. Each time Veronica did, though, the guilt she felt at the deaths of her victims weighed on her soul. My lover silently strolled hospital wards, taking her meals from the terminally ill while vanquishing their pain and bringing them peace. She told me about other vampires she'd encountered doing the same, bringing them peace. I, on the other hand, couldn't kill the mortals I fed on. Something in my nature made me unable to, and that also set me apart from other vampires.

"I'm sorry, Brenna. I didn't mean—she didn't mean it. You know how she feels when you talk about killing other vampires. It reminds her of Devon."

"I know, but I wasn't talking about you. You don't toy with your food. You bring them mercy. This poor girl was torn apart with nothing left for her family to bury. It reminds me too much of...him. That's all."

"What do you want me to say?" Veronica asked as she resettled in her chair. "I—we—miss him. It's crazy, I know, but Devon created me. As much as I hate him, she misses him. I can't explain it. But, I just got back, so let's find something else to discuss. I'm not saying you shouldn't do anything about the girl, but let's wait and see if there's another killing, all right?" she asked as she saw I was about to protest.

I nodded. There was no way I could say no to her.

"So, how's the Tearoom?"

"Fine. Zach came in looking for money again. I turned him down, but he just doesn't get it."

"I thought you were going to fire him. If he hasn't changed in these past eight months, why do you think he's going to now?"

"I don't know. I—"

A loud crash interrupted me as a man pulled down a game of Scrabble. The game fell, spreading little letter tiles all over. The man struggled to find all the pieces with no one helping him. I scanned the rest of the room, noticing there really weren't as many people as when we'd first entered. A table of six was the final destination of the Scrabble game. A table of two leaned in close to one another, sharing intimate secrets as waves of their bliss ran over my mind like pink fuzz. In the next aperture over, I saw a pair of legs stretched out on a table. Itching started back up again in my mind. I swept my eyes over the pair of jeans, wondering who owned them, but Veronica stopped the premonition before it started.

"You still think of Zach as you did when you were human. You see him as mutable because that's what humans do, they change. But we can't. We'll always look and act the same. Give up and let him go. You can find another psychic at the drop of a hat. All you have to do is reel one in, or head up to Salem. Didn't you tell me once there was a huge population of psychics there?"

I shook my head while swallowing my tea. "No. Well, yes. There are lots of psychics there, but mostly there's a big Wiccan population. What does that have to do with Zach?" I snapped.

"Nothing. I was just suggesting maybe you should look there for a psychic. That's all. I didn't mean anything by it. What's the matter with you? I go away for a few days and you turn into a raging bitch? What's up?"

The affects of whatever Azrael did had worn off, but had been replaced by a small burning in the pit of my stomach that slowly eked into my veins. The blood of my last victim passed out of my system quicker than the one before. Or maybe Azrael's power had sapped the last of my reserves? I'd never dealt with angelic power before. I'd have to feed within the next couple of days, or my hunger would get the better of me. I didn't know what would happen then—I'd never let myself get that far.

Starving vampires were not pretty sights. They foamed at the mouth as their teeth cut into their lips. Once a vampire reached that point, the beast inside had total control until it fed. Since I had no beast, I didn't know what would happen to me. I was still formed from demonic blood, though. The hunger was proof of that.

"I've been dead for over two hundred years. It gets lonely watching your family die. Especially when you caused their deaths. You haven't even been dead a year. Haven't watched anyone you love perish. You're so close to mortality, you haven't experienced what it's like to lose that which you hold dear. To have your breathing shut down automatically because you're becoming something else. Soon, you'll have to think about breathing, about trying to appear human. Then you'll realize how much you've truly left behind."

Veronica smiled, but I saw tears in her eyes. To destroy her ties with humanity and sate her newborn hunger, Devon had made her kill her sister. Then her parents. Deep down, she knew that if she'd never let

Devon into her life, her family would have lived and died normally, and she, like them, would have been dust. I reassured her that her actions weren't her fault. Devon seduced her by using his powers on her.

A chill ran down my back as Veronica discussed death. I never really thought of myself as being dead, as my heart still beat and I still breathed. Also, I felt my purpose in my new existence was to help humanity. That was one reason I wanted to find the thing that had shredded Haley.

My teeth ached to tear the bastard limb from limb, but Veronica didn't fully understand my feelings. I honestly didn't want to involve her in my reasoning. All I could do was see if any other vampires knew about the asshole. But my Master had a point that appealed to my rationality. Wait and see if there were more murders. Gathering information wouldn't hurt, even if it meant slumming, interacting with the very creatures I hated. I'd have to go to the Black Rose. It was the only place I knew where vampires hung out.

"Oh my God!"

"What?"

"Nothing." I realized what Azrael had meant when he'd mentioned dead flowers. Of course, I had no fucking clue about the rest of what he'd said, but that was the way things were with him.

I was about to suggest we go to the Rose that night, but Veronica ran her finger up my arm. The little hairs stood up, and I felt myself growing moist at the thought of the night ahead. Even the slight separation we'd endured was long enough. My heart still wasn't healed from our six months apart.

You want to get out of here? she whispered in my mind.

Sure, I answered back, entwining my thoughts around hers.

We got up, leaving our cups on the table. She grabbed my hand, leading me to the door. Desire rose in me as we walked out. I glanced at the pair of legs I'd noticed earlier. In the alcove was a man with blond hair and pale skin. Something was very off about him, something that made the warning lights turn on in my mind. But before I could examine him, my lover wrapped her arms around my waist, pulling me into her as she nuzzled my neck. I smiled, losing my balance. Veronica caught me, whispering her secret longings of what she would do to me in the hours to come.

4

CHAPTER FOUR

My name is Miranda.

After closing my book, I rubbed my eyes, rejoining the real world. I'd been so lost in a fictional reality that I'd forgotten what time it was. At first I assumed we were still open, but after seeing no one, I suspected we'd shut down for the night. Gina would never leave without tugging my arm. Glancing behind the counter, I heard my roommate and the other staffers in the kitchen eating some of the leftover cake. It was a nightly ritual.

My friend had a wonderful way with everyone as she chatted with the staff, motivating the employees. Most stayed away from me. They thought my obsession with vampires was strange. I never let on about it. Even though reading about the beasts helped the thing in my head, I didn't think that was the main reason I loved the undead. I traced my interest back to something I'd learned when I was a child, before my mother died. She'd told me stories about an ancestor, a prostitute, who'd been attacked by a vampire and then saved by the innkeeper. The innkeeper had destroyed the creature and married my great-great-whatever. I thought it was a love story, but I secretly wanted the vampire to claim his prize.

Now, I stretched and walked into the kitchen to join the rest of the crew. Gina had her mouth full of chocolate cake and gestured to the last piece. She knew me too well.

"You decided to join the land of the living, I see," Gina giggled, wiping whipped cream off the top of her lip.

"Yeah. Well, those books suck me in. I forget how time flies," I said while taking a bite of cake. My stomach rumbled as I munched.

"The others and I were talking, thinking about going to this place up the street to get our fortunes read. Linda was just there, and we thought maybe you'd want to go," Claire suggested.

I eyed the three of them, wondering what they plotted. Seeing a psychic? "You guys have got to be kidding. You want to have someone steal your money? Tell you you're going to meet a tall, dark, handsome stranger who will cheat on you and leave you for the next teenybopper that comes along? Sorry. Doesn't sound too appealing."

"Come on. It'll be fun. Maybe they'll help figure out who's haunting your dreams. A few psychics have been known to be reputable, and Linda says this place has been around for a while," Gina lectured as she gathered the rest of the plates and stuck them in the dishwasher.

By looking at the mess, I could tell we'd been extremely busy. Actually, things had been going so well, I'd considered hiring another part-time employee. I'd have to bring it up with Gina first. She did the books and knew the finances better than anyone. Tomorrow was Sunday, and we'd be closed. Gina had argued once that we should be open for the tourists. I'd told her if she wanted to open she could, but I had to have a day when the café was closed. If God rested that day, then so could I.

I glanced over at my friend, knowing she was set on taking me to the psychic. Maybe a psychic would hold the key to getting rid of my nightmare, giving me a night when I didn't have to think about seeing the demonic face or feeling him waiting in the doorway. That would be a wondrous thing. Then I could look forward to resting instead of staying up all night, drinking tea and praying the Sandman wouldn't pay me a visit. I didn't give psychics much credit. I'd seen the 900 numbers on television; the fortunetellers were phony as three-dollar bills.

I ran my hands over my arms as a chill passed through my bones. Hugging myself, I looked down. The burn scars were visible, but maybe, just maybe, I wouldn't have to think about them anymore. Maybe I could be free of those memories once and for all. The heaviness of sleep weighed on my eyes, begging to drag me under.

"The psychic was awesome. Some of what she said already happened. The other stuff won't happen until six months from now or something. Her name was Raven. You really should go and see her. It was like she knew every—" Linda stopped when Gina shot her a look.

I suppressed a laugh. Linda was the newest member of our little family. She was a freshman at Suffolk University and way too enthusiastic, reminding me of a younger version of Claire. But appearance-wise, Linda and Claire were opposites. Linda was short and chesty, where Claire was tall and overweight. I glanced over at Linda and saw the shushed conversation ready to burst forth. This girl was no one to keep a secret. As I looked at both Gina and Linda, I knew I wasn't going to get out of going to the psychic. Gina was my best friend, and I couldn't disappoint her.

"Fine. I'll go. But you're paying."

Gina gave me a huge hug.

"Hey. Whatever happened with that guy you went after earlier? The one you thought was eyeing me?"

Gina gave me a blank stare, as if I was talking about a ghost. "What guy?"

"What guy? Come on. You know what guy! You thought he was a huge hunk, blond hair, pale, kinda built. Great eyes."

The others' eyes darted between Gina and me, wondering what the hell I was talking about. Gina always shared her latest fling when she wasn't mentioning how great Jeremy was in bed.

"You don't remember?"

"No. I think I'd remember a cute boy, Miranda. Maybe you dreamed him up from one of your books?"

I chuckled. It was unlike Gina to forget anything. God forbid I forgot to write down a little expense. Then she would be on my ass for days, telling me how important it was to write it down. But I knew this boy was real. My memory was bad now and again, and the lack of sleep really wasn't helping, but he had been here.

"Maybe you're right. Not sleeping is catching up to me. Why don't we go home? Claire, would you mind closing up?"

"It's Saturday. We could be busy in an hour or so. We are open until two, right?" Claire pointed out.

"Thank you, Claire. I realize that, but there's no one here," I snapped. "It's okay to close up."

Claire glanced at Gina, wondering what to do. The confused look made my blood boil. I hated when Claire did this. Sometimes I wondered if people forgot I also owned the place. I opened my mouth to say something, but Gina jumped in.

"Miranda, let's let Claire and Linda close. I'll go home with you. You need sleep. Come on." Gina headed for the door. The other two nodded as Gina led me out of Crimson Liquids.

We got out onto the street and walked down to the entrance to the T, the subway, when Gina stopped me halfway down Park Street. She examined me. I wondered what she thought. She was rarely this quiet. Usually, my friend talked my ear off so much I couldn't hear myself think.

She and I had met when we started college. I'd been wandering down the halls, looking for my room, when I bumped into her. My load of boxes had scattered everywhere as both of us collapsed on the floor. Gina looked the same now as she had in college, and we'd become instant friends, realizing we lived right across the hall from each other.

"What's with you, Miranda?"

"Nothing. I'm just tired. I haven't slept more than two hours consistently for the last month. It's getting to me. I haven't had this much trouble since I was a teenager, but at least this time I'm staying away from matches." I rubbed my arms unconsciously.

Gina smiled and gave me another hug. "I'm just worried about you, that's all. Maybe the psychic tomorrow can give you some insight into how to get rid of your dreams. For good this time."

"Tomorrow?"

"Yeah."

"I'm going to kill you, but now I'm too tired to care."

5

CHAPTER FIVE

My name is Brenna.

I'd had a bad feeling when I opened my eyes this morning. I was sure something was going to go wrong today, but nothing had happened. Yet. I sat back in my chair. It was Sunday, and I didn't have any appointments. Veronica planned on meeting me later.

I sighed, remembering last night. We'd been up for hours playing. Just thinking about her got me hot. It had been wonderful to have her back in our bed. Today, she would be back in to watch the Tearoom, as I had to feed tonight. My body had started pulling itself apart piece by piece. Whatever Azrael had done to me had affected me more than I thought, and I didn't like it.

Part of me was still frozen from his touch. So cold I feared it was empty, as if he'd planted a piece of himself inside me. My mind was clouded with thoughts of blood and hunger, and I was becoming slightly irrational. I licked my lips in anticipation of the human blood I'd consume. The psychics in the Tearoom were tempting, but I'd never think of feeding off of them. They knew nothing of what I was, and I wanted to keep it that way.

"Raven."

A hand came down on my shoulder. The pressure was light. The energy mixed against my aura, feeling like warm sunshine. It was Sophie, a soft-spoken but very energetic psychic. Only she and Peter had shown up today. Zach was absent, which was unlike him, even if he was on his latest binge. Honestly, I was tired of wondering where he was. This was the last straw. Favor for Edmund or not, Zach was gone.

"What is it, Sophie?" I asked, irritated after being disturbed.

She shouldn't have interrupted me. She'd been in the middle of a reading, as had Peter. Two women had come in while I was out getting some tea. Peter was doing his reading while both laughed and joked. If Sophie was out here, then something was wrong.

"I can't connect with her. I've tried everything, but it's like pounding my head into a brick wall. What do you want me to do?" Sophie asked in her soft voice, which was even quieter than usual, as she didn't want the client to overhear.

I glanced past her to see her reading, watching us intently from the doorway of the Water Room. She was twenty-seven or so, but could've looked younger if she wore makeup. Her blonde hair hung loose around her shoulders, and her clothes were wrinkled. The scent of coffee and cinnamon hung about her as if it were ground into her pores. She was my height, five-eight, with average-size tits and an okay body. But it was the bags under her eyes that showed her story.

I sighed. The woman didn't seem angry. An air of disdain hung around her like she really didn't care one way or the other. I extended my mind, trying to learn her secrets, when a rush of images hit my psyche. Pools of blood on a tile floor. A shadow standing in a doorway. The scent of sulfur filling my nose, and then burning flesh. I surveyed my own skin and saw the hair igniting, charring under the heat. The tissue turned red and then black, blistering until pain shot up my hands and arms. Then there was overwhelming sense of desire. Absently, I licked my lips as my heart sped up. Images of the ocean and a small, quaint house entered my thoughts. The clanging of spoons and bells, along with pictures of books and romantic notions of vampires came as well. This woman owned Crimson Liquids.

I blinked, aware of myself again. The woman who waited was in a lot of pain. I understood why she didn't want a reading, as she hid her true feelings behind a wall to keep everything out while sheer exertion of will kept her going. Beyond that, I was surprised she wasn't ill, but there was something else I just couldn't place, so I moved into her mind using my vampire abilities.

In some ways, my vampiric talents were different from the other gifts I possessed, but in so many ways they were the same. My vampiric abilities allowed me to do telekinesis, alter memories, and enter a mortal mind and flip through it like a photo album. My psychic talents were more abstract. I'd connect with a person by feeling their emotions, getting flashes of things, events, sometimes pictures or symbols. I'd get names at times that were given by my guides, the beings who helped me through my daily life. Their presence always surrounded me, but I'd learned to ignore them. Since I'd become a vampire, they came around when I did readings, but usually, they stayed in the background. At times, I missed their closeness; in my mortal years, they'd been there when no one else was.

Now, in the client's mind, I found everything I would in a normal human's: her worries, cares, and memories. As I delved deeper, something ceased my progression. A barrier was thrown spontaneously around a certain part of her thoughts. The makeup of it was something akin to my own power, but not nearly as strong. This was strange. She was mortal and shouldn't have had this ability. Nothing like this had ever happened with me before. I wondered what it was or how she put up the wall to keep me out. What was she protecting?

Centering myself, I pushed into her thoughts harder, hoping she wouldn't be aware of the intrusion. It's not possible. She's not a vampire. But does she truly know?

I examined her intently and decided that no, she didn't really know what was going on inside of her.

"Raven, what do you want me to do?"

"Bring her over. I'll do her reading." I was surprised to hear myself say that.

Sophie looked at me as if I'd gone insane. Normally, I only did readings by appointments; Sophie had found that out the hard way.

I'd been in a particularly dark mood. The Tearoom was busy and I was in the middle of looking over the payroll when Sophie tapped me on the shoulder, presenting me with a client. I glared at her, sending a bolt of energy at her hard enough to make her wince. My reading astounded the customer, but that didn't surprise me. When the place calmed down, I took Sophie out back and screamed at her long enough that she avoided me for a month. I felt bad later, considering she'd just happened to be the punching bag that got in my way after I'd fought with Veronica. Now I tried very hard to keep my temper in check.

"Are you sure?" she asked meekly.

"Go get her." I smiled at the woman, motioning her over since Sophie made no move to do so. She sat down before me. The other psychic glanced at the unwitting client and me. There was something seriously wrong with my customer. As I flicked through her mind, trying to figure out what plagued her, I discovered her name. Miranda.

"Sophie says you and she weren't connecting. I can give you your money back, or I can give you a reading."

Miranda weighed the two possibilities. Since she hadn't paid for the reading, she didn't give a shit, but her friend would be disappointed if she didn't try. Honestly, she was too tired to think of any creative lies to explain why she shouldn't have her cards read.

"Sure, whatever." She yawned.

She was sure I was a crackpot, someone who would tell her about a tall, dark stranger who would abuse her, cheat on her, and then leave her for some bimbo. Her irritation poured from her into my brain. Truly, she wanted to say fuck it and go home and sleep. The longest she had slept was three hours since she was awakened by her nightmare, something she'd been weighed down with for years.

"Let me see your hands."

She hesitated, wondering what kind of spell I was going to cast over her, but after a moment, she gave in. Circular scars covered her arms along with other small puckers of flesh. I smiled, knowing the wounds had been the result of cigarettes and matches.

My eyes closed to hone in on her vibration. As my breathing slowed, my heart ceased to beat. The heat of Miranda's skin sunk into my cooling palms. Meanwhile, golden light flooded my being, filling me from the top of my head. The world around me burst to life. Temperature shifts pressed on all sides of my body as a frigid breeze from nowhere floated through the Main Room. Shadowy ghosts came out of the walls, vying for my attention, whispering in my ears like a distant waterfall. I ignored them.

In my mind, I saw all the different levels of existence like wide steps on a never-ending staircase. My guides stood on a higher point, away from the earthbound plane. Silently, I acknowledged them. A rush of warmth enveloped me, as if they were hugging me. For a second, I basked in their kindness. I was aware of everything on the other side even while I was inside Miranda's mind.

Through her eyes, I saw how she perceived me. Clutching her hands lightly, she sensed the energy burning my body as it transferred between us. My head had slumped forward. My client wondered if something was wrong with me, if she should pull her hands away and call for help. Miranda tried moving. I grabbed tight. My nails sunk into her skin. She didn't flinch.

My eyes snapped open. I stared through her, into her mind, her future, her past, her present, and all of her emotions. Words formed in my thoughts as the heat intensified, increasing my awareness and making me one with the environment. Molecules of hair and dust floated past me. The elevator whirred. In the club downstairs, someone stripped the floor. The tailor next door watered his plants. Peter talked with his client. His aura never wavered. It was calm and silent as a blue endless sky. His client was Miranda's friend, Gina. Her aura was like an annoying yipping dog, bouncing up and down, bright yellow. Words tumbled from my mouth, and I was unable to stop them.

"Dreams have plagued you nightly since you were a child. A shadowy figure stands in a doorway, waiting to ask you a question. You feel no fear at first, but he lunges at you, snarling like a demon. You don't know where he comes from, but you know he desires you. Pain made you stay awake. Matches and lighters, anything that burned. Blood dripping on the floor, forming a perfect pool. Your hands reach out as something, a garbled whisper, tells you how warm it is. You crave it even now, but deny your urges. For now, your demons are under control. You tell yourself you're crazy, haunted. But you aren't. Whatever plagues you is a throwback from a story. It comes through the door of your mind when you're under stress; its presence is old, but weak. You have nothing to fear as long as you are in control.

"Now you're concerned with the future. Friends will be wiped from your life while you find yourself falling in love with your destiny. Beware of the man who follows you, watches you. He seeks another whom others have sought to control. It's only by accident that he stumbles upon you. Remember. The closer you get to the truth, the more you'll discover that—"

I was slammed back into my body. My guides had disconnected the energy flowing through my head chakra. The abrupt shift caused my whole body to quake. The jar back to physical reality made me wonder what my guides were trying to protect Miranda from. I was getting close to uncovering what was after her. Tears leaked out of the sides of her eyes. My mind was still attached to hers. She now knew I wasn't pulling her leg or trying to cast a spell on her.

As I surfed through her mind, the barrier I'd discovered earlier remained. I wondered what I'd said to her. Even though I'd done the reading, it was like being in the passenger seat of the car. I hadn't paid attention to where I was going, so now I didn't remember.

"Are you okay?" I asked.

"Miranda. My name's Miranda. How did you know that stuff about me?"

"It's what I do."

I got up and grabbed a few tissues from the host station. She wiped her eyes. A sudden urge came over me. I wrote my home phone number and the hours I worked on the back of my business card.

"Take this in case you ever need to talk. Or if anything strange happens. My name's Brenna. Raven is just the name I read under. Call me anytime."

Miranda took the card, not knowing what to say. She sat on the couch, stunned, waiting for her friend to finish. As she sat down, one more message pushed into my mind.

"Miranda, one more thing. This doesn't make sense. Most of it normally doesn't. Past blood is awakening as old stories are made true. Beware the night dweller out for blood and ward off the sleeping beast."

Fear passed through her eyes, and she was about to question me when Veronica glided in. I glanced up and smiled. Patting Miranda's knee, I got up and embraced my lover, but she didn't return my affection. Her dire expression alerted me that something was terribly wrong. The horrible feelings I'd fended off all day washed over me.

Shit.

"What is it?"

"Can I talk to you outside?"

"What's the matter, Veronica?"

"I think we should discuss this outside, Brenna."

"Just tell me!" I clenched my teeth.

Veronica sighed, running her hand through her hair. "Zach's mother called me at home. He never came home last night. The police knocked on her door when she was on the phone. They found Zach. There was hardly anything left of him. They only knew it was him because they found his wallet."

I slammed my fist into the wall. Some of the plaster fell from the ceiling. My fingers grew, hardening into talons. Teeth elongated as my rage bled my eyes black. The skin along my back danced as my wings pressed under my flesh to emerge. Everything in me desired to transform and find the thing that had butchered Zach. The woman had been one thing, but Zach—this was personal. He was one of those I protected, and his death would be avenged.

"Get a grip," Veronica whispered as she pulled me into the hallway.

I glared at her coldly, fury burning through me. The need to slash something overwhelmed me as the vampire blood screamed for vengeance inside me. My fangs shifted in my mouth, growing longer and then shorter. I clenched my fists, feeling no pain as my sharpened fingers pierced my skin.

"Do you still think it was a mortal, or a pack of wild dogs?" I growled.

"No." She shook her head, taking one of my fists in her hand. She brought my wounded palm to her lips, licking the blood away and sealing the wounds. Her tongue felt like sandpaper, reminding me of her caresses from the night before. Slowly, she sucked my fingers clean, trying to get me to relax as my fingers returned to normal. Veronica smiled and gave me a quick kiss.

"I believe you, but don't rush out. Calm down and rationalize. There's only one place you can go, and you don't want to go there half-cocked. You don't know what the Rose is like."

I sighed as she referred to the Black Rose, the place Azrael had suggested. Veronica was right. I had to be composed when we went there. I'd have to pretend to be one of them, playing their games. That was something I hated.

6

CHAPTER SIX

My name is Miranda.

Gina came out of her reading just as Brenna came back into the Tearoom. I smiled weakly as she walked by. Everything she said swam inside my head like a lost goldfish. There was no way she could have known so much about me. She knew everything about my burns, my nightmares, about my stint in the hospital and my obsession with blood. The most astounding thing was that she knew about my nightmares. She knew how the demon haunted me even while my eyes were open.

My eyes watered as Gina and I stepped onto the elevator. We stood in silence as I thought about what had just happened. Brenna and I had had an instant connection. She was a real psychic.

Now, as I listened to Gina rattle on about how wonderful her reading was, I didn't want to tell her anything. I fingered the business card Brenna had handed me. I had no reason to call her and didn't think I ever would. She'd told me these wondrous things I doubted would come to pass.

Gina would never believe me. She was too wrapped up in her own life.

Then I remembered the last part of Brenna's reading. A chill ran down my spine as we exited onto Winter Street. Her cryptic message somehow reminded me of the story my mother used to tell me about my great-great-whatever grandmother, the prostitute. She'd only had one child, and my ancestor had died a few years after it was born. The story had hypnotized me at a young age. When I was four, my nightmare had started. My mother had thought it was her fault I had the dreams. I knew it wasn't, even after she died when I was ten.

Gina continued rambling on about how great Peter was and how she would have to go back in another few months. This surprised me. I never thought my roommate believed in the supernatural or psychics. Apparently, there were a few things even I didn't know about her.

"So, what happened? Was it great or what?" Gina asked as she fished a cigarette from the crushed pack in her pocket.

Could I truly tell Gina what Brenna had said? Would she understand? I noticed her tousled platinum hair and the pink shirt she wore with a black denim skirt. Her sense of style was nowhere near mine. After knowing each other for eight years, she knew everything: my dreams, my hospital stays, and even my burns. She'd put up with my fascination for the undead and my unwillingness to date for the past two years. Yet, my instincts told me that, this time, my best friend just wouldn't get it. Even I didn't fully understand the information I'd received and the connection I'd felt with Brenna. I shook my head quickly and smiled as we walked across the street to the Park Street T-station.

"You all right?"

"I'm fine. I was just thinking about going up to the shop to check on the inventory. You go home. I'll meet you later."

"You? Work on Sunday? You sure you're feeling okay?"

"I'm fine. Now go home," I told her as I began walking away, but then I turned back around. "I did have fun though. Thanks for the reading."

"Did she help you?" Gina asked, the concern on her face genuine.

"She helped a little, but she couldn't really suggest anything about my dreams. Now go on." I shooed her away.

Gina smiled and strolled down into the subway as I climbed up the hill to Crimson Liquids. A wave of dizziness overwhelmed me as I fumbled with my keys. I dropped them, and they hit the stone step with a heavy thud. The doorframe caught me as my head spun. I closed my eyes, just trying to make the spinning stop. The splinters of the old frame caught in my hair. The lack of sleep was catching up with me. Along with the spinning, I felt a slight pressure in the center of my forehead that I'd never experienced before. I opened my eyes as the hazy feeling passed. In front of me was a handsome stranger offering me my keys.

"Are you okay?" he asked.

His eyes were Siberian husky blue and had a familiar look to them. Even his presence was calming as I lost myself in his gaze. His pale, pink-tinged face was crowned by tousled blond hair, which flew all over the place as he waited for me to respond. All I could do was stare like an idiot with my mouth slightly open. I blinked, coming out of my stupor while taking my keys from him.

"Yes. Fine. Thank you. I—um—didn't realize I'd dropped them. Thanks."

His smile hit me head on and made the dizziness fly from my mind.

"You're welcome. I'm Julien," he said, extending his hand.

His skin was hot against mine, as if he were burning up, but as he took my hand, a feeling of tranquility descended over me. I almost forgot what I was going to do, his eyes were so compelling. I felt that somehow, if I let him, he could solve all my problems and drive away my age-old demons. His arms would be strong as he held me away from the cold world. In him was salvation.

I blinked and shook my head. The strange thoughts faded like the dawn light, and all I saw in his eyes was my reflection.

"I'm Miranda."

"Remarkable," he whispered softly.

"What?"

He smiled again. "You're name. It's beautiful, and you're beautiful. I think it's love at first sight."

I giggled and got the door open. *Love at first sight, my ass. But he's cute and I'm tired of being alone.*

"That's a sucky line, but I think it worked. Want some coffee?"

"Sure, if it's not an inconvenience."

I shook my head, and he walked in. The door closed behind me and I locked it again. I walked around the coffee bar and flicked on the lights. One of the coffee machines was always ready to go. I scoped the kitchen and saw it wasn't that much of a mess from the night before, but it wasn't as spotless as I would've liked. The coffee beeped, alerting me it was done. Grabbing a cup, I filled it and threw a tea bag into a mug for me. I brought them back to find

Julien admiring the posters. He turned around when he heard me come back out.

"This place is wonderful. I love the décor," he said as I handed him the coffee.

I gestured to a table in front of the window that overlooked Beacon Street. We slid in together and I knocked my knees on the legs, but I didn't notice the pain. I just watched as he glanced over at the floor-length shades that blocked the view from passersby and kept out the hot sun. The other four street windows, which faced Park Street, were also curtained.

Julien was dressed casually in a red pullover sweater and black pants. He looked comfortable enough to go out to dinner or just hang out. He was slender but well built, and he had a great smile. No specks of dirt clung to his fingernails, which was a plus. Gina would have said he was gay, but my radar wasn't going off. Instead, I sensed a subtle air of calmness and authority around him. As I drank my tea, I basked in the warmth of his presence, forgetting everything Brenna had told me. Then, I realized why this man was so familiar. He was the guy Gina had pointed out to me yesterday, but I assumed it would be too weird to ask him about her, so I let that detail slip from my mind.

"I didn't think this place was open on Sunday?"

I blew the steam away on my tea. "It's not. I was going to do inventory. Where you from?" I hoped he would say somewhere close by. It would be my luck that I'd meet a guy and he would be flying out tomorrow.

"Worcester, actually. I'm trying to locate someone I haven't been able to get in touch with. Right now, I'm staying with an old friend. She's thinking about selling me her club, but it's still up in the air. How long have you been in business?"

"Almost five years. Is this person an old girlfriend? The one you're trying to find?" I smiled, trying not to sound too nosey.

"No," he chuckled. His teeth were perfect, and his look caused a flash of warmth to run through me, touching parts that hadn't been caressed in a while. I squirmed in my seat.

"I'm glad to hear that."

"Just someone I need to acquire something from. The thing is, I think I found her after months of searching."

"Good."

"And you? Is there anyone in your life?"

"No." I blushed.

"Maybe there can be. If you want."

I tried to hold back my shocked expression, but my efforts weren't successful. So I sipped my tea and just nodded. "That would be nice."

We chatted for what seemed to be only a few minutes, but I ended up drinking four cups of tea and he had five more cups of coffee. After my last cup, I realized it was growing dark and I should be venturing home. Inventory would never have taken me this long, and I knew Gina would be wondering where I was. She'd tried calling several times while Julien and I talked, but I wasn't going to break the mood.

One reason I didn't want to answer was that I learned Julien's friend owned some club over in Cambridge. He'd been in and out of Boston over the past month-and-a-half following leads on the woman he'd been trying to find. With the information I learned, I wondered why someone like him would be interested in me. He was clearly well off, financially speaking. He was handsome and could have any woman he wanted. I just wondered why he searched for this mysterious woman.

I'd rattled off about college. I'd even felt compelled to tell him how I was hospitalized as a teenager. I'd even told him about Ruth committing suicide, but I'd left out the blood fetish. That was a bit much on a first date. As I'd told him all these things, I'd gotten the sense that he wouldn't judge me for them. He'd just nodded, which was amazing.

Now, as I emptied the remnants of the coffee into the sink and washed the pot, I figured Brenna could keep her cards and psychic mumbo jumbo.

Maybe she did have some weird insight into my life, but it was all a fluke.

She was just a fake. She'd made a lucky guess. That's all, I thought. I don't need her cryptic messages to run my life. *Here's a man that's nice, well off, and handsome. She should've seen that, but she didn't. All the dark stuff is crap.*

I finished drying the coffee urn and refilled the filter so it would be ready for tomorrow. Julien waited for me as I clicked the lights off, immersing the café in darkness. The only light that snuck in underneath the shades came from the streetlights and cars that turned down Park Street.

Stepping out from behind the bar, I looked for Julien. At first, I saw nothing but his outline. He stood in the doorway, just a silhouette against the glass in the ominous blackness. My heart picked up speed. Images from my dream flooded my psyche. A lump rose in my throat, and I felt the tea churning hot in my stomach.

Breathe, Miranda. This is real life, not a dream. Julien's not some nightmare monster. He's real, he's cute, and he's interested. Don't scare him off just yet.

"Miranda, you okay?"

"Ya-yes," I stammered, trying to calm my rushing heart. "I'm sorry. I haven't been sleeping well lately. The darkness distorts things. I don't like it much at times."

"There's nothing to fear. Nothing lives in the dark except legends. Would you like to go?" he asked softly.

"Yes." I sighed, feeling tension drain from my body. Home and bed sounded wonderful, but then again, so did a night in this man's arms. I stepped forward with that thought on my mind when he stopped me.

"Answer one question for me, and then we'll go?"

My dream overwhelmed me. I waited for him to lunge. Waited for his lovely face to turn into a monster's. Instead, his hand caressed my cheek as he brought my face to meet his lips. They were soft; kissing them was like kissing a flower petal. He pressed his mouth into mine as the tip of his tongue parted my lips. It ran along the top of my teeth. I moaned against him, and my hands rubbed against the material of his red sweater. Before I could respond, he pulled away.

"Can I ask you something?" he asked again.

Yes, I will marry you. Yes, I will crawl into bed with you and let you sleep with me. I'm yours. All you have to do is ask me.

"Yes," I breathed, caught in whatever web he'd woven, already anticipating the feel of him inside me. The feel of waking with sore muscles. Of just sleeping in his arms and being protected after a long night of magnificent sex. It'd been way too long since I'd gotten laid.

"Why do you like vampires so much?"

I froze. All the thoughts of going back to his place vanished. Why had he asked me that? Then again, it wasn't that strange, since one could tell I was obsessed, and I had mentioned them a few times while we were talking. Hadn't I?

"They make me feel better."

His fingers brushed my cheek as he gazed deeply into my eyes, searching for something. The look made me weak in the knees again, and I knew I was just waiting for the word again. Whatever it was, he didn't seem to find it.

"Come on. I'll walk you to the T."

I nodded, following him blindly and locking the door behind us. At the subway entrance, I waited to feel the softness of his lips. Instead, like a gentleman, he took my hand, placing a kiss on the inside of my wrist. My heart leapt at his touch as the disappointment of my daydreams came crashing down.

"I'll see you soon." He winked.

"All right," I squeaked.

He smiled and then turned, whistling down the street. I stared after him until he was swallowed by a crowd of college students coming up Tremont Street. Then, I headed underground. I wondered when he would next grace me with his presence, or when I could crawl into bed with him.

I smiled slyly, thinking of my great-great-what-ever and wondering what she would have done in the situation. Then again, she'd probably have fucked him and already moved on to another client. I wasn't anything like her, but with him, I would be whatever he wanted. My mind was already set on that.

7

CHAPTER SEVEN

My name is Brenna.

"Brenna, you can't go. You don't know who this vampire is or what it looks like. Even if you go to the Rose, it's unlikely they'll let you anywhere near the Elder. Not without me," Veronica said as I dressed.

"Then why don't you come with me?" I snapped.

We had argued on and off about going, and she wouldn't go when it was vampire-only night. But I had to go while the trail was fresh. I needed to speak with the Elder of the City.

I'd learned that news of any new vampire or major happening among the undead never escaped the Elder. Veronica didn't want to get involved in the politics of the vampire world. If they discovered she was a human lover, a meat-lover, then they would kill her. I was just going in blindfolded, hoping I would sense their power to get an idea of their age. It was only a hunch, but I assumed the murderer would be at the Black Rose, considering the despicable things that go on there when the club's only open to vampires.

I glared back at my lover as I put on black fishnet stockings, thigh-high stiletto boots, a red miniskirt, and a black corset. Over that I threw on a black suit jacket to cover my tits, which spilled over the top of the corset. It had been a while since I had worn these clothes and my reflection smiled back at me.

I'd been so caught up in the Tearoom these past eight months that I'd toned down my appearance. I still listened to Goth music and dressed in black, but it'd been a while since I'd worn a corset. My body hadn't forgotten, though I felt like I'd lost touch with my gothic dark side.

Dark side, I thought. I was the dark side, and to lose touch was to forget part of what I was.

"You've never been to a vampire club when it's only open to our kind. Things are different when the undead's rules apply. If you piss off the wrong vampire, you're dead, no questions asked. The older ones will be on you like hyenas since you don't have your master with you. Besides, you don't even know who the Elder is. There are rules in our society. Just because you think you're different from us doesn't mean you can simply barge in there. Remember when we went to find Devon."

"That was different. Screw the rules. Whether I'm a true vampire or not, I won't be like them. I have to find out what happened to Zach. Even if it wasn't in my nature, I'd want to find out who killed him. He was one of my own. What if someone is after us? Or after me? Wouldn't you want to find out everything you could?"

"If you go in there, you could end up a slave, or worse." Veronica grabbed my arm and squeezed.

She was afraid I'd be caught up in the vampire lifestyle. Deep down, she didn't understand the creature I'd become. Veronica sympathized as I tried to figure out what kind of being I'd turned into, but she was even more worried that I couldn't handle myself in the undead world. She was terrified they would discover my difference and kill me as well—in that world, anything different from the norm was killed.

"I was human last time we went to the Rose."

Veronica laughed. "Exactly—you were human. Without me, you'd never have gotten out alive. Now lay off the power trip. Just because you think you're a breed apart doesn't mean shit. If you go, you could die."

"Veronica, I'm going with or without you. Now let me go." I snarled.

"I won't allow you to," she growled. Her voice was gravelly. Ronnie merged with Veronica's personality.

I turned slowly from my reflection. Her features had twisted, full of anger and hatred. Her chin had elongated. Her skin took on a waxy pallor as the beast surfaced. The look in her face reminded me of Devon, but she wasn't him. I wrapped my fingers around her wrists and tried to pry them off me. Her grip began to cut into my skin as her fingers morphed from flesh to bone. I tightened my hold, but it did no good. My physical strength was nothing compared to hers.

"This is not the time to be playing Master, Veronica."

"I'm not playing." She yanked me into her. "You're my child, and I'm not letting you go. You have to learn to obey your Master. You seem to forget who pulled you from death. It was I who gave you blood," Veronica said, throwing images of me lying on the floor with Devon hovering over me into my mind. I'd barely been alive, lying in my own blood. Veronica poured her feelings into my thoughts, letting me feel how she'd worried when she found me with the candlelight reflecting off my skin.

I tried to shake these images, but she kept the onslaught coming before I could erect walls around my psyche. She showed me pictures of Devon with his mouth covered in my blood. His eyes were black, red pinpoints burning in the middle. Talons had curled around my throat, ready to kill me. I had suckled from her neck and transformed.

Even though Veronica tried to use these images to guilt me into staying home, she just made me angrier. I had things to do. I shook my head and erected my shields as though I were putting on a suit of armor. Then, I pushed a rush of energy into my lover's mind. It was intense enough to fry her circuits; she let me go and reverted back to human form. Rage burned in me. Never before had she invaded my privacy and forced herself on me. Mentally, my abilities were stronger than most vampires, even some of the older ones.

Ignoring Veronica, I went back to the mirror to adjust my corset, since my tits had fallen out. I would go back to the Black Rose and discover the beast behind the killings. No one laid a hand on my friends. The Elder would talk. The thought of ravaging the beast that killed Zach was something I could focus my temper on. My anger called to the traces of demonic blood in me, building in my veins with my rising hunger. My eyes were turning black while their usual silver shade was wiped away.

The thing was going to pay.

I closed my eyes, gathering my thoughts and cooling my rage. I had to stay focused. Veronica wasn't helping. I pulled energy around myself, starting to shield when her hand slid around my waist, gliding over the boning of my corset.

My eyes snapped open. I tried to worm out of her grasp, but her strength was ironclad. One hand slipped underneath my jacket. Her fingers were cool as they circled my nipple. It hardened with her touch. She squeezed hard enough to elicit a moan. The pleasure of her caress drove away some of my anger. The thought of staying with her tore me in half, for I wanted to please her. Veronica's other hand went underneath my skirt, massaging my clit and making me wet. Her lips suckled at my throat, sending shudders through me as her tongue flicked over my skin.

"I don't want you to go." She purred and nipped my earlobe.

Everything in me wanted her. I leaned back, but I didn't want to encourage anything, even though I wanted nothing more than to throw her down and ravage her. Although she had made me, I could dominate her, since it was in her nature to give in. I remembered how it had felt when Devon forced himself upon me. I'd wanted nothing more than to have him fuck me. That momentarily loss of control was something I'd never let happen again. Now, Veronica was pissing me off, and that was not a good thing.

"Veronica, I have to go." I sighed. "I don't want the whole staff picked off. I can take care of myself.

You know that." My anger dissipated as she rubbed me harder, and I trembled against her as I held back my moans. Veronica knew what she was doing, but she wouldn't break me.

"Come…with…me." My voice shook as I neared climax.

She didn't answer me as her mind fluttered against my shields. I lowered them slightly and let her wind her thoughts gently around mine, weaving our personalities together. Her fear of losing me raced in my mind. I saw myself through her eyes, beautiful and dangerous. I also saw a loneliness that had never been there before, and something else—a slice of herself she'd kept hidden from me since her return from New Orleans.

Before I could discover it, she sunk her fangs into my throat, and I came. She swallowed a few mouthfuls while I shook in her arms as the orgasmic high left me. I realized a piece of her soul had been fractured with Devon's death. It had been months since her return. She'd never spoken about the time we were apart. Not even when I asked. Her mind begged me to stay, but I wasn't broken.

Her violet eyes shone in the half-light as I stared at her reflection. She wiped the blood from her lips with the back of her hand. "Stay with me," she moaned in my ear.

"I can't." I turned in her arms, seeing how beautiful she was. I moved a piece of her hair away and admired her. "I'll be back. Don't worry about me." I gave her a quick kiss on the lips.

"You're my child. I don't want to lose you. I love you more than the family I sacrificed. I want to spend as much time as I can with you," she said with a sad smile.

I looked at her questioningly. "Veronica, what's wrong?"

"Nothing." She smiled. "I'm just worried."

"I'll be fine," I reassured her. As I backed away, the emptiness in her eyes struck a chord in my soul, but I couldn't think of that now. I pushed her out of my mind and ran for the window, holding my jacket so it wouldn't get ruined.

Air ballooned around me as I was caught in a vacuum. The ground neared. My skin danced as my wings pushed on the inside of my flesh until the skin stretched and they burst out, drenched in mucous and dried skin that floated away as my wings caught the air. With the wind in my face, I forgot about my arguments with my maker. My instincts took over, and my rage was strengthened by my hunger. I would feed soon. Very soon, but first I headed for the Black Rose.

I LANDED OUTSIDE the club near the gated door. I tugged on the gate, but no one answered. Music blared through the brick walls, so I walked around the building. My wings sunk back into my flesh as I threw my jacket on. I found the stage door. The music was deafening, so I pounded until someone let me in. A vampire dressed in drag pulled open the door. Muscles the size of basketballs bulged from underneath his leopard-print dress. A blond wig hung on his head as tacky, large gold hoop earrings dangled below the fake hair. His lips were red, but I doubted it was lipstick that accentuated them. The aroma of blood scented his breath as booze did a bum's. I curled my nose at the scent.

"What do you want?" he asked as he examined me.

I showed him my fangs. "I'm hungry."

His mind tackled mine, sifting through my surface thoughts. I let him rifle, but I didn't dare raise my shields. Any sign of mistrust would have been bad. His mental abilities were crude, childish, but I doubted that was why he guarded the door. Just by the sheer size of him, I knew he could bend me in two. I didn't want to piss him off.

The bouncer stepped aside, and I walked past him into the music-filled club. I emerged downstairs, underneath the main room beside the coat check. The place was only half-full, and from the quick mental scan I did, I could tell no one present was powerful enough to be the Elder of the City. It was still early.

At the coat check, I handed my jacket to the boy behind the counter. The chill of the club hit my tits, but at a thought, my body temperature regulated. The stench of rotten garbage filled the air. The place teamed with other vampires, but there was something different about the boy. He was human, but with the taint of the undead on him. I looked closely and spied healing bite marks on his neck. He was marked, an undead-wannabe-junkie who would probably never see an eternity, just death. I held in a shiver at the thought of him wasting his life. I forced a smile as he gave me my claim ticket. I drew up my leg, resting it on the counter and winking at the boy as I placed the ticket in my boot.

"You should be careful who you hit on around here," a voice behind me chimed.

Glancing over as I put my foot down, I saw a woman leaning against the wall next to me. She was only five feet tall, slender and of some Asian descent with dark, blue-black hair spiked into a mohawk. I brushed my mind over her, but was surprised to feel nothing to indicate a vampire or any being even existed in her place at all. Intrigue and fright raced through me. I didn't know how powerful this tiny girl was, and I hadn't sensed her before. If she could hide herself from other vampires, then she was truly powerful indeed.

"Thanks," I muttered.

"No problem. Why don't you come upstairs? You'll find more appetizing meat there. Besides, if Zhen catches you with him, she'll skin you. Frankie is one of her favorites." She extended her hand.

Her nails brushed against my skin, sending an electric charge up my arm. She led me up a flight of stairs to the main room. The dance floor was filled with dry ice and smoke. A song by Siouxsie and the Banshees played on the sound system as a few vampires danced in the center of the room. In the far corner, a little dungeon had been set up with humans manacled to the wall. Undead gathered around them, flicking whips at reddened skin. The mortals enjoyed themselves, all wanting the monsters to suck and fuck them. A young woman writhed in her restraints as a female vampire brushed her long, black, forked tongue along the ridge of the victim's face while she attached clothespins to the girl's nipples. The human tried to cry out, but she had a ball gag in her mouth. A talon sliced along the girl's chest, a straight line down over her heart like an incision, and the vampire waited while blood dribbled over the wound, then began suckling.

This sight disgusted me, and I tried not to cringe. If I could have, I would have freed all the mortals from the clutches of the vampires, but if I tried, they would discover I was unlike them. I let my fingernails grow as well as my teeth. I had to let them think I was like them. Now was not the time for me to be a hero. I had to play with the demons to get close to the devil.

My host led me through a small doorway into an adjoining room filled with couches and chairs. A few more vampires filled this room. Some reclined on the settees and in each other's laps. I heard them snarling and growling as they made out. Their teeth clicked against one another as they tongued.

My host led me over to the corner behind a pool table, underneath a television that played random snippets of Japanese animation. Once in the corner, I had a good view of the room. I tried memorizing some of the vampires' faces in case I ran into them on the street. I tried to study them to see if any of them might be the Elder, but my host's presence was too pressing and forced me to focus on her.

"You're new, aren't you?"

I nodded, not sure if she meant to the club, or new to the vampire race. Probably both.

"I was hoping someone could help me," I pleaded, lowering my voice and keeping my eyes downcast. I tried being the submissive newborn she assumed I was.

My guide waited as I felt her hard stare. "Are you looking for your Master, little one? Because you don't seem to have a host."

"Yes, Mistress. I lost him. But I know he's in the city. I've heard of his kills. I was hoping the Elder here could help me." I put a lost child whimper in my tone, hoping it would be effective.

"I know nothing of kills in the area, or any new vampires. Trust me, I would know. And what makes you think you'd be able to speak to the Elder? Stop trying to fool me with stories of killings, child. I think you're just looking for companionship and don't know how to ask."

Her hands ran over my corset as her nails dug through the cloth. I caught her wrists and smiled seductively, but nothing about her truly interested me. Her lips ran the line of my jaw, making me shiver as the little hairs on my neck stood alert. Her mouth was soft, but cold and clammy. Her breath smelled of old blood. One hand worked under my miniskirt, trying to get to my nether regions. I tried to push her away. She reminded me of a sculpted doll waiting to be posed. A scowl crossed her face when she realized I wasn't going to return her advances.

"No one denies me," she whispered. A look of hatred crossed the vampire's face. Her skin rippled, forming the mask of the beast for a split second as she shifted quicker than I'd ever seen. Brown fur poked through her skin as muscle and bone rear-ranged itself into a flattened forehead, long ears, and stretched skin. Her eyes bulged and reshaped. Her lips thinned and her forehead pushed out, but the rage in her eyes died as the beast hid beneath a human façade.

"Forgive me," I said, lowering my eyes. I craned my neck, knowing that I had to play their game. She was the dominant one. I was a fledgling and had to be the submissive, as all good vampires were sup-posed to be. Moreover, if I didn't play by their rules, I'd end up dead.

Part of me wanted her underground, and that was what kept me going. Her lips touched my neck. Her teeth nipped my skin, and she drew a small amount of blood. She paused as she savored it. I waited for her to take a chunk of my throat, but instead, her hand came up under my chin, lifting my head so my eyes met hers. Vampires never did that. They always dominated others and never treated them as equals or showed any gesture of kindness.

"No, child. You demean yourself by looking away. It's obvious you're not like the rest. There's a spice in your blood I have tasted once before. It intrigues me. Now, tell me what you really came looking for. Maybe I can help if you won't accept my hospitality. I can guarantee the Elder will listen to you."

I stared back at her. Why did she want to help me? What did she mean, saying that my blood intrigued her? I wasn't going to pass up the opportunity either way. "How can I know that the Elder will listen to me?"

She chuckled softly and brushed a piece of hair from my face with the back of her nails. "Child, who do you think owns this place? Who do you think runs Boston? Nothing happens here that I don't know about."

I stared at her and backed further into the wall. "You're the Elder?"

She nodded and crossed her arms over her chest, waiting for me to respond. I knew not to let our little conversation go on too much longer. I was already in way over my head. If she was the Elder and I hadn't felt her downstairs, then how was I to know that she hadn't already been inside my mind? She might already know I was different from the rest of her kind. Why hadn't I listened to Veronica? Scratch that. I knew exactly why I hadn't listened. I was being my impulsive self and getting into deep shit.

I swallowed, knowing that I couldn't break the charade now. "A mortal I protected was slaughtered, and I want the vampire's head."

The Asian vampire clapped her hands. "Retribution. Oh, goodie."

It was my right to ask for vengeance. Humans marked by other vampires were off limits, just as the coat check boy was. I hadn't cared about him, but she didn't know that when I was down there. Even though I hadn't marked Zach physically, he was still mine. Other vampires bit humans to claim owner-ship. I protected humans, and that in itself was a rare thing. It was within my right to want the head of the one who had mutilated Zach. Sure, I was going to fire him, but I didn't want him dead. Now I had my chance to discover the location of the tyrant.

The Elder grabbed my hand and pulled me back into the room we'd emerged from. She led me through the crowd of vampires on the dance floor and went up onstage. The music stopped as all eyes turned toward her. I observed the room as she put up her hand to get attention, which she did only for effect, since her mind had already gathered all the other vampires like a fisherman casting a net. For some reason, her power didn't snag me. As I gazed around, I eyed about thirty of the beasts. If I screwed up, I'd be food real quick.

Scanning the room, I did notice another vampire in the corner with the shadows clinging to him. There was something oddly familiar about him. He had blond hair and was quite attractive. My hackles rose as my eyes swept over him. Warning bells went off in my mind. I should have been able to place him. He looked my way, sensing my interest, and smiled enough so that I saw the glint of his fangs in the black light.

"Children, there is one among you who seeks justice. Do we give her what she asks?"

There were murmurs among the crowd as the other vampires looked at one another. I sensed their enjoyment. They hissed at one another, laughing in their own perverted way. The Elder chuckled—some of her children must have been feeding her ideas of what to do with me. A sense of dread began to spiral in my mind.

Play the game, I reminded myself. *Just play along.*

"What shall her payment be?" the Asian vampire asked the brood. Her eyes slid over to me as I stood off to the side. Her mind played on mine as she kept the attention of the others. She was trying to get my take on the situation, and I was trying to keep my mind as blank as I could.

I obviously intrigued her, but I didn't need to pique her interest any more than I already had. Her mind wove into mine. As soon as it did, I knew she could cut down my shields without a second thought. She was that powerful. She showed me images of being tied down to a mattress. She was on top of me with my blood coating her mouth. A rush of pleasure moved from her into me. She assumed I would feel privileged that she had me in her view. However, that feeling never came, and I glimpsed all the humans she had tortured. Mental connections were a two-way street. And when I didn't react the way she wanted, her anger ignited.

What was I thinking? Of course, she's like the other vampires. If I want anything then I have to pay for it. It could mean an eternity of service. Fuck.

"Ask your question, child. I don't bite," she half-growled as her fangs grew. The hissing from the other vampires intensified.

"What kind of payment would you require?"

She studied me. Her thoughts sliced my mind and narrowed—she knew better now than to be hasty as she assessed my abilities. Possibilities of what to do with me ran through her mind. This vampire was older than any I'd ever dealt with, and I'd stepped into the center of her nest. Funny thing was, I never remembered seeing her before when I was a human. Then again, it was no problem for her to be invisible.

My eyes darted around the place, looking for possible exits. There were none except the way I'd come in. The blond vampire stepped up on stage and whispered something into the ear of my host. She nodded and smiled. I didn't like the gleam in her eyes.

"Payment can always be negotiated. Now what is it you came here for?"

I sighed. She'd forced me into an even deeper corner. How could I refuse her help now that I was in the middle of the lion's den? "There have been two murders. One was a mortal I protected. I came here seeking the beast's head."

The vampire's face remained blank, but a few grunts and groans came from those around me. The blond's face remained the same, but something in his aura shifted. He caught my gaze for a split second, and he knew I sensed the difference in him as he corrected the oversight in his energy field. His shields were erected so I couldn't read him. The change was quick enough to make me suspect that he knew something.

Many of the others laughed, hissing as their vocal chords shifted. I wanted to ask the blond what the hell he was whispering about, but to ask him anything would overlook the power of my host. I'd already pissed her off enough by rejecting her. I should have known I wasn't going to get anything out of them. She was just playing with me, as most undead did. I should have listened to Veronica. If she'd been here, my inquiry would have been taken seriously. The skin on my back danced as my wings wanted to unfurl and help me escape.

The rogue can wait. I can find Zach's killer without the help of this fucked-up brood, I thought.

Silently, I yearned to whack my head into a wall.

I glanced at the Asian undead once more, then at the blond leaning into her ear. Both of them were casting glances at me, and she smiled more devilishly than before. Her mind was gathering thoughts from her children in the audience. Her full attention wasn't cast on me, so I took a chance. I turned my back on her and pushed my way past all the other monsters in the room. No one said a thing, hardly believing I was behaving in such a manner. It was unheard of. Disrespectful. I didn't care.

I gave a side-glance to the humans in the dungeon. The girl I had seen earlier was dead. Guilt hung in my heart because I couldn't free her and the others, but I was outnumbered as I moved through the club, and I'd learned from my past to pick and choose my battles.

Never disobey the Master, the vampires' thoughts whispered against my mind. *Especially an Elder. Bow down and show your respect. Never turn your back. It goes against everything we are.*

I didn't care. Before they could break their stupors, I leapt over a bench and went subterranean as I landed on the hard concrete of the basement floor. The coat check boy stared at me. I smiled for a moment and thought about retrieving my coat, but that was foolish.

Screams of rage sounded from upstairs.

"Find her!" My misbegotten host screamed mentally as well as out loud. Her rage seethed in my mind, almost knocking me out, but I pushed it off and made for the exit. The drag queen from before was sucking the dick of some human. His head snapped up as I went by. The queen made no move to come after me. He was high on blood as it oozed out between the corners of his mouth like fake blood on a Halloween Dracula. The human had his eyes rolled in the back of his head, enjoying the sensation of being sucked and fucked. The greatest quickie there was.

I ran out the door as a thunder of vampires came rushing down the stairs. My wings burst out as soon as I hit the alley. They were coming for me, but I'd be ready. No matter how many of them came after me, they were all going to pay.

I flew until I reached Boston Common and was surprised to find that only two of the vampires from the club followed me. I'd assumed the whole lot was coming. Maybe the queen bee hadn't wanted to waste all of her good soldiers. Fine by me. Of course, that didn't mean I was free and clear. If these two were as old as the Mistress of the club, I would be dust. Still, I decided I'd take my chances as I landed by the Frog Pond.

The pond was a wonderful place for children to wade and splash in. During the winter, it froze over and was used as an ice skating rink. I'd never done either.

Slowly, I scanned my surroundings. There weren't many places to hide in case I got into real trouble. Oak, willow, and cherry trees dotted the landscape. Over to my left was Beacon Street with cars traveling down it as lights twinkled in windows. The full moon shone overhead. Soon it would begin to wax. The temperature was moderate. A slight wind blew twigs and leaves around the sidewalks. People strolled arm in arm as they went to their nightly destinations or caught a late movie. Pigeons pecked at the ground looking for crumbs. Squirrels chirped in the trees as they munched on stores of nuts, and now and again, I heard the ducks squawking over in the Boston Garden.

Even as I awaited the vampires, I wished part of me could enjoy the beauty of the park as I had when I was human. The only supernatural creatures I worried about then were the ghosts that lurked in the shadows.

A slight chill tinged the air as I thought about Azrael. My eyes settled on a shadow that seemed darker than the rest. Was it him, coming to watch the fight? Considering his macabre ways, if he wanted to watch, then so be it. Then I would ask him what the hell he'd meant by sending me to the Rose. But that would have to come later—the two goons had arrived.

I hid myself from human sight. Instinctively, I gathered my energy like a second skin, but the vampires still saw me. It was the only drawback to this kind of ability. One of the undead monsters was the drag queen I'd met earlier.

I growled, showing my fangs. It was the typical predatory thing to do, and I was one of the monsters anyway. The other was a black vampire. His skin was like polished ebony, and he wore nothing more than leather chaps. His nipples were pierced and connected by a fine silver chain. He was taller than me, probably six foot something. I couldn't help but laugh at the pair. They were the ones she'd sent after me. They were no match for me. This was why I had been born. To destroy creatures like them who thought humans were nothing but fuck toys.

The drag queen's fingers changed into talons. His red pumps split in half from his toe talons. He ran at me, but I anticipated his movement and jumped out of the way, landing a few feet from him. Then, the black dickhead tried. He circled, swiping at me with his claws. I jumped back each time, feeling as if I was in a bad gladiator movie. As I leapt back,

I didn't know what hit me until I felt hands enclose around my stomach. The drag queen had me in a bone-crunching bear hug, lifting me off my feet, trapping my hands. He pressed hard enough to crack my ribs. Pain shot through me as I coughed, struggling to take a breath. Blood trickled down my chin.

The queen tried squeezing the life out of me while the other grabbed my face and held it in his talons. His claws sliced my cheek and thin, red ribbons joined the dribbles from my mouth. The black vampire smiled. He brought a curved talon to his lips, licking it clean.

Shit, I thought. I tried moving again, but the drag queen hadn't relinquished his hold and had me too close for me to extend my wings. The ebony vampire slowly unhooked my corset, admiring my body. He got the garment off, cupping my tits in his palms. He weighed them in his hands. As he did, my nipples grew erect as he rubbed and pressed his thumbs into them, using them like elevator buttons. He looked into my eyes, waiting for a reaction.

"You feel good, young one. Good enough to fuck right now. Mistress will be pleased that we caught you. No one runs from her. You're lucky she's showing you mercy and doesn't want us to kill you. But first, we'll indulge ourselves."

His jaw stretched as it made room for uneven teeth. His nose flattened into something akin to a bat's; his ears grew pointed on both ends as well as furry. Coarse black hair sprouted through his skin. He shrank as his knees buckled to hold the excess weight of his wings, which creaked like trees in the wind. His toes extended and sharpened as his chaps fell away, revealing a hard, furry penis that rested against my leg.

Fumbling with my miniskirt, he ripped it off, and my stockings, as well. While all this was going on, I stopped struggling and closed my eyes to let my blood awaken. My hunger surged forward, giving me strength. My nature rippled through me like a fireball. My own mouth extended, allowing my double set of canines to fill in. My shoulders broadened as my wings pressed against my skin, but I kept them inside. My fingers grew, hardening to bone, sharp enough to slice through anything. My eyes bled black. The vampire pressed his cock against me. That was when my trapped hand found the chain connecting his nipples. I pulled, ripping the nipple rings off, and then kicked him in the balls. With that, he crumpled to the ground like any normal human male.

The drag queen dropped me, surprised his comrade had gone down. I turned on him, quickly slashing his throat, leaving half of his neck. The wound wasn't enough to kill him, but it would take him a few minutes to heal. Blood poured out of the open wound, black like oil as he slunk to the ground, giving me time to deal with the other one. The black vampire was getting up.

As he checked his companion, I grabbed one of his arms, raking my talons down his back, exposing his spinal cord. He screamed in rage and lunged after me. His claws caught my tit, slashing half of it away. As great as the pain was, I pushed it aside and let it, and anger, fuel me. Blood poured out of my wound, and the air stung the open tissue. I wasn't worried. I would regenerate with sleep and blood, but first, I had to dispose of the asshole in front of me.

He wanted to rape me. That was against his Mistress' rules, if she wanted me intact. If she wanted me so bad, then she would have to get me herself. It only took one to send a message. This one truly pissed me off. How dare he attack me?

The black vampire came at me again, decking me in the cheek. Another crack. I felt a bruise forming where the bone had fractured. Now I couldn't even move my jaw. I sunk to my knees from shock as all the blood in me rushed to the different parts that were hurt. The bleeding at my breast had slowed to a trickle, but my rib wasn't healed. Now my cheek tingled as the bone began to sink back into my skin, but it was still exposed. My attacker smiled.

On the ground, I waited. I called in all of the energy I could hold, even reaching into the environment. Momentarily, I even tapped into the other vampire. The extra energy flooded to my wounds and helped heal them. My temperature rose, expanding my aura. I felt like the center of a candle that kept growing bigger, burning brighter.

The black vampire was coming. His heartbeat thumped erratically in his heightened state. I sat, bowed almost in a ball. My fingers touched the ground, waiting for him. As he came close, I sprang. My claws dug into his exposed abdomen. I clasped them together, shredding any vital organ I could. The look of shock on his face was tremendous, but he still wasn't dead as he collapsed on the ground. His body was relentless, already starting to heal. As I got up, the heat diminished, giving me the strength to stand.

I glanced over at the queen. He was weak after losing so much blood from a near-fatal wound. If I'd gone deeper and severed his spine, he would never have regenerated. The black vampire held in his intestines as he tried to stand, but I saw his dwindling energy flowing to repair his injuries. Before he could do any more damage, I straddled him, grabbed his neck, and spun it around. To make sure he was dead, I rolled him over and reopened the wound in his neck, this time separating the vertebrae.

For a moment, nothing happened, then his body darkened and everything in him collapsed into a puddle of ooze. I winced at the stench that was left behind. Then, I turned to the drag queen, who was just beginning to come after me. My anger flared and I decked him, throwing him off balance in his weakened state. He folded on the ground and I placed my stiletto boot on his stomach as he looked up at me like a pinned bug. His leopard-print dress was smeared with blood and grass stains.

"Tell your Mistress I belong to no one. If she sends any more after me, I'll kill them as I did the other," I said, well aware my jaw creaked.

He said nothing, but reverted to human form. He was pathetic. The Elder had sent two vampires after me, and both had failed. When he returned without me, he would be humiliated. Maybe even killed. He was nothing. I could take his life if I wanted, and that knowledge filled me with pride and power. The heat in me surged forward.

The drag queen cringed and covered his face. I grabbed his wrist, wrapping my talons around it. Steam rose from the place I touched, as if someone had placed a hot poker on his flesh. He screamed high enough that some of the glass broke across the street. He got enough leverage to push me off so I landed on my ass, wondering what the hell had just happened.

He stood in shock, gazing at me in terror. Both of us watched as his tissue bubbled away. I saw the white bone clearly underneath his skin, and then his hand fell away. I stared at my hands. How could I have done that? It was impossible for a touch to eat away a vampire's hand. The only thing that could do that was exposure to the sun.

His appendage fell to the ground and lay against the coarse grass. It moved a few times before it went still. I glanced back at him and saw his stump. It was raw and burnt. There was even an indentation where my fingers had wrapped around his arm. The other flesh below his wrist was unscathed. He ran away.

The only marks on me were the ones that had been inflicted during the fight. I stared at my hands again, wondering what new power had emerged that had enabled me to do such a thing. It added to the mystery of what kind of creature I was.

I returned to a normal state. Pain shot through me as my injuries became more apparent and the adrenaline rush stopped. My body needed blood, but my first instinct was to fall into a deep, comatose sleep. In unconsciousness, my body could find salvation.

8

CHAPTER EIGHT

My name is Miranda.

The train ride home passed swiftly. I caught the last subway home on the Blue Line, as I normally did after my shift at Crimson Liquids. The smell of the salt filled my nose and clung to my skin as the sea breeze sank into my flesh. It woke me up a little after the ride home, but all the way, I thought of Julien and when I would see him again.

All night I looked for him, but he never appeared. I kept telling myself he was busy. He was probably looking for the mysterious woman he sought, or just doing business. Maybe he had led me on? Maybe he was actually dating the woman he was buying the club from. But I gave him the benefit of the doubt, and my thoughts drifted back to his kiss. He'd made me realize how lonely and how silly my life was; I was living in fear of a nightmare.

Julien wasn't a creature from a dream, but a living man who liked me. I'd forgotten what it felt like to have someone hold me.

I smiled as I unlocked the door and slammed it shut. It swung out of the jam, as it had been doing for years. So I rammed it with my shoulder and locked it so it would stay closed for good.

"Gina," I called as I flicked on the lights, looking for any signs of my roommate. I glanced at the living room and saw the pillows askew and figured Jeremy was probably over. Gina was a free spirit and never committed to anyone. She'd gone through five guys before she met Jeremy.

As for me, two years had passed since my horrible breakup with Gary. We'd dated for three years and had planned to get married. After leaving him, I'd been driven into a depression. My dreams had consumed me, but only for a little while, until Gina pulled me out of it. From that point, I swore off men, and now I realized how much I missed the physical contact. Not so much the sex, but actually being able to do things with a normal human being.

"Gina." I banged on the door that led to the basement. I heard laughter below, but to be sure, I opened the door a little. Punk rock music blared from her bedroom as I caught a moan or two. I closed the door and headed to my room, changing into my nightgown and hoping the memory of Julien would drive away the demons as it had the other night. It would be nice to have another night of dreamless sleep.

I padded into the bathroom, glancing into the mirror and wondering what Julien saw in me. Permanent bags were etched into my face. My blue eyes were tired and my blonde hair lank after not being washed for a couple of days. I turned on the water, but stopped when I heard a door creak open.

"Gina," I called again, sticking my head out of the door. I listened for a moment longer and heard nothing. My imagination was getting to me. I tried the water again when the floor shifted. Sticking my head out of the bathroom once more, I was met with the darkness of the hallway. Shadows created by passing cars moved along the wall. I shook my head. My dreams were getting to me.

I opened the medicine cabinet and took out the bottle of sleeping pills I kept for emergencies. Even when I took them I had nightmares, but I would sleep until the day greeted me. I couldn't rely on a natural night's sleep, so induced was what I got. That was one of the things Gary and I had disagreed on. He saw my solution in drugs, and I didn't.

After opening the bottle, I shook out two of the pills and placed the rest back in the cabinet. As I closed it, I grabbed my chest when I saw a reflection in the mirror. A scream rose in my throat, but it never escaped. There, standing in the doorway, was Julien, dressed in a black shirt and jeans.

"How did you get in here?"

He smiled. "You left the door unlocked. You should know better than that," he cooed.

My shoulder still ached from ramming it into the jamb.

Shit.

I swallowed while my hand fumbled for a nail file, tweezers, anything. I didn't take my eyes from his reflection as he looked at me, coolly savoring my fear. Suddenly, I realized how transparent my night-gown was.

"Gina," I yelled.

"She won't hear you. She's a tad busy." He closed his eyes, inhaling deeply. "She's wearing lavender, and he has something with a strong musk on, but the scent of their blood is even better. Their sweat gives their odors an even more magnificent and sticky consistency, so it sticks to my tongue like honey."

My eyes widened. He shouldn't know that. How could he know that?

"How do you know that?" I asked. My fear of him still ran through me. As it raced through my body, I became aware of the thing in my brain stirring. It was intrigued by the mention of blood. With that in the mix, my heart slowed a moment, and I wondered why he was there—and so did the other part of me.

Julien stepped out of the doorway, offering his hand. Tentatively, I took it. Part of me wanted to slam the door in his face and call the police, or escape out the bathroom window, but the other half, the hidden part, was in control.

Julien smiled as I followed him into the darkened living room. He sat on the couch, inviting me to join him. I did, but still stayed on the end of the couch. Moonlight streamed in through the windows, catching his skin and casting a gleam that shouldn't have been there. He was more alluring than he'd been the other night, as if he gathered power from the moon.

"What do you want?" My voice quivered as my fear crept to the surface. Whatever part of me trusted him slowly retreated. The comfort I'd originally felt, ebbed like the tide, replaced by pure terror. I shifted uncomfortably in my seat, getting ready to bolt.

His smiled faded as he sensed my fear. I stared at the door. It was still ajar, blowing in the wind as the sea breeze caught it. Before I could think of what to do, I jumped, but he grabbed my wrist, yanking me around so that I faced him. One hand came around my waist, and he pulled me into him and forced me to sit on his lap. His hands glided over my nightgown, taking in my body.

As his hands slid over my breasts, my nipples poked against his fingers. I kept my head down; tears streamed down my face and my heart thumped against the inner wall of my chest. I waited for him to do something—slit my throat, rape me—but he did nothing save run his hand along the side of my cheek and down my neck. He raised my chin to meet his eyes. He wiped away my tears with the back of his hand. His touch was soft.

This isn't supposed to be happening. He kissed me. We talked. He was supposed to be normal. What does he want?

"I won't hurt you," he said as he searched my eyes.

His expression gave me some relief. I sensed that what he said was true. With that, the other part of me surfaced again.

"Now, tell me again why you like vampires?" he whispered in my ear.

"They h-help me," I answered.

"Ahh, yes. They help you deal with the demons in your mind. But you don't know what true demons are. Now, tell me the truth. What is it you like about vampires?" He kissed my neck lightly and released his hold.

I melted as his lips touched my throat.

"My mother used to tell me a story about my ancestor. She was attacked by a vampire and lived. I've been fascinated by them ever since. Is that so bad?" I asked.

Julien chuckled. "Mortals are such fools." His eyes turned from sea-blue to steel gray. "Sometimes stories aren't just fiction; sometimes they're real."

He wound his hand in my hair, jerking my head back. I screamed then, hoping, praying Gina would hear me.

Don't fight him, a voice whispered inside my head. It came from behind the mental walls that had fallen when he arrived. But I couldn't listen. The voice was just the demon of my mind. All it wanted was for me to give up control.

Fuck off! I shrieked to the back of my head.

It was too late. As I screamed at my own mind, pain erupted in my neck and I lost consciousness. Before the darkness took hold, I heard laughter rising in the depths of my thoughts. Whatever I'd kept behind barriers was now free to roam whenever it wanted, and that filled me with an even greater fear.

THE NEXT MORNING, I awoke on the couch, wondering how I'd gotten there. I glanced over at the door leading to the cellar and saw it was open, and I heard cups rattling in the sink. I stretched and went into the kitchen.

"Hey, Gina. I was wondering if—"

I looked and saw Jeremy standing in his boxers doing the dishes.

"Hey, Jeremy," I said as he turned around. I padded over to the refrigerator and got out something to make breakfast, but as I bent over, a wave of nausea hit me. I came up fast and grabbed the door so I wouldn't fall over.

"Miranda, you all right?"

"Yeah. Why?"

"Shit. Can't you feel that? It looks like you got mauled by a huge-ass spider." He brushed the hair back on my neck.

At first, I didn't feel a thing, but when his fingers grazed the wound, pain shot through me, almost knocking me off my feet. My eyes widened as I flashed back to my dream. Julien had been there. We'd made love, and he'd held me until the sun came up. In my dream, he'd bit me as I came, but it hadn't hurt.

I figured all my thoughts of him the night before had manifested into one hell of a wet dream. The spider must have gotten me good. I rushed into the bathroom and flicked the lights on. The glare hurt my eyes, but I dealt with it, and pushed the hair back on my neck. What I saw was no spider bite. As I stared at the reflection, I got flashes of something else.

The memory was hazy. I had come in to get sleeping pills and seen Julien reflected in the mirror. Then I was on the couch and the thing in my mind was there, telling me to trust him. Julien attacked me. The rest of it was fuzzy. We were kissing. We were having sex, but he was gentle with me and something about him made me feel so safe. I shook my head as I realized my dream had never happened. Maybe I'd finally put a face on my nightmare demon. Panic overwhelmed me. What the hell was I going to do?

I rushed into my bedroom where I'd dumped my clothes from Sunday. Rummaging in my jeans pockets, I found Brenna's card. She'd told me this would happen, and I'd doubted her reading. I should have listened. I flipped the card over and studied her number. Maybe now she could tell me what to do.

I grabbed the phone, barely able to dial her number because my hand was shaking so much. The phone rang about ten times before a very drowsy someone picked up. I didn't recognize the voice.

"Is Brenna there?"

"She's sleeping. Who's this?"

"I need to talk to her. It's important. Can't you wake her up?"

"I'm sorry. No, I can't do. Who is this?"

"My name's Miranda. She gave me a reading the other day and gave me this number in case there was an emergency. Please. It's very important. You've gotta wake her!"

Silence greeted me from the other end as she contemplated what I'd said. "Fine. Wait a minute. I'll see what I can do."

I heard her put down the phone, and then some whispering on the other end. There was a long pause and the rustling of sheets, then another voice.

"Hello...umm...Miranda."

I barely recognized her voice. It sounded like Brenna, but it was garbled and sleep laden. "Brenna, I need your help. Everything you said was right. Something happened last night, and I need to see you. I need to know what to do."

Brenna groaned. "You sure picked one hell of a day."

"What?"

"Nothing. Today really isn't good. How about tomorrow?"

"No, it has to be now—today. Please!"

She sighed. "Shit. Fine. Meet me at the Tearoom around three. Will you be fine until then?"

"I—I think so. Thanks. Thank you very much."

I WAITED AT the Tearoom, watching the clock painfully ticking past three-thirty. I waited an hour for Brenna to show up. None of the other psychics knew when she would be in or where she was. They tried the house and got no answer, so I waited, impatiently looking over the store and drinking enough water to float away. I glanced over the variety of crystals, incense, books, candles and other paraphernalia far too many times until I sat back on the couch and rested my eyes.

But all I saw was Julien, or whatever he was. Then, when I thought of him, the thing in my mind stirred, so I tried to think about something else—but that was hard.

"Miranda, sorry I'm late."

I opened my eyes to find Brenna standing over me. She smiled. Dark glasses covered her eyes. An oversized sweatshirt and baggy jeans with holes in the knees seemed to enshroud her, hiding something. This was not the woman I'd met the other day. She took off her glasses and looked like shit. Her face was gaunt, as if she'd been bled. The veins under her eyes stood out. There were faint pink marks along the sides of her cheeks, as if a cat had scratched her, and the angle of her face was wrong. In her hand, she had a large cup, and the contents smelled vaguely like coffee.

She signaled me to follow her out back. I got up, following her into a small room where she shut the door behind us. We settled in on two high stool-chairs next to a glass table. There was a bookcase in the back with a table on the side. The room was a bit cramped and made me feel slightly claustrophobic.

"What's so important that you dragged me out of bed?"

The annoyance in her voice was clear. Instantly, I felt bad for waking her up, but she had given me her number and said to call her if anything strange happened. Well, something had happened. But, just by looking at her, I knew her night seemed to have gone as wonderfully as mine had. I didn't think I wanted to know.

"What you told me the other day was all true. You said to beware of a night visitor. Well, he visited last night and…oh God…" I collapsed and couldn't hold back the tears any longer. I'd tried to keep them hidden at home as Gina thought I was going crazy, running out of the house still in my nightgown.

Then I'd remembered that I needed clothes before I could hop on the subway. All the way into the city, I'd prayed that last night's events were a hallucination, but when I felt my neck, I knew they'd been real.

Brenna reached over, taking me into her arms, and held me, but only for a moment. Then, she shoved me away. When I looked up, her eyes were closed and her fists clenched in concentration, like she was fighting against an internal monster.

"What happened?" she asked through gritted teeth.

I recited my story, starting with how I met Julien, then going on to yesterday when I went home and he'd showed up at my house. I told her what I remembered and then showed her the wounds. Brenna seemed more interested in what he looked like and what he said than the bite marks.

She traced the wounds ever so slightly. Her touch was like ice that numbed the wounds for as long as she fingered them. Her face was grim when she glanced back up at me. She sipped her drink and sat in silence. At this point, I didn't care what it was. I would believe anything she said. She put down her coffee and stared deeply into my eyes.

"Miranda, do you believe in vampires?"

9

CHAPTER NINE

My name is Brenna.

The look of shock I expected to see on Miranda's face never came. She just gazed at me as if I'd told her something she already knew. So I waited a few more seconds, and still, she said nothing. I looked away, taking another swallow of my tea. The slight taste of blood in it helped tame my burning hunger, which raged through me hotter and more painful than I'd ever known. I kept chewing my lip to keep from crying out, to keep my secret from being exposed. Veronica had wanted me to stay home and let my body finish healing when Miranda interrupted my sleep. I should have stayed with her, but I knew that if Miranda was calling, then something was terribly wrong.

Veronica had woken me with Miranda's call and, to make sure I was all right, she'd given me some of her blood. I only took a swallow or two to fall back into the death-sleep, to let my body repair itself. I only went into a half-sleep, though, aware of all the hammering and drilling in my house because of the carpenters, the cars on the street, even the yipping dog in the house next door.

The light mode might have helped if I'd fed and had minor injuries, but after what I'd endured, it did nothing except help preserve my energy. My cheekbone had healed some, but the wound made my face look crooked, and a few scratches remained. My ribs were still broken with a few pieces of bone lodged in my lungs. It didn't hurt to breathe, not that I needed to, but I'd been spitting up blood for an hour, which was why I was late.

My breast was just a mass of tissue as it reformed, and half of my nipple was still missing. My tired body kept trying to heal, but I expended a lot of energy just to stay conscious, fight my hunger, and move around.

Being around Miranda and the other psychics was excruciating. Their heartbeats pressed against my skin, pounded in the back of my mind, vibrating against my teeth and keeping time with the throbbing hunger. I sighed, trying to hold it together. Never before had I been this hungry, and it hurt worse than I'd ever thought it would. My nature might not have let me kill humans, but my hunger was at the point where I might kill if my control slipped. That was why I had to hold it together. I didn't need any ghosts haunting my conscience.

When I'd arrived home the night before, Veronica had been livid after I'd told her what happened, and then she'd seen my wounds. She'd quieted and helped me into bed. There'd been no reason for her to voice I told you so. My words had been only half-discernable, my body already shutting down because I'd reached sanctuary. I should have waited to go with her when the club was open to the public on Wednesday, Goth night. Thankfully, she'd saved the lecture for when I was better.

"Why do you ask me about vampires?" Miranda asked hesitantly. I noticed her clenched hands on the table edge. If she had my strength, she would have cracked it.

"Because that's what attacked you," I said, running my hand through my hair. My nails scraped along my scalp, bringing strands with them. I looked at them and then shook them off, watching as they fell to the floor and added to the dust. "What do you know about Julien? Have you seen him before? Do you have any idea why he's following you?"

Panic appeared in Miranda's eyes as her fingers absently ran along the puncture wounds. I wanted to enter her mind to discover what she wasn't telling me, but I didn't even have the energy to use my vampire abilities, let alone my psychic ones. I was useless; I felt completely human, and it had been a long time since I'd felt that way.

"You never answered my question. Do you believe in vampires?"

Miranda nodded. "Ever since I was a child, I've had this dream in which one comes at me. He looks like a demon. It was like Julien came out of my nightmare. I read vampire novels to help keep the dreams at bay. They seem to help, but what does that have to do with Julien? Why does he want me?" Miranda asked.

"It sounds like your dreams are premonitions. Once a vampire picks a victim, it keeps coming until it claims you. They're demonic freaks that get their rocks off by tormenting others. Once you see them in full transformation, they'll haunt your nightmares."

I sighed and got up. The closeness of the room was getting to me. Miranda's heartbeat pounded in my ears, and the scent of this Julien clung to her pores like old shoes. When they bit their victims, vampire's saliva, their essence or whatever it was, fused into the prey. Especially if the wound was only a day or two old, other vampires could detect the scent. It was just like any other dog marking its territory.

"So what happens now? Is he going to come after me again?" Miranda asked. She tried to keep a straight face, but the fear in her voice was very apparent.

Miranda is helpless if Julien returns. I can't do that to her. She's an innocent victim, not one of the junkies who beg for it, I thought.

No matter how much I disliked getting involved, I couldn't leave innocents to the hands of the undead unless it was their choice, and obviously, it wasn't Miranda's. Dreams and nightmares may have plagued her since she was a child, but this particular beast wasn't going to claim her.

A knock erupted on the door. "Who is it?"

The door swung open, and Veronica stuck her head in. "Brenna, can I talk to you?"

I sighed and got up slowly. My bones felt like lead, and I swore I was one-hundred-and-twenty years old all of a sudden, growing weaker with each passing moment. I hoped my strength would get me through until nightfall.

"You look like shit." My lover gathered me in her arms. The lavender of her perfume lifted my spirits some. The color of her face drained as she felt my forehead and then my cheeks. "You have to feed, love. What are you doing with this mortal? What is so important that I woke you up, hmm? Why did I ever let you come out today?"

I kissed her lightly on her lips, feeling their warmth, well aware that my skin was cold and looked like frozen wax. "I'll be fine. And, yes, it was important. Now, what did you want?"

She handed me an oversized manila envelope. "I found this at the door this afternoon. It's addressed to you."

Inside was a red invitation with silver writing. On the bottom of the stationery was a black rose. I grinned. This was going to be fun. I read the invitation and then handed it over to Veronica.

"What do you think?" I asked as she passed it back to me.

She drew in a breath. I could hear the hollowness in her lungs as she inhaled. She wasn't happy.

"You can't go, but if you don't, then the Elder will come to claim you. What did you do to piss her off anyway?"

I smiled slyly. "Nothing."

"I'm going with you this time. You aren't being summoned until tomorrow night, so you have time to heal and feed. I would give you my blood, but it won't help much. Take it easy, and no buts. I'm your Master. You must do what I say, but I know you. Now why did this chick drag you out of bed?"

"She's been marked. She needs a place to stay, Veronica, at least until we can figure out what to do."

A scowl appeared on Veronica's face, but she wouldn't deny me and send Miranda away. It was against her nature, and she also knew how determined I was.

"Fine. She can stay with us, but only until you figure out what to do with her. We already have enough problems, or at least you do. I don't know how you got yourself involved with Zhen. Devon mentioned she was an Elder and said it would be a death wish to fucking deny her. For him to say that was something, since he was—" Veronica stopped.

My eyes grew wide. Of course, only I would get involved with a maniac undead. I shook my head. "I had no idea."

"What did you do to piss her off?"

"I turned her affections away."

"Shit, Brenna. You never…look, we'll deal with it later. I have to get home because another carpenter is coming by. I'll wait for you to get Miranda."

I went back in the room. Miranda would be safe with Veronica until I figured out a way to find Julien and dispose of him. "Miranda, I want you to meet Veronica."

I motioned her outside and introduced the two of them. "If you go with her, you'll be safe. You might even be able to sleep."

Miranda flung herself into my arms and gave me a big, long hug. I held the embrace for as long as I dared. Veronica looked at me, but I just smiled as she began talking to Miranda.

"How do you know so much about vampires?" asked Miranda.

I swallowed. "You could say I live with one." I eyed Veronica.

Miranda glanced over at my lover and giggled. I grinned stupidly at them until they went into the elevator, then I collapsed on the smoking couch.

PETER SHOOK ME awake. Opening my eyes, I focused on him the best I could. My vision blurred, and I felt as I had in my human days when I'd worn contacts. My body was eating away at itself. In short, I was dying, but I didn't plan on seeing the inside of a coffin any time soon.

"Raven, it's time to close up."

"Hmm. Yeah. Why didn't you wake me earlier?"

Peter smiled. "I tried to, but you sleep like the dead. I didn't think it would be such a good idea. Veronica said you weren't feeling well. You look better than when you came in, though."

"I'll survive." I got up slowly. My bones creaked and my head spun. Peter saw my difficulty and lent me his arm. I took it gratefully, feeling very feeble.

As he helped me up, he lost his balance, falling back into the sofa. I ended up falling back as well, landing next to him. My head settled directly on his neck. My lips were inches from his skin. The mixture of salt, sweat, and alcohol made for an interesting aroma. His pulse beat near the surface, and I focused on it intensely as he breathed. I licked my dried lips. My nails grew a little sharper as I wrapped my hand around Peter's shoulder and pulled him into me. My tongue met his skin as stale smoke filled my mouth, along with the faint hint of blood where he'd nicked himself shaving. My senses came alive as adrenaline rushed through me.

Peter shifted and tried to get away, but my power flooded his mind, pinning him like a bug. Whatever was in my nature not to kill was thrown to the side as the demon rose in my blood. Hunger was all I knew. I pushed back his personality so he was only an observer. Sharp teeth pressed against his flesh with the vibration of his life pounding against them. Panic flooded my friend's brain. I purred. My mouth opened wider to bite.

He would be a wonderful kill to renew my battered body, but as I anticipated the taste of his fear-filled blood, his feelings raced through my brain. The warmth of his friendship blanketed me. The panic in his blood lessened as he realized what I'd become. My hunger abated even though I was starving. I wouldn't take him. I couldn't kill him, even though he was willing to sacrifice his life just because he understood I needed it. This was too much.

I shoved the psychic away and darted to the other side of the room, pulling my mind out of his as he looked upon me with a startled expression. We assessed one another, and I understood how far I truly had fallen from humanity. My heart sank as Peter smiled as if nothing had happened. Fear still lingered in his eyes, but there was also a light of acceptance. I could never take blood from my friend.

I sank to the floor. Pain flooded me as a little bit of death crept into my limbs. It would be better to die than take advantage of one I loved. I cried. Even though it had been my destiny to become what I was, it would have been easier to remain human. Veronica was right. My existence was hard, and I didn't want it anymore. I'd almost killed my friend, and I'd vowed I'd never do that. I'd sworn I'd never taste blood from those I protected. I didn't need to kill— that was what separated me from the others.

"Raven." Peter knelt next to me.

"Go away. I can kill you quicker than you can light your cigarette. Just go away." I sniffled, finally having the heart to meet his eyes. He put his hand under my chin so I saw his warm smile. The heat of his flesh felt like a burning ember. Hunger scorched the back of my throat like hot bile. With all my inhuman strength, I was too weak to break his grip.

"Raven, stop blaming yourself, and don't let your vampire nature control you. You're better than your hunger."

That wasn't the answer I'd expected. As I searched Peter's eyes, I found comprehension. He knew what I was, not from just now, but from before.

How is that possible?

Psychic or not, I would know if he were in my thoughts. I shook my head and was surprised as a sense of serenity came over me. Peter was my friend, and he would never betray me. I wouldn't take those I loved. Somehow, I found renewed strength from his kindness and acceptance. My hands slid along the wall as Peter offered his hand, but I ignored it and walked into the main room, fighting off the dizziness and chill that was working into my skin. My vision was blurring and my thoughts hazy, but I waited as Peter shut off the lights.

"Do you really know what I am?"

He smiled warmly. "You're my friend, and that's all that matters."

I waited for him to say more as we rode the elevator down in silence, but he didn't. He strolled past the bouncers and the short line of patrons waiting to get into Charlie's. The cool night air helped clear my head a little, bringing my senses around to stop the insanity and hunger spreading in my body. The darkened sky held a few stars through the dim glare of the city lights. The moon was hidden, but its silvery light warmed my skin, infusing me with its silky power while the scent of the metropolis made me feel more alert. It wouldn't cure my ills, and soon my body would stop working, giving me a valid reason to see Azrael.

But I wasn't going to let that happen. Death wasn't my goal at the moment. Miranda needed my help, and I had to find the thing that had murdered Zach. Not to mention I had to clean up the mess I'd made with Zhen, which in the end might spell my demise as well.

Hmm… I weighed the options. *Death by starvation, or having my mind and body flayed by an ancient vampire.* Neither was appealing. Besides, there was still a lot of ass to kick first.

My face turned to the wind, catching the scent of mortals on the street. Wine sweated from a woman rushing to meet a discarded lover. Several teenage boys, college freshmen trying to score, strolled by talking about their next kegger that coming weekend. The pungent scent of an unwashed homeless man huddled in the stoop across the way came to me. These were only a few of the bunch, and all were appetizing, almost like I was at a Chinese buffet. A buffet where I wanted everything, but could only have what was on my plate. My hunger surged forward, and my teeth lengthened. Blood sang in my ears while a death rattle played in my body.

My ears perked up as I heard the distinct clicking of metal on metal and the faint hiss of spray paint. I even caught the hint of voices of two males in the nearby alley. Vandals having a night on the town. I licked my lips and felt my teeth tingling. I took a few steps forward, following my nose, as instincts began to take over.

"Raven."

I heard my name. My eyes fell on a human. Meat! The hunger almost had me. *No.* I knew that voice.

"No!" I screamed internally. I wasn't like my counterparts. I didn't need to kill. I forced the hunger back and stared at a blurred image of Peter, who smiled calmly at me.

"No matter what happens, you and I will always be friends."

I couldn't help but voice what I was thinking. "How do you know?" I was bewildered by his discovery.

"Edmund always said that if you ask the universe for something long enough, you'll get it. And you asked for years."

I chuckled. "You're right, but you're still full of shit."

He took out a cigarette, lit it with shaky hands, and took a short drag, enough to illuminate the ember and let it die. He said, "Veronica told me the whole story at lunch. She loves you very much. She asked if I believed her. I told her I suspected one day you'd get your wish, since you'd always carried on about vampires when you were younger. You wanted it so much, you were bound to discover the underworld of the supernatural."

"You're a good man, Peter. Everything in me says, don't tell. Humanity can't know. Thank you for that." I glanced down at the bricks, not able to look at him. "You've always been someone I could talk to."

"Like I said. There's a purpose for you being the way you are. You'll fulfill your destiny, whatever it may be. It's time good things happened to you. You had a shitty upbringing, but what we go through prepares us for our paths in life. Now go and have a good night. I suspect you'll be getting more action than me."

I smirked, letting Peter see my extended canines, and turned toward my prey. Veronica had told Peter for a reason, but it troubled me that she hadn't told me. There was much she kept from me. Her past hadn't been the best. Devon had practically used her as a chew toy while they were together, trying to make her into his perfect image. Sooner or later, she'd share. We had an eternity of nights to look forward to. Usually, whatever Peter told me came true, but tonight, his advice was just as vague as Azrael's.

I sighed, still lost in a sea of gray and wondering where to go. It was comforting, him knowing.

I smiled again and shook my head, thinking of how innocent I used to be. But that was a lifetime ago. Ages ago, vampires existed only in books for me. Now I was one. It was nothing like the books. In so many ways, it was better, but literature knew nothing about the true hunger threatening to consume me.

All my time of stalling was over as I found the source of the hissing I'd heard moments before. Two graffiti artists spray-painted their tags on the wall, hoping the dimly lit passageway would shield them from the passing beat cops. Silently, I made my way into the alley. I caught the first one and dragged him into the shadows as his buddy got high off the fumes.

I held him from behind, covering his mouth with my sharpened nails, and sunk my fangs into his jugular before he let out a muffled scream. I was so hungry I could barely contain myself, and his blood hit my throat like mulled cider and warmed red wine. My parched veins sucked it up faster than I took it. My senses returned to normal and my dizziness instantly vanished. Blood rushed to my wounds, healing the fractures in my ribs and fixing the angle of my jaw; I heard it clicking back into place. His heart thundered in my ears. The urge to keep drinking was overwhelming, but it was like a wall fell around me, and I had to pull away. I dropped the boy and left him unconscious in the shadows. I looked up and realized I was only partially healed.

I descended on the other man, who made a strangled sound as I took him. People who strolled by saw us in a lover's embrace and never noticed his prostrate friend. His blood scorched my throat, laced with the giddy rush of alcohol. My hunger demanded for me to drink him all in, like it had with his friend. His heart reverberated in my mind, and as much as part of my nature demanded I drink him dry, I couldn't. This was what truly separated me from my vampire relatives. I couldn't kill. Peter had been right. Why would I want to turn back the clock? This was what I was meant to be! This was my destiny. It was time things started to go my way.

I laid the tagger next to his friend in the darkness, knowing they would wake up semi-sober, wondering what had happened.

I leaned against the wall and let my senses readjust to the night. Everything was crisper. The blues and greens of the graffiti tags blared out like neon signs. My heart beat at a normal human pace, giving me the body temperature and pink appearance I was accustomed to as a mortal.

In the far distance, the static of the stars crackled faintly in my ears, or maybe it was only some white noise, but I wanted to believe it was the distant jewels in the night sky. I was free of all inhibitions that bound me to the mortal coil, and that made all my efforts worthwhile, all my struggles to deal with the remnants of the vampire race in me.

The night air caressed my skin with molecules, passing over it and invigorating me. The moon overhead hummed a silvery lullaby only night creatures could hear. Car breaks squealed as they stopped and started, getting caught in the tail end of rush hour. Nearby, Chinatown was bordered by the local fish market, which stained the very buildings and streets with its harsh aroma. Coffee wafted down the street from the nearby Dunkin Donuts, which was on every street corner in Boston.

I pulled myself out of the glorious wonders that surrounded me.

I had let my shields down, so people saw me. For once, I was just another body walking the streets, and I was content. Thoughts from the crowds of people pounded against my mind, but I pushed them aside, used to all the psychic noise. If I wasn't, I would have gone crazy long ago. Even though I wasn't cloaked, I still felt the cold presence that fell in step with me, calming even as it was harsh.

"Hello, Azrael."

He said nothing at first, but walked with me a few blocks. I didn't think much of it, considering he would make his intentions known when he wanted. His silence was just another anomaly about the angel I'd gotten used to. Ignoring him for the moment, I focused on Miranda and what to do if Julien returned. He was powerful, but I had a feeling the vampire was careless. If that were the case, then it would be easy to take him out. After that was done, I'd explore the nature of what had killed Zach and have my revenge.

Sometimes, Brenna, the answers to what you seek are right under your nose, the Angel of Death spoke in a whisper in my mind. I had never heard his true voice.

"What does that mean?" I glanced over, but didn't break stride. Conversations with the angel were always interesting. His face remained impassive and, if anyone saw me, they assumed I was talking to myself.

Brenna, I know you think my purpose is to deliver cryptic messages, but did it ever occur to you that I'm here to help? Even I cannot give you all the answers you seek.

He grabbed my arm, forcing his cold power over me so I had to stop. I stared at him. He wore his usual trench coat and suit underneath. His eyes always filled me with awe as they held countless stars in them, like mini-holes into space. His dark hair was swept back into a ponytail, glittering as if stars had been sprinkled over it. He held my gaze for a while, searching for something. I felt his ominous mind touch mine and flutter on the outskirts.

I held my breath and waited for the blow he'd dealt me before. Instead, his hand came to touch my face, but I shied away. Fear surged from me to him. I didn't want a repeat performance from the other night. An odd expression of sadness crossed his face. It was the first emotion I'd seen him express. He pulled his hand away, as well as his mind, creating a welcoming space between us.

"I don't know why you show up, Azrael. I should be thankful, but every time you give me advice, something bad happens. I went to the Black Rose to gather information as you suggested and nearly got killed. Then there's this girl I'm protecting, and I don't know where to start with her. What am I supposed to think with you popping in?"

Azrael sighed. His wings brushed against my aura like a sea breeze on a warm day. *Why do you care so much about mortals?*

"Why do you care?"

He glanced at me, and I knew to answer his question and not ask my own again.

"My instincts say humans are food, but deep down, I have this overwhelming need to help them. They're blind to the world around them. They don't see spirits or your kind. Hell, most don't believe in them. Sometimes I want to shake them and say, 'I'm real. Everything you dream is real. All you have to do is wake up and see. All you have to do is believe.' But they're blind and deaf to the world I live in."

That's not the typical answer vampires would bestow. Not even your beloved Veronica thinks that of humans.

She sympathizes with mortals, but leaves them to their own discretions. She feels no kinship or overwhelming desire to be known or recognized. It isn't because she's older than you. Do you know why she feels this way?

I sighed. My viewpoint was different because I was a different ilk than the woman I loved. Veronica was a meat-lover, a vampire who hated to kill. If the other undead discovered that, she was dead. It was a kill-or-be-slaughtered society, so around other vampires, Veronica acted as they did. I learned to project my energy field to pass like one of them. It was a matter of changing the harmonics of my aura to resonate like the rest of them. It wasn't hard, just taxing. But I fooled many a vampire, or at least I thought I did.

It was true I was different from Veronica, as she was different than the other undead. She saw mortals as food. Devon forced her for years to hate and slaughter humans, but she despised doing so, and now she didn't know how to act among mortal society. I'd always desired to help others. Being psychic was the way I contributed to the universal kindness bank. Now, after being turned, I wanted to make humans more aware that there were other sides to reality. I just happened to belong to a darker one.

"What does it have to do with me?"

Brenna, it's part of who you are. It's not in your nature to kill. No souls have come to me by your hand. You must be aware that sometimes the ones you chose to aid are not always what they seem.

"Are you saying Miranda is a threat? That I'm going to get hurt? I can handle myself, thank you." I took a risk getting involved with anyone I helped, especially one sought after by a vampire, but I wasn't about to let an innocent be hurt.

The Angel of Death said nothing, but took my hand, bringing it to his lips, brushing the surface of my skin lightly as if he were touching a flower petal. My heart fluttered as he kept his gaze on mine. It seemed, for an instant, that the world ceased to exist and I could lose myself within him. Questions I wanted to pose to him moved over my mind. I took in a deep breath and tried to understand what the angel was doing. The look on his face was beyond passion, even though he barely touched me and kept his eyes locked to mine.

"Why?" The word slipped out, but then, as usual, he vanished.

I sighed. I stayed stuck to my spot and passed my hand through the space he'd occupied. There was no sign that he'd been there. A sharp pain moved through me from a semi-born emotion I wasn't sure I was ready to accept. A moment later, the bats in my stomach settled, and I ventured home. I couldn't think about Azrael. Miranda was the priority, and maybe, just maybe, I could get to the bottom of things.

10

CHAPTER TEN

My name is Miranda.

The scene hadn't changed as I peeked out the window for the millionth time, hoping Brenna would stroll up the stairs. Pedestrians sailed by with shopping bags, leading children on plastic leashes, all on the way home to a life without monsters or nightmares.

I'd taken to counting the leaves on the shrubs outside. All afternoon I'd been in the house, waiting, but Brenna still hadn't returned. Even though I was being stalked by a monster, there were other things I could have been doing.

The house was a little drafty, but the afghan around my shoulders was warm enough. Scaffolding along the stairs and kitchen surprised me. Blue plastic tarps covered most of the furniture and lined the floor. Veronica gave me a tour, explaining they were fixing the house up so Brenna could sell it if she wanted. I asked her how long Brenna had owned the house, and Veronica chuckled. I'd assumed Brenna would live in some New-Age, semi-posh Beacon Street apartment with crystals and a variety of multi-colored scarves adorning everything. But this home had a country feel to it.

The couch was leather and squeaked as I moved around. Veronica and I talked, and we got along fine. After a while, it was apparent that she wasn't happy being my babysitter, and I wasn't the happiest being cooped up either. I had a café to run. My hostess asked me a few questions about how I'd met Julien. She seemed interested in my dreams and wondered how I had functioned on two or three hours of unin-terrupted sleep a night. I wondered that myself, but it seemed that years of not sleeping had made me immune.

Every time I caught Veronica's eyes, I felt a little more worn out until a calm descended on me, and all I wanted to do was surrender. Veronica promised me I would be free of dreams if I slept. I was skeptical, but I trusted her somewhat, so I closed my eyes. Blackness came over me. I drifted into a void I hadn't known existed in a long while. One without night-mares, claws or bogeymen. I was safe.

IT WAS DARK out when I awoke. I'd slept long enough to have dreams, but none came. At least that was a godsend. My body was so exhausted from everything it had gone through lately, I figured I'd blacked out. Streetlights illuminated parked cars, and the house was dead. Nothing stirred. I doubted even a ghost would want to live here. A chill rushed through me as an impending sense of doom raised the flesh on my arms.

"Veronica?"

I heard a muffled moan as something fell upstairs. Then, silence.

Fuck this.

I waited a few more moments and, hearing nothing more, I decided no one was home save the shadows. I was glad to be free of my nursemaid. Veronica was nice, but there was something a little off about her. I couldn't place what it was, but I wasn't sticking around to tell her.

Screw it. If Brenna isn't here by now, then she must not care. I'm not waiting here any longer. Okay, so a monster attacked me. But if he's coming back, then I want to be on my own ground, not this strange place. Besides, Brenna is just a regular person, and I don't want to put her in danger. It's better if I leave.

Everything in me agreed. I'd gone to Brenna for help, and she'd left me like a cast-off blanket. If I was so easy to get rid of, then fuck her.

165

Jeremy's and Gina's cars were in the driveway outside my house. The light was on. The door was slightly ajar, but that was nothing new, since it never closed properly. As I walked in, I wrapped my arms around myself and glanced around the darkened living room, seeing nothing except the open basement door. Pushing through a beaded curtain downstairs, I tried to ignore the Day Glo colors of my friend's room and the heavy scent of pot that clung to the air and carpet, and which, by now, was imbedded in the walls.

Gina's blue bedspread was in a heap on the floor. The bright yellow sheets were tangled on the bed. I switched off the stereo, shutting off some punk band, and my foot caught on the blanket. Tripping, I landed on the orange shag carpet and, when I looked back, I screamed.

This is not real. None of this is real!

The thing in my mind stirred again.

It's real.

No. No. No, I said to it and myself.

Shaking, my hand reached out and clutched the blanket. For a moment, I prayed, and yanked. I screamed again.

This was real.

Jeremy lay on his back, staring up at the drop ceiling with a vacant look in his eyes. A frightened scream twisted his features. Gina was next to him with a twin expression. Hopping over the bodies, I ran upstairs. I had to call the police. I had to get a knife, or something big and heavy, but the idea of a weapon blew out of my mind when I found Julien sitting patiently on the couch.

Julien smiled, showing perfect teeth.

"I knew you'd be back," Julien purred. "I've been waiting for quite some time, but then again, all I have is time. I got a little hungry and found your friends to be quite entertaining, especially the girl. Don't look so shocked, Mira."

Oh, God! Why is he here?

"You know exactly why I'm here." His eyes reached into my soul, trying to take hold, but I began backing toward the door.

If I can make it outside, I can get to a car. I can go back to Brenna. Why did I ever leave? I should have waited. Should have known he'd be here waiting for me. Why did I leave?

Why do you think you left? The thing hissed in my mind and I realized it had made the decision to leave the safety of Brenna's house. It wanted this.

"Naughty, naughty Mira. Trying to run from me." He was behind me, even though I hadn't seen him move from the sofa. Before I reacted, he picked me up by my neck so I couldn't get away, but his hold wasn't quite enough to choke me. He dragged me over to the couch. I propelled myself off the seat, not caring about anything except getting away.

He shook his head as if he were dealing with a disobedient child. "You realize I'm not going any-where."

I stared at him, looking at his fishnet shirt, blue jeans and bare feet. His toes were grotesquely long with translucent nails, and I wondered if he could hold on to a tree branch with those babies. Oddly enough, I wanted to laugh in spite of the seriousness of the situation.

"What do you want?"

"You," he stated plainly, vaguely annoyed. "You're mine." He studied me. "Didn't you feel our connection when we were at your shop? I know I did. I thought you'd been lost, Mira. But here you are." He half-smiled and ran the back of his hand along my cheek. I swallowed as I watched him draw a line across his wrist with a sharp nail. Blood welled up.

Something in me stirred; I licked my lips absent-ly. My nerve endings ached like little spiders crawl-ing inside my veins. For an instant, I looked at him differently. He wasn't the killer who'd taken my friends. His words made sense. I'd known him in the café. Something deep down had recognized him as one who could make me understand what I truly was, what had awoken inside my mind. The thing inside of me stretched and stared out through my eyes as we shared the same space, the same existence.

I watched him lick the wound clean with a black forked tongue between two sharp, pointed canines. The awakened part of me cheered.

After so long, it's time.

"Time for what?" I asked.

It smiled. Its sharpened teeth pressed against my brain. *One of my kind.*

My heart jumped into my throat. What exactly was this thing inside of me? What had been born the night my roommate committed suicide?

Desire for the blood spread through me. I tried to pull my gaze away from his wound, but I wasn't in control. Everything in me yearned to take his wrist as he offered it, but I fought the urge, tearing my gaze away, and stared at the floor. Disgust and sadness washed over me. My friends were dead because of him, and the monster wanted me next.

This isn't happening. Monsters only exist in movies. I'm not a monster. Whatever is inside of me isn't like him. It's just some repressed part of my consciousness. Maybe I'm some kind of homicidal maniac, and this is the voice they talk about?

"Child, why are you confused? Why do you fear what you are? Your senses tell you I've come for you. Your dreams were a beacon that foretold my arrival."

I looked at him blankly. He knew something about the thing in my mind. I began to shake as everything I knew fell apart. *Gina is dead. Brenna told me about vampires, and now one is in my living room. How can I ever be normal? Hell, my whole family is fucking crazy. Mom died trying to have my sister. Grandma was insane, muttering about beasts trying to tear her apart in her dreams. I was too little to remember Mom much, but Dad always said Mom wasn't right in the head sometimes. That she'd go off on tangents about evil inside of her and how she was unclean. He thought I'd be fine until I showed signs of not sleeping. Why hadn't I listened to Brenna? Why hadn't I stayed at her house?*

"I don't know what you're talking about." My voice quivered. "Kill me, rape me, just fucking get it over with."

I expected him to laugh, but he took my face in his hands and kissed me. I tried to pull away, but the thing in my head took control. His tongue pushed into my mouth, and the forks caressed mine. His grip was gentle, with his fingertips hooked under my jaw. The monster worked down my neck to the spot he'd bitten before. The wound became inflamed as his lips locked over it and his fangs reopened the punctures. Everything in me sang that this was right. This was how it was supposed to be. I felt a cold sting above my heart as he pulled the life from me, and whatever bliss I'd been trapped in stopped. I screamed. Brenna was right. He was a vampire, and I was in deep shit.

He downed a couple sips of my blood, leaving me faint from the loss and unsteady on my feet. Then, he patted my cheeks, looking at me lovingly, as if I was the greatest thing that had happened to him in the past hundred years. He smiled as I fell back into the couch. I tried to scream again, but he waved his hand and all my muscles froze. The thing inside me shrank, but not in fear.

"Silence, child. It's time for you to come home."

He bit into his thumb. A crimson drop balanced on the tip. He pressed it against my lips, which I pursed together, but the smell enticed the thing inside me. I squeezed my lips harder, but the drop went between the crack and onto my tongue. It was warm and tasted like sour milk. Another came, and another. As each drop settled, the taste changed from bad dairy to liquid sugar.

Tentatively, I dragged my tongue over the wound. His eyes were obsidian black as he watched how it affected me. The thing sharing my mind shoved me aside. Sucking desperately, it tried to drink in as much as it could, but the blood wouldn't come out fast enough. I cringed inside my mind, as part of me was doing this and enjoying it, until he pulled away.

"More," I heard myself whisper. I screamed, struggling to take charge of my body, but I couldn't. It, the beast, was in control, and I was being dragged along for the ride.

11

CHAPTER ELEVEN

My name is Brenna.

Strolling back to the house, I enjoyed the night, looking forward to seeing Miranda. I hadn't meant to be gone for so long, but I hadn't planned on being on the verge of Death's door. Then he'd showed up, lecturing me about how I should be careful who I got involved with. I hated being reprimanded, but he was right. I normally jumped into things without thinking, and honestly, something about Miranda didn't set right. It was the otherness I sensed inside of her. My heart told me to be compassionate while my mind echoed a warning. My heart was what I listened to most.

The conversation between the angel and I was the most normal one we'd ever had, almost like a conversation between humans. Moreover, he'd shown something new, an emotion.

Truthfully, I knew nothing of what angels' roles were in mortal society. I assumed everyone had some type of guardian angel, but I'd never really been sure. My experience with the celestial creatures was minimal. The only thing I knew was that Azrael took souls to wherever it was souls went. I didn't know if Heaven or Hell were even a factor in the scheme of things. And I wasn't going to find out anytime soon.

Still, something else bothered me about our meeting. I tried to block it out, but my thoughts were muddled. Something about him called to me. We'd never really spoken more than a few words to one another, yet his power over me was magnetic. I shivered as I thought about him and could easily see myself in bed with him. But my attraction to him was more than just physical. It wasn't pure lust that spiked through me when he appeared. It was a deeper emotion that only my soul seemed to recognize.

I sighed and unlocked the door of my home.

I walked past the scaffolding, pushing some of the blue tarps out of the way. The construction guys had started on the ceiling two days ago, and dust was everywhere. The tarps were meant to catch debris, but they didn't seem to be doing much good. Searching the kitchen, I ran my hand over the wooden countertop. My palm caught on the remnants of the knife blade embedded in the wood. The knife had once held a message for Veronica. It brought back a few memories from when I'd been human.

Veronica and I had been asleep. Devon had come shortly after sunset and kidnapped me. He'd locked me in my mind to silence me. I'd been so afraid, mentally calling to Veronica, but she'd been lost in the deathlike sleep of the vampire. Devon had dragged me to the Tearoom, draining me to the verge of death as he waited for his former protégée to arrive.

Devon, my would-be Master, had lined my lips with his blood so my soul became trapped in my dead flesh, allowing my heart to beat for the few precious moments it took for Veronica to rescue me. Then, after Edmund had encouraged her, she'd changed me.

I always wondered if Devon's blood had affected me somehow. He had fooled me into thinking he was human, calling himself Cain. He used his shape-shifting ability to trick me into loving him. It took enormous amounts of energy to accomplish the feat of complete physical transformation. Most undead took on their normal appearance, wiping their prey's mind or cloaking themselves, but older vamps loved to show off.

The undead also had another face besides the human one they presented to the world. That of the demon with brown fur. The face of a bat. A snout of a dog with jagged, sharpened teeth. Toe and finger talons as hard as bone, and wings like old leather that creaked when they flapped. Vampires could also change into a gargoyle-dog akin to a hellhound. It was part of the makeup of the demon. I had these characteristics as well, but I'd never tried to change into the Hellhound. I never saw a reason to.

My other appearance wasn't as demonic as the others, though I had toe and finger talons, but my mouth only extended some, giving me room for four daggered teeth. My wings weren't leather, but fine bird down, black as night, and I never sprouted fur. This was because I was set aside from other vampires. It was also what saved me from having to kill humans in order to live, thus separating me from the demons.

As I remembered the vivid events of my own transformation, I understood what Miranda had been through.

Heading into the living room, I couldn't find either inhabitant. Miranda's scent permeated the space. The blanket was askew on the sofa with the curtains pushed back over the window as if someone had been watching out of it. I listened, hearing two heartbeats upstairs. One barely beat. Veronica. The other raced along like any normal human's. The panic in me lessened, but to make sure, I ran up the steps two at a time. The bedroom door was slightly ajar, so I poked my head in and saw Veronica on the bed.

She was on top of a man, riding him like a deranged bull. The scent of blood rose off the both of them. Her lithe body remained free of sweat, and her full breasts rubbed against her meal's chest as she fed. The sight of them held me spellbound.

The man had his eyes closed, lost in the pleasure of the feeding. He panted, on the verge of orgasm as Veronica rode him. I watched them a moment longer and noticed the flesh dancing on Veronica's back. This wasn't typical of my lover. She fed on the dying, and nothing about this man suggested he was sick. Ronnie must have gotten the better of Veronica and taken over. If Miranda had woken and found Veronica gone and me not there, she'd probably thought I'd deserted her and gone home. If she had, then she was in danger, as I had a nagging feeling Julien would be waiting there for her.

There were hundreds of possibilities as to what could have happened, but my gut said she'd gone home because she felt safe there.

"I can't believe you!" I screamed.

My lover stopped in mid-thrust, unhooking her fangs from her meal. Blood was smeared on her mouth and her eyes were blacker than volcanic ash. It didn't bother me that she was sleeping with the man. It bothered me more that she'd gotten careless.

"Brenna, why did you interrupt me?" She glanced at the man under her.

"Miranda's gone."

Realization crossed Veronica's face, and only then did she climb off her prey, wiping the blood from her lips, leaving crimson smears on her pale skin. "Brenna, I'm sorry. I made her sleep and thought it would last all night, or at least until you got home, which was supposed to be hours ago. I wasn't going to force her to stay. You look better, by the way. I'm sure Miranda's fine. If there's any trouble, then she'll come back. Don't worry. Besides, she's marked. She already has a Mas—"

Before I could think, I slashed at Veronica. I couldn't believe she'd leave an innocent to one of them. My fingers sliced her cheek, leaving thin rivulets of blood running down her jaw line, but they disappeared as the wound turned pink, sealed and vanished, as if no damage had ever been inflicted.

"You of all people should know better than to say that. How dare you?"

The look on her face rolled into rage as she fought to keep control. I growled. My fingernails sharpened, but I clenched my fists. This was getting us nowhere. Miranda was the priority. I didn't have time to play petty games.

"Enough, Ronnie. I don't have time for this. I'm going to find Miranda. Thanks for all your help."

I turned and walked out of the room. I was going to explode, but it was best to do that when I found Julien. I'd trusted Veronica to watch out for my charge. But, no, she'd chosen to fuck someone instead.

I unclenched my fists, closed my eyes and concentrated on Miranda. My instincts told me she'd gone home. I remembered the house I'd seen when I first met her. I saw the overall landscape and what the house looked like. I smirked. The neighborhood was familiar. It was Revere, a place where I'd lived for a year with Edmund, but that was a different lifetime. The house Miranda lived in wasn't far from the old place I'd inhabited. As I double-checked the picture in my head, hands wrapped around my waist.

Veronica's tongue flickered against my flesh, but she still wasn't my Master. It was the other trying to entice me to stay. I unwove myself from her grasp and left the house. As I jogged down the street, I cloaked my appearance and flipped off my sweatshirt to allow my wings to emerge from underneath my skin.

Flying as fast as I could, I followed the Blue Line subway into Revere, praying Miranda was all right. Once there, I took in a long breath out of habit, enjoying the salt air. The house was painted sky blue, with a small front yard with brown crab grass sprouting through the lawn. Porcelain garden gnomes dotted the lawn, and a small bird feeder dangled above a shrub in a window. It was quaint. The driveway held two cars, and the outside light was on with the front door open. I pulled the screen door slowly. The scent of stale death filled the room, along with the smell of dead fish. A vampire had been here.

Damn.

There were no heartbeats here, but Miranda wasn't dead. The smell of her blood didn't scent the house. Besides, she was too valuable. I just had to figure out what the monster wanted from her. All vampires had perverse reasons, but Julien's were different because Miranda was unique.

I opened my senses and picked up two humans downstairs. I didn't need to go into the basement to know they were dead. A cry of anguish ran through me. If I hadn't gone to the club last night, I might have helped Miranda escape her demons rather than having to face her nightmare. All this had happened because I'd been my usual impulsive self.

I slammed my fist into the chair, and my nails got stuck, but as I pulled my hand out, some of the foam stuffing came with me. Mentally, I scanned the rest of the house and found nothing, though I'd been hoping to find some kind of psychic impression of what had happened. But nothing lingered. Miranda was lost for now, but not forever. I didn't know where to start.

I sent a questioning thought to my guides to see if they had any insight, but all I got back was silence. I was on my own. Glancing around the house, I wondered where Julien's nest might be. If he'd left these corpses behind, then I knew his lair wasn't close, because he didn't fear discovery. I sighed and left; there was no more I could do here. The leads were as dead as the bodies in the basement.

So many things swam in my mind that I became confused. I walked out of the house and across the street to the beach, wondering where to start. Zhen would have my hide or something even worse. But I had to finish what I'd started or else Veronica would be involved, and I didn't want that.

The sand felt good under my feet as the sound of the waves soothed my rage, but they also made me remember everything I'd left behind. There were days, when I was a child, that my grandparents and I had strolled for shells. Days I spent with my father bowling, or just loafing around on a Saturday watching television before my music lesson. I'd had all of this before I was transformed, before I cut all ties with my family save the occasional brief letter letting them know I was all right.

They didn't know their daughter was a walking corpse, a demon that wasn't really a demon. The loss of my humanity troubled me. I'd never really dealt with the fact that I was dead, that I'd left another life behind. Everyone thought I wanted nothing to do with them. I continued as if life hadn't stopped and I hadn't changed, but I had. Images from my sharpened memory floated before me. Collapsing on the sand, I began to cry.

Twice in one night. This might be a record.

I looked up and saw Azrael sitting next to me on the sand. His wings weren't visible, and he wore only jeans and a black T-shirt. No trench coat or suit. He looked more comfortable in the suit. His hair was pulled back in a ponytail. Strangely, he seemed more approachable. This time, when I looked into his eyes, I saw myself reflected as in any normal human eyes. My heart caught in my throat, and I swallowed an undefined emotion. His presence allowed me to forget some of my woes and, for once, there was no coldness around him.

"Hello," I sniffled.

He smiled and stretched out his hand to wipe my tears away, but I shied out of his reach, remembering what had happened the last time he'd touched me. A look of dismay crossed his face, but he didn't take his hand away. It was apparent that he ached to touch me. But the fear still lingered in my being, even though my instincts told me that if he touched me, it would be sweeter than anything I had ever known. I took in a breath and wondered what magic he was working on me. Since he was an angel, he could do anything he wanted.

"I will not harm you," he whispered without using his mind. His voice was soft and low. At first, I thought it was the wind. "The other day in the café, you were irrational. I only wished to calm you. I never intended to cause you harm."

The sincerity in his eyes was overwhelming. I didn't know if he could lie.

"It was so cold. It felt like you were pulling out my soul—"

His fingers brushed away my tears and then his arm wrapped around my shoulders, pulling me into him. "I wouldn't do that unless there was just cause. Do my actions wound you now?"

"No," I whispered as I nestled in the crook of his arm. The fragrance of frankincense and lilies surrounded me. The scent of funeral homes, of churches. The aroma of death. The breeze lessened as the angel's wings encompassed me, protecting me from my internal storm. It felt so right to be with this strange creature who could kill me with just a simple gesture, and I trusted him completely.

"You must stop condemning yourself for all dire events, for what you left behind. You made a choice before being born to this existence. Yes, you miss your innocence, but that part of your life has fallen away like childhood does. I feel how your heart suffers, but you made your decision. As much as it would please me to help you unearth the answers you seek, I have obligations, and there are times I can't just appear on a whim. But it seems I can't resist you, and that is an enigma to me."

I looked at him quizzically. Why was he so concerned? I had nothing to do with the mortal coil. I was on the other side of the spectrum from him, which was one reason I wondered why I was reacting to him so strangely. The demon in me told me to shun him, but the mortal side trusted him, and was the part of me that reacted to him like he was a shelter amidst a stormy sea. If I trusted him, I could tell him all my secrets, and he would understand with no questions asked.

"Azrael, why are you here?"

"Why is the sun suspended in the universe? Why are the stars arranged in the atmosphere? That is a question only the Divine Source can answer."

I sighed. This was the typical answer. His voice was smooth and calming, and I felt more relaxed than I had in months. With him, I didn't have to think about blood or killing. He offered me his arm and we stood upon the sand. I wanted nothing more than to try to figure him out. What made him tick, but the more time passed, the more I knew he was right. I couldn't blame myself for everything that had gone wrong. Even if part of me mourned my humanity, I did choose this existence and everything that went with it. But I wasn't ready to look back and embrace my past.

Miranda had chosen to leave the house, and I had to find her. It was my responsibility since she'd come to me. It was my duty to help others. Veronica filtered into my mind. Her call got past my blocks, pulling me home. There was sympathy in her summons. Much of me yearned to be in her arms with her nipping at my throat. With her breasts pressed against mine as they'd been so many times before. The image danced through my mind, and I smiled.

But another part of me could easily have turned around and tried to seduce the angel who protected me from myself. It would be so easy to make that turn and brush my lips against his. To feel my hands wound in his hair and prove that it was made from threaded silk. My fangs tingled as I thought about him. I wanted to explore every inch of the creature before me, but I shook my head. That wasn't a possibility.

It was then I realized I was topless. It seemed sacrilegious. I grew self-conscious and crossed my arms over my chest, trying to hide my breasts. For some reason it felt wrong to be half-naked while I was with the angel. I doubted he cared, but I did.

Azrael noticed the change in my demeanor and laughed. Without saying anything, he pulled his shirt over his head and gave it to me. I couldn't help but stare at the smoothness of his chest and the subtle rose color of his nipples. He looked as if he'd been carved instead of David. There were no flaws, no scars on his skin. I wanted to run my hand over his formed torso and see if it was real.

Before I could stop myself, my hand touched the flesh above his heart. I never took my eyes from his. Thoughts of what could happen with him slid through my mind as easily as we might slide between satin sheets. But the angel just stared at me. A look of wonderment painted his features. He wasn't used to being touched. He was used to being feared.

His eyes changed color from black to deep purple. There was no heartbeat underneath my hand, just the subtle rise and fall of his chest as he breathed in and out. He met my gaze, almost challenging it. I wondered what was going through his mind as we stared at one another for a frozen moment. Angel and vampire locked together in eternity while the planets spun and the universe was all but silent. His silken lips were inches from mine, close enough that I felt his warm breath on my face. It smelled faintly of roses.

My heart skipped a beat and thundered in my throat. I drew in a ragged breath, feeling that I should be cowering in front of such a magnificent being. A knot formed in the pit of my stomach. Something bloomed in me, and I didn't know if what I felt was true. My skin was alight with fire and cold all at once. His power pulled me like the tide, and I lost my sense of self. The sound of the sea was silenced. Even the salt air didn't penetrate our moment. We were in a soundless vacuum as his wings enclosed fully around us. I felt his hand on mine. Every atom in me was aware that he touched me. It was as if his hand had brushed my face or my lips. The caress zinged inside me, making me shudder.

I held in a moan as my insides quivered. I bit my lips so hard with my regular teeth that blood seeped into my throat. I swallowed as the angel moved my hand from his chest. The moment was slow and fluid at the same time. I didn't resist as he moved me away, but somehow, I sensed reluctance in him. I let out a breath and blinked. Reality set in as the angel drew back his wings and backed away a few steps. The spell over me was broken, and the fleeting moment in which time had been suspended had passed.

Part of me cried out when we parted, for I was no longer in the protective shelter of his wings. I blinked, as we weren't on the beach any longer, but standing in front of my front steps on Beacon Street. I was wearing his shirt. His display of power was marvelous, leaving me a little dizzy. His eyes were still dark, and his fingers clenched. He glanced away, and his breath was labored as he tried to regain his composure. So much of me wanted to breach the distance between us again and soothe the angel.

"How?" I whispered as his star-filled gaze turned on me again.

He smiled. The atmosphere thickened behind him. A dark blue haze twisted behind him like a mini black hole. Shadows elongated and wrapped around him, pulling him into them. "You shall unearth what you seek in the dungeons of the abandoned ancients," he said softly as the hole swallowed him up.

Dungeons of the ancients?

I shook my head. That was the angel I was used to. He was a strange being I didn't understand and probably never would. In his own way, he guided me through life in its darkest times, and being a pain in the ass seemed to be a prerequisite. But still, something about our most recent encounter continued to throb deep inside of me. I doubted I would ever be the same again.

Now that the angel was gone, Veronica's cry exploded in my brain. The feel of her arms would chase away the haunting feelings Azrael had left behind. Still, as I climbed the stairs, I knew I had Miranda to worry about. There was nothing I could do for her right now. I would try and find her tomorrow night after I went to the nest. Hopefully, Zhen could provide me with the information I needed about the thing that had killed Zach and the other woman. I hadn't forgotten about them. Things had just fallen to the back of my mind.

I felt itching in the back of my skull, but I dismissed the beginning of the premonition, knowing it would be all doom and gloom. I'd had enough for one night. Besides, Veronica's smiling face was more important than my guides.

"Hi." Her lavender eyes looked lovingly at me. "I've been calling—I thought for a moment—I couldn't feel you. I didn't want to assume the worst, but—"

The look on her face was tragic. I let her take me into her arms and lead me upstairs. My troubles could wait until tomorrow, when the monsters of the night had fallen into their slumbers and the sunrise drove away all the evil spirits.

12

CHAPTER TWELVE

My name is Miranda.

It was cold and damp when I opened my eyes.
Rough rope scratched against my skin as I tried
wriggling my hands free. They were tied together in
front of me while I sat on an old mattress. I scanned
the room, wondering how I'd gotten in this small
concrete cell. Papers were strewn on the floor. Small
trickles of water ran down the walls. Pieces of disinte-
grating cardboard littered the floor, along with some
other indescribable material.

I stood up, trying to walk, but sank down on the
mattress again, losing my balance because my head
swam like a washing machine on the spin cycle. I'd
gone home from Brenna's and when I'd gotten there,
I'd found…

Oh God! They're dead!

The image of my friends' bodies haunted me. The contents of my stomach came up. I wiped the back of my hands over my mouth to be rid of the remains and walked over to the other side of the room to get away from the stench. My hands trailed over my neck, locating more wounds.

Pain jogged my memory a little. I remembered the taste of Julien's blood. The recollection alone awakened the thing in my mind, bringing it up to the surface along with a terrible thirst. The other seemed stronger than before. It was more aware, pushing against the back of my eyes, waiting for a moment when it could pounce and take control completely. However, I was still the one ruling my body. I ran my tongue over my lips. They had never been so dry. I needed something to quench my thirst before the parched feeling drove me insane.

Searching the cell frantically, I saw the water on the wall, but from the dank smell of the room, I knew it was foul. Footsteps crunched down the hall. It was Julien coming to finish the job. My heartbeat quickened, but the thirst remained.

Calm down, it whispered in my mind with more definition than it had ever had. *He won't hurt you if you obey.*

Obey? I didn't think so. *I need to get out the hell out of here,* I thought. *He's a nut, and I'm not going to die.*

I scanned the room. There was no way out, just the dim light seeping through the glass window, which was now blocked by the shadow of a man. The door creaked open, letting in a blast of even colder air. The man outside stepped in. His presence filled the room. I stared down at my feet, trying to avoid his gaze, but my mind took over.

I smiled seductively even as I feared him. He was irresistible to the thing inside of me. It recognized him on a deeper level than I understood. We didn't share the same thoughts, but we were connected to one another. He watched with interest as he knelt beside me and returned my smile. I tried to become part of the wall, tried to will myself home in my bed, but Julien reached out and stroked my cheek. I shied away, bringing my knees up close to my face. My heartbeat drowned out what he whispered. Instead of hearing my own heart, I heard the other whispering inside my mind.

He spared your life. He won't hurt you. He won't hurt us.

Shut up! Leave me alone. You're nothing but a hallucination trying to drive me insane.

Laughter filled my thoughts, echoing into every fold of my brain while my thirst spread into my veins. I gritted my teeth against the pain, trying to think of something soothing, a cool breeze, water lapping at the sand. Even as I did, the thing in my brain stirred, expanding underneath my skin like snakes fusing with my muscles. I tried to fight it, but the slightest movement made it more determined, causing my body more pain.

"Please stop," I whispered to it.

"I can make the pain go away, Mira," Julien answered.

The coolness of his palm felt good on my sweaty cheek, helping calm my burning veins. The snakes ceased winding around my bones. I looked into his eyes and saw my reflection. I was sweating, begging for release.

If you accept him, I'll stop. Deny him, and you'll writhe in agony for an eternity.

Of course I want it to end. I want everything to stop, but he is the cause of the whole mess. He kidnapped me, then awakened the thing in my mind and made it stronger. He killed Gina and Jeremy. Doesn't that mean anything to you?

What the fuck do I care about a couple of slabs of meat? They were only human. Don't you want to discover where I came from, why you and I are so close?

I don't give a shit where you came from. I just want you out of my mind, and I want to get away from him. I'll never let him take me.

With that thought, the thing redoubled its efforts to merge with me, and I felt like a corkscrew was slowly pushing into my veins. I doubled over, falling into my captor's arms. The intense heat increased and my vision blurred. I bit down hard on my tongue to keep from screaming, but I couldn't fight it and agony washed over me as the thing burrowed its way into my bones like termites into wood.

My heart picked up speed as if I'd run a marathon in a matter of seconds. The air grew heavier, and my eyes fluttered as I tried to stay conscious. As I closed my eyes, I glimpsed the face of something I'd thought was only in my dreams. It was a demon, just as Brenna had described it. Dark hair, large leather wings, a black, forked tongue. Internally, I screamed, but even as terror filled me, somehow this creature felt familiar, as if it had been with me all along, waiting to break free of its chains.

Stop fighting. Accept me and this can all be over. Accept him and both of us will be free. Its voice was as persuasive as the pain was crippling.

I wanted the pain to end, and the only way to make that happen was to give in to one of them. I fought to open my eyes and felt Julien run his hand across my forehead.

"Help me," I whispered.

"I can only help if you answer my question. Tell me the truth this time."

A question. He had to be fucking kidding. What could be so important when I was dying in his arms? My lips were shrinking and cracking, my tongue expanding and making me gag. My organs stuck together as if all the water inside me was draining away, leaving me like a dried husk.

"What q-q-question?"

"Why do you like vampires so much?"

I'd already answered that. What else did he want? "They've always been around me, inside of me, it seems." Another shudder seized me.

Julien held me down as it ran its course. I bit down on my tongue, taking a chunk, and felt blood trickle down my throat. It was mine, but it tasted good. "They help settle my dreams. My ancestor was attacked by one, long ago, in France. Please—I don't know what else you want." I screamed as another tremor coursed through me. The thing under my skin started snaking around again, delving deeper.

Julien kissed my forehead, his lips cool as I now lay on his lap. "That's good for now, Mira. You're not yet far enough along to give me the answer I desire. Drink—it will ease your suffering."

Blood dripped into my mouth, tainted at first, then growing sweeter, reminding me of honey as it had the same texture. It went down easier this time, and as soon as it hit my stomach, the pain evaporated and the thing stopped worming around in my body. The yearning for more made the thing surge forth, pushing me aside.

My mouth opened wider and pulled Julien's wrist into our mouth—my mouth and that of the thing—and drank, taking in his life. Even though it had shoved me aside, I desired blood with it, not knowing why or how. My other merged with me, bringing me into its embrace. Our reasons fit together like a puzzle, different parts of the same soul, as if we were always meant to be together. We took a few more swallows, and then Julien pushed us away. When we looked up at him, he showed his fangs. As he did, we didn't fear him any longer.

"Hello, little one. It's good to see you again."

13

CHAPTER THIRTEEN

My name is Brenna.

When I awoke, Veronica was nowhere to be found. I mentally scanned the house and found only the carpenters who pounded on the stairs and ceiling. They'd only just begun working and I already wanted to throw them out; they were annoyances, like some of the mortals in my shop. We had to be careful around humans, we had to watch what we said and how we acted, but Veronica was set on redoing the house.

Stretching, I put on a pair of jeans and an oversized T-shirt and began brushing my hair, sending static electricity sparking though the room. Outside, rain poured and thundered on the glass panes. The noise was like drips on a drum, pounding, insistent. Most thought the rain was horrible, but to me, this was a beautiful day. I loved cloudy days the best, because the clouds blocked the sun.

I think the sudden outburst of rainstorms was what I missed most about New Orleans since I'd moved back to Boston. At times, parts of me longed to go back there, but now that was impossible. My life was here, running the Tearoom, fulfilling some part of my destiny.

I focused on my body, feeling the blood I'd taken in last night surging through me, giving me life. I was satisfied and wouldn't have to feed again for another three weeks, but I hungered for something else, something solid. Maybe I'd munch on something light, an apple maybe, considering food sat in my stomach until I thought about it and made my body digest it. When that happened, the food came out within a matter of minutes as solid waste had when I'd been human. The process might have been the same, but I rarely ate anything except on social occasions or when the desire to overcame me.

Normally, we kept the refrigerator stocked with a few things, but Veronica hardly touched it. She told me I would eventually lose my taste for food, but on occasion, I caught her munching on cheese or chocolate. Even though human fare sat in my belly, liquid was a different story—I could drink whatever I wanted, and it was absorbed right away into my system just as blood was. I hadn't figured out how or why that happened, but then again, it was probably one of the anomalies of being undead.

I stared into the mirror, noticing that there were no longer any pink marks on my cheek, my jaw was back to normal, and my ribs had completely healed. I pulled the brush through my hair one more time and then put it up into a ponytail. My reflection stared back at me, and I wondered if I had the capacity to actually change my physical appearance like some of the other vampires I'd encountered.

I stared hard, not really knowing what I wanted to change. My eyes were dark brown with silver flecks that ignited when I was aroused, but why not green, the color I used to pretend they were when I was human and wearing contacts, imagining myself a vampire? I concentrated, seeing the change in my mind and, when I opened them, they were actually evergreen. The change had worked, but they faded back to brown again. Shrugging my shoulders, I figured I had all the time in the world to master the technique.

As I stared at my reflection, something caught my eye. It was the directive from Zhen. She wanted me to meet her inside the subway station at South Station. From there, I was supposed to look for a black rose on a doorway. I was being summoned an hour after sunset, and Veronica was supposed to go with me, to put on the show that I was being humble,

that I'd done wrong being so young and disrespect-
ing to the Mistress and Elder of the City.

If I went, Veronica would be in as much danger
as I, and I couldn't have her in the middle of everything. I gritted my teeth and made up my mind. Now
or never.

I was counting on the fact that the beasts were
sleeping, or holed up in the nest. I didn't know how
regular vampires were, but Veronica slept most every day for a bit, just to get her strength back, but not
for very long. I hoped the other vampires would be
the same way. While most undead hated the light, I
assumed Zhen would be very volatile since she was
so old. Hopefully, she'd despise the sun as Devon
had. I never saw him in full sunlight, just inside, and
even then, the filtered light hurt him.

Yes, I would have to go now and destroy the nest,
or at least get information out of Zhen about Julien,
as well as Zach's killer. Hell, a few less vampires in
the world meant less for me to worry about. But, after
this, Miranda was the priority. If I didn't get her, then
Julien would transform her into a beast. She'd become his paramour, knowing nothing of her former
life, and even if she were lucky enough to hang onto
her humanity, she'd struggle for the rest of her im-
mortal existence, fighting the monster bonded to her
and trying to escape from her beloved Master.

Veronica had told me stories of how Devon forced her to do his bidding when she disobeyed. He'd starved her, letting her body eat away at itself so bugs settled into her rotting flesh, worming around inside of her as if she were nothing more than a corpse. In truth, that was what she'd become with no blood to restore her. Those memories always made her shudder, and I didn't blame her. Devon was a bastard, so I could only imagine what Julien would do to Miranda if she woke as a newborn and refused to be his devoted follower.

I sighed. Veronica was at the Tearoom, the best place for her considering she wanted to accompany me. She'd figure out something was wrong when she realized I wasn't at work. I had appointments all day and was supposed to break the horrible news, but I was sure she'd tell the staff about Zach if they didn't already know. Hopefully, my lover would only assume I was late, thinking I wanted to sleep in. Veronica knew me better than that, but I could still pray.

As I left, I spied the T-shirt I'd thrown aside last night; the one Azrael had given me. I picked it up as an afterthought, remembering how he'd held me in his arms. My heart lightened at the thought. Last night was the first time he'd showed interest in me aside from giving me cryptic messages in his silky smooth voice.

The aroma of lavender and frankincense filled my nose. His scent reminded me of crypts and the hallowed halls of churches. I rubbed the shirt against my cheek, feeling the otherworldly material, just like cotton. I smiled, then put the shirt in my drawer. The next time I saw the angel, I'd return it, but for now, I had other scores to settle.

There were three outside entrances to the subway at South Station and another inside the main station where the Commuter Rails connected people to the outside world. I strolled into the station and was assaulted by the aromas of flowers and the leather from the suitcase stand, as well as the eateries in the back.

I wove in between the public coming off the Commuter Rails, but this level wasn't the one I wanted, so I stepped on to the escalator and went down into the bowels of the subway. As I went, I wrapped my power around me. Humans saw me fade out as if I were a ghost deciding to evaporate. An elderly woman crossed herself, saying Hail Mary as if her path had been traversed by a demon. I guess, in some way, it had.

I walked a few steps down a ramp and then jumped over the turnstiles. The subway had been under construction because of the Big Dig, with many of the old entrances bricked up, but the one in front of me was hidden by a fraying blue tarp. It reminded me too much of my house, but at least here the work seemed to be done. Wind from the passing trains caught the tattered tarp, and I saw a blob that could have been taken as a rose in black paint. It was faded, but my intuition gave me the creepy feeling that this had to be it.

They're not going to know what fucking hit them.

The good thing about me venturing into the nest was that it was still daylight, but I was counting on the vampires being asleep. If they were awake, I was going to become a very tasty meal. Taking a deep breath, I said a silent prayer to whoever listened. Gathering my energy even closer, doubting even a fly could survive in the vacuum, I knew there was no turning back, no way for me to get out of this. The only way out was to pay a visit to Azrael, and I wasn't ready for that.

The door was locked, of course, but that didn't deter me. I slammed against the steel, very well aware of the noise I was making and the people who gathered to look at what kind of invisible force was crashing into the door. I broke the lock. To the audience, it seemed that the door flew open on its own.

As I stepped in, I noticed the dent that I left. It was a pretty good size, and I was going to have a large bruise on my shoulder. But, hell, what was pain after everything I'd been through?

The hallway was lit only by jaundiced emergency lights throwing shadows around the room as if moths clicked against the lights. They flickered as the trains rumbled underneath me like miniature earthquakes. It was hot and muggy, and the air was hard to breathe. The exhaust fumes from the trains were thick as they gathered underground. I walked a few feet, wishing that the light was either on or off because the flickering obscured my vision—my eyes didn't have time to adjust to the abrupt changes.

The scent of decay lingered at the top of the staircase. It wasn't the heady, damp smell mixed with trash or urine that accompanied subways, but rather the smell of death old and new, the pungent odor of rotting flesh layered with the undertones of parchment-dry skin. The scent of fresh earth was also there, as if the whole place was some type of newly dug grave. All the aromas signaled vampires. I walked down countless steps until the only places left for me to go were blocked off by the Big Dig from the turn of the century.

I had to walk the old subway lines where the Green Line had originally been built. All that was left of the old track was the hard, packed-dirt floor with bits of concrete here and there, crude pieces of tile still stuck to the walls and poking up through the dirt like finger bones.

The temperature increased dramatically as I descended to the lower levels. I walked silently, hearing the trains roaring above me as they sped to their destinations. The stench of rot grew stronger as I walked along the deserted tunnels looking for any signs of vampires, but it seemed there weren't any, which was odd—this was the perfect place for a nest. Dark, dank, and creepy as hell.

I shivered at the thought of being taken by surprise. There was nowhere to hide, and the nearest exit was half a mile up. Still, I rounded the bend, and each whiff reassured me that undead creatures were here.

Maybe Zhen knew I was coming? I shook my head. She couldn't know. *Maybe she anticipated my coming here, but then she'd have guards. Wouldn't she? Or is she so confident she doesn't think I'm a threat? God, I hate these undead assholes.*

Rats squeaked and cockroaches scurried on the dirt floor, attracted by other scum lurking in the dark. The vermin came up to my feet, crawling over them, aware that I was there, which I found interesting because I was still invisible to everything. But I guess the rats and insects had assimilated the identification of vampires into their own special frequency. Nature was marvelous that way.

I came to the end of the tunnel. There was nowhere else to go.

"Shit." I kicked the wall, figuring I'd hit concrete, but my foot passed through it. I lost my balance and fell through the illusion, landing hard on my hand. A dust cloud exploded around me as I spat out dirt and saw that I'd landed face first into a crowd of about forty vampires in various stages of vampiric transformation. Many appeared as demons covered in brown or black fur. Others were in human form sprawled out on the earthen floor. Slowly, I stepped through them, trying to find some sort of path. They were in a hive mind, so if one of them woke up, then they all would, and that would alert their mistress.

Carefully, I tiptoed, wondering if Zhen was the Maker of all these creatures, or if some were strays who swore a blood-oath to her, which was almost the same as her being their true Master because she could summon and control them just as their original Maker would have done. This would only happen to the weaker undead whose Masters had cast them aside or died.

I glanced back at the entrance that was so far away now and saw that it was a concrete wall again—a very good illusion. I'd only seen one other vampire accomplish this feat. Malachi had been an ancient vampire living outside of New Orleans. His illusion had been a huge plantation house in which everything was solid and perfect, as if it were real.

After his pet werewolf devoured him, the house collapsed in on itself.

I'd barely made it out alive because the werewolf decided I was dessert as he latched onto my ankle, but Aria helped me out. She'd taken me there to kill Malachi, as that would have made Devon even more powerful, since Malachi was Devon's master. They chose me as the instrument to destroy Malachi, since Devon was too chicken-shit to do it himself. Devon thought he could own me. He almost had until I overcame his influence and slaughtered the fucker. But, that was the past.

Gingerly, I stepped over the last of the vampires and ducked under a curtain where there were piles of bones in one corner. Along the opposite wall, mortals were tied up with bite marks over every major artery. All of them were near death and had a bluish tint to their skin; their lips were purple and their breaths shallow. It was impossible for me to save them, even though my heart cried out to do so. I placed my hand on one woman, her blonde hair lank and hanging around a sharp face. As I touched her, she opened her eyes a slit and began to moan.

"Help me," she whispered.

I stared into her eyes and pushed my mind into hers, but I was hit by a huge psychic wall, basically saying *no trespassing*.

"I'm so sorry," I answered, bathed in the energy of the one who claimed her. Because of it, I was able to follow the energy like a trail of bread crumbs to the source, and I realized Zhen had psychically tethered all the humans to her in case they decided to escape. If they did make it past the nest, she'd find them and torture them until there was nothing left. My heart cried out for the victim, but there was nothing I could do. I knew better than to tamper with another's property, especially the Elder of the City's. I could only imagine what would happen if I insulted her again. She'd fry my mind.

I followed the psychic leashes through another deserted tunnel littered with more vampires and various body parts, bringing the total number of undead to about one hundred. If I was caught now, I would never see daylight again.

I pushed aside a sheer gray curtain. The scent of oranges wafted in the chamber as shadows flickered from candles on a bedside table. A large, canopied bed with curtains tied to the posts was placed in the middle and housed two vampires. Zhen lay next to a younger creature, her hand thrown back over her head, long, black hair stretched on the pillow like someone had spilled a bottle of ink, not styled for the night in her usual mohawk. The other vampire was fairly new to the life of darkness, and if it was sleeping next to her, then it must have been one of her new protégées.

Slowly, I made my way to the bed, observing how pale the elder was, almost as white as her sheets with a silent heart in her chest. The ancient didn't have to breathe since she was beyond that fact of life; she only did so when she made her body remember how to do it, like Veronica. After passing through the stage where we forgot, we were able to smell things on our tongues like a snake. I could do it now, but I was still human enough to breathe unconsciously, even though I didn't have to.

As I watched Zhen, heat rushed into me; my head chakra opened and I connected to the cosmos. My skin and muscles hardened as my fangs grew; my eyes opened as the warmth found a home above my heart. It rushed through me, settling as it had done the other night when I'd fought the two goons. This time, it was stunning, and I felt I'd been thrown into a fire.

Zhen opened her naturally black eyes. A dark, amused smile spread on her lips and she vaulted, wrapping her fingers around my throat, digging her nails into my skin. Even though she was shorter than I, she was able to hold onto my neck and throw me on the bed, knocking off her sleeping child.

"I should have known you'd come early," she purred, glancing past the sheer curtain and mentally checking on her other children, surprised to sense that they were still sleeping and there had been no bloodshed. "You got past my children, and in full sunlight. Impressive, but foolish."

I met her eyes from the velvet comforter and saw calm, cool patience as she stood with her arms crossed against her chest. She was testing me, waiting for me to do or say something to reveal my true nature, but I doubted she expected me to be honest. Slowly, I rose, never taking my eyes from her. I'd learned my lesson on that one.

"You invited me. Besides, you promised me information and I never got it, so here I am."

She chuckled. Her laughter was rich and held the wisdom of ages as it echoed through the hallway. I almost expected the other vampires to wake, swarm in and defend their mistress, but only the one on the floor stirred, as he hadn't even woken up from the impact of his fall. All, like him, were under her spell.

"You puzzle me, child. You kill one of my best soldiers and permanently maim another. By law, for that alone, I should kill you. But there's something about you that intrigues me. I tasted it in you the other night, as if we have something in common. Maybe a distant bloodline, but I'm sure we can discover that later. And you were ever so sweet. I could offer you the pleasures of the night that no other has given you." She paused and sat down on the bed.

Me, have something in common with this bitch? I fucking doubt it.

She ran her hand over my knee, and her nails dug into my jeans. I tried not to shudder at the death on her breath. "I acted hastily the other night. It's obvious that you don't know many of our ways. I have survived over four thousand years, living off the blood of humans and vampires. Many beings have crossed my path, from fairies to trolls, angels and unicorns, which sadly have died out. But you puzzle me. I've seen thousands of vampires in my day, spawning many of them as you see here, but this is only a portion of the nest. It runs under the city and all of its catacombs. My children are all over the world. But with all the vampires I've made and seen, I can tell you're not exactly a vampire, now are you?"

Unicorns, trolls. Either she was out of it, trying to impress me, or she was telling the truth. True, she'd seen a lot, but then again, legends had to be started somewhere. How much did she know? Maybe, just maybe, she knew what I truly was?

"Don't look so surprised. You seem as any other newborn and feel almost like any other vampire, but the vibration of your aura resonates a little higher. The harmonics are off. Most of our kind would never notice, not even the older ones." She smiled.

I tried to keep my face blank, but the shock in my eyes was evident.

"You wonder how I knew. At first, I didn't, but then you got mad and the taste of your blood sent chills through me. Your lack of control gave away something in your energy signature. And then Robyn came back with the burn and told me how his hand had melted off. His wounds haven't even scabbed over yet, and they still bleed occasionally. That's a unique thing. Not many beings have the power to overcome a vampire's healing capabilities. So you see, child, I respect you. And it's not every day I give someone my respect. Mmm, the spice in your blood makes me think of happier times. And you're just my type, so it's a shame you have a mistress waiting for you at home. It was wise of you not to bring her. I can see how much you love her, which is good. As much as I would love to play with you, you're here for other reasons."

"If you know why I came, will you help me?" My instincts told me she'd be playing a very large role in my destiny, but I only wondered. I didn't want her interfering with me and Veronica. It was bad enough that she was flirting with me now. It was also a little disconcerting to think I was coming to a vampire for help, considering I wasn't part of their race.

She remained silent, contemplating something. "Everything comes with a price. In choosing this life, we must sacrifice our families, watch loved ones die, and embrace a beast some call a demon. But the benefits are worth it: longevity, freedom from sickness, and our powers. The sun is our pain, and our drive for blood is our price. My help also comes with a price."

She and I both knew I'd pay anything. I'd swear a blood-oath and be bound forever to her if she gave me what I needed. My fingers shrank, and the heat inside of me evaporated as I released it. My connection to the cosmos was severed.

"I'll do whatever you want," I whispered, "as long as I get what I need."

"You shall. As for my payment, that will come when I deem it. Agreed?"

I looked away, wondering how Veronica would take this. I'd never wanted to betray her, but in this instance, it seemed like I was. Even though my heart said no to the thought, my instincts screamed yes, letting me know it was the only thing to do. Even though my guides were screaming at me for making a bargain, I knew it was the right thing to do. The only thing to do if I wanted Zhen's help.

"Agreed?"

I met her eyes and swallowed, and I knew I'd sold my soul. The devil comes in many forms, and I'd just met mine.

"Yes."

"Then tell me what it is you want."

I sighed, wondering where to begin. "A vampire marked a human who came to me for help. Now she's been taken, and I need to know where she is, since it wasn't her choice to go. And one of my friends was murdered, as was another human woman. I want the beast that killed them."

Zhen nodded and closed her eyes as energy gathered around her. No sound could be heard from her, not even the faint whisper of blood in her veins. Her olive-bleached skin grew cold as she did some form of remote viewing, sending her soul out of her body to see things far away. More time passed uneventfully, and nothing happened until her color was that of a bleached bone.

She took in a long breath, forcing her lungs to inflate with a sound like crackling leaves. She opened her eyes, which were as white as if she'd been blinded, and when she spoke, it wasn't her voice, but the garbled, gravelly one of the beast.

"The creature who murdered your friend no longer dwells in the city. The scent is gone. He's back with his Master. The thing that killed your protected is not our kind, only a servant. We know the one you seek. You've seen him; he was at the club. His lair is in an abandoned nursing home in a city west of here. It is there you must go if you wish to reclaim the human that was taken. Remember, she is marked, and by our law, you have no right to claim him unless an injustice has been done to you," the beast said.

I smiled. This was exactly what I needed. I'd deal with the price of her advice later. Now, at least, I knew where Miranda was—or at least what city she was in. She was in Worcester. It was the only place near enough for him to take her but still close enough to Boston, a place where he didn't have to worry about the police tracing any murder to him. Then there was the thing that killed Zach. If my fears were correct, then I had another vampire and his pet to deal with, but I'd get to them after I rescued Miranda.

"Thank you," I whispered, and rose from the bed.

"Wait," the beast growled, wrapping its talons around my wrist in a vice grip. "If you choose to rescue the one he covets, then you must destroy the would-be Master, as he has been a thorn in our side for eons. But, if you don't kill him, then your destiny and his become intertwined, for he has been on your path for months. He has heard the rumors and wishes you for himself. He knows you are not like others and, like myself, he would have you for his harem. But be wary and do not get caught by his mind, for if that happens, then you shall lose your soul. Kill him and you are free with us."

Kill him. I could deal with that. He was dead anyway, considering murdering him had been my original plan. But what did she mean, saying he'd been following me? And how could I lose my soul?

The only being who could take my soul was Azrael, and he wasn't about to condemn me. Then, it dawned on me why the blond vampire at the club seemed so familiar. I'd felt his presence at the Tearoom and Crimson Liquids. What rumors were going through the undead community about me? Maybe Devon had bragged before he died, and that was how this vampire had traced me? Or, maybe it was just the fact that I'd killed Devon, and even though I hadn't killed Malachi, I'd defeated him and pushed him aside, proving I was more powerful than him. Any of these could have been the reason this vampire was following me.

Great, more of what I need, another vampire who thinks he can rule my world. But then, why did he go after Miranda if I was his goal?

Something about Miranda didn't set right. She'd been having dreams of Julien since childhood, and only a twist of Fate had made our paths cross. Of course, it would be Fate detouring my life again, seeing what other troubles I had to deal with.

"Consider it done," I said, and headed toward civilization. I didn't wait to see Zhen come back to herself as her power extended before me like a carpet, showing me out. As I walked out of the subway, toward daylight, a feeling of dread, as well as other premonitions, washed over me. My guides were trying to tell me something, probably that I was getting in way over my head. No shit.

14

CHAPTER FOURTEEN

My name is Miranda.

Julien came into my room again undoing my bonds. I looked at him complacently as he led me out of my cell and into the hallway. The stench was horrible, like stepping into a compost heap. The dank and cold permeated my bones as he led me slowly, stopping so I could step over a few random pipes protruding from the floor. Without him, I was virtually swallowed by the blackness around me. Here and there, enough light flickered to show many shadows, but most sockets just sparked as currents raced through them. Strangely, I wasn't scared as he guided me through the infinite blackness. Oddly, I was content, even though part of me knew I should have been running in the opposite direction.

As Julien escorted me, the thing sharing my mind slept, purring in the back of my consciousness. It was content to have fed on his blood, and even as it rested, some part of it wrapped around my awareness, incorporating itself into my thoughts. I figured that was the reason I wasn't exactly afraid of Julien anymore. It was so strange. It was part of me and I was part of it, part human and part other. Still me and not we. Now that I thought about it, the thing in my mind was more solid than it had been hours ago, having been nourished by Julien's blood.

Through a heavy steel door, we stepped into what used to be an old room, but had been transformed into a bedroom. He brought me to the bed and sat me down. Gazing at me, he waited for my reaction, but I didn't think I knew how to react anymore, how to feel. Everything felt numb, as if I were lost, swimming in the dark abyss of my mind. And then, he kissed me.

His lips were chilled as I felt every little indentation against my own. His tongue pushed into my mouth, caressing my teeth as his hands trailed underneath my shirt and over my bra. He paused, and with one finger, sliced the garment in half, slipping the remnants off, pulling my shirt off with it. His nails trailed between my shoulder blades, sending shivers through me. The cold air hit me as hot flashes burned inside. He nuzzled my neck and, the more he kissed me, the more alive I became. The thing in my mind still slept, but I was coming around.

My hand slipped under his fishnet shirt, feeling the hardness of his stomach and his chest. His skin was cool, and I wanted to warm him. My lips found his nipple through his shirt as I explored the ridges of it with my tongue, taking it between my teeth. He moaned, pushing my head into his chest and encouraging me to continue.

I slid one hand down, undoing his pants. His dick sprang out, hard and ready to fuck me. He was smooth as silk, but cold as steel. His purple head was plump, waiting to go into my pussy. His eyes closed at the light pleasure of my touch. It had been so long since I'd done this, been with a man, but every fiber of me wanted to be used.

He pushed my head down as I went to my knees, and my tongue flicked over his cock, tasting a slight coppery taste on his skin as a drop of cum glistened on the tip. He encouraged me to take him so I could taste more, and as I sucked, he groaned louder, his hand forcing me down even more. My tongue ran up and down his shaft. My hands fastened on his hips as he bucked under me, releasing into my mouth.

The first taste of cum was like the blood I'd taken earlier, and it made me suck on him even harder, trying to get as much as I could. As I drank him in, my hunger for blood awakened, but the desire had nothing to do with the other that shared my consciousness. The fire of lust and blood burned inside me, and I wanted to take all of him in, drink him in to satisfy my buried desires. I got the sense that I could sate all my hungers with him and he would never tell me to stop. I could bathe in blood, and he would join me.

He pushed me away so that I landed on the bed. He looked at me and I smiled, licking the rest of his cum off of my lips.

"How do I taste?"

"Good." I ran my tongue over his lips. He opened them for me as he slipped all the way out of his jeans. My tongue moved against his teeth as they lengthened. I caressed them, remembering the pain of them in my throat and how good it felt when he sucked. My insides grew hot as my whole body ached for him.

I shoved him down on the bed, exploring his body with my hands, loving how it contrasted with the burning heat of my own. My lips found his neck and began to bite. My tongue licked up and down his jugular vein, and I craved the feeling of biting and taking his blood. As that desire spread through me, I felt a shifting in my mouth. My teeth ached and pressed through my gums as they grew, but just a little, getting baby points. They scraped along Julien's throat. He jumped, pushing me away, and I smiled, showing him my infant fangs.

"Soon you'll be completely mine. My one and only true child. Does it frighten you to be truly awakened?"

Why would I be scared to be with him? He'd shown me a reality I'd never dreamed about. I wanted to believe that was why I'd been so terrified of my dream for so many years, that I denied the part of myself that craved blood. If I'd known it was going to be like this, then I would have indulged in it long ago. Brenna had been wrong. She may have had encounters with vampires, but she knew nothing of the ecstasy I felt right at this moment, listening to his heart beating faintly in my ears, hearing mice scurrying down the hall, smelling the dank and rot and the mold as it grew along the walls, just being alive. This was what I was meant to do. To become. This was what I wanted.

As I thought about it, the other part of me awakened, but decided not to merge with me, just to observe, looking out through my eyes as if it were a tourist.

"No. It's what I want."

"Good."

His lips curled as he pulled me down on top of him. His lips were hungry, seeking out every exposed piece of my flesh. His nails dug into my back, and everything about me wanted him. He must have sensed my desire, because he rolled me over so he was on top of me, kissing me, running his tongue over my teeth. His obsessed hands groped my tits, massaging them, pinching the nipples between his thumbs and forefingers hard enough to leave snow-flake bruises. His sharp nails cut into my chest as his tongue shifted, growing long as he smashed his mouth into mine.

I moved my hands along his back, feeling the skin moving; the muscles underneath were bunching, as were the bones. All over his body, his joints snapped like broken chicken wings. I closed my eyes, enjoying the experience as he pushed himself into me, but soon his dick grew bigger, colder, and it was too much.

I moaned as he pounded into me, making me come as his lips sought my neck. With each thrust, his entrances were more painful; with each move-ment, the beast was taking over. He moved with me as I came. Still, tremors racked my body, coursing through me as he pushed, each stroke hurting more than the last. The thing in me wanted to enjoy it, but my senses and my rationality were returning. This wasn't what I wanted. I didn't want to be his forever.

What the hell had I been thinking? He was noth-ing more than a monster, but at this point, I was fucked, literarily. I beat my fists against his chest, but he didn't stop. I opened my eyes, ready to beg him to stop his assault, but when I did, I was met with everything I'd ever seen in my nightmare.

He had the muzzle of a wolf with thin black lips lining a maw of sharp teeth, a flattened nose that reminded me of a bat, and ears that had grown furry and pointed. His black eyes looked on me with astonishment, as if he was surprised to see I was afraid. How could I be complacent as he ripped me apart? I was his bitch as he plunged into me, and all I could do was thrash and scream against him, trying to get away and not lose myself in whatever sick fantasy he thought we were enacting.

Once he realized this, his lips curled back, exposing all his teeth, and his eyes ignited with hell-red intensity. He growled something unintelligible, and I felt some sort of buzzing inside my head as my other tried to come forward, but then came a surge of pain.

And then—
Nothing.

15

CHAPTER FIFTEEN

My name is Brenna.

I flapped my wings, cloaked from humanity on the way to Worcester. Circling the city, I looked for the abandoned nursing home. The more time I spent searching, the longer Miranda was in danger and the less daylight I had left. Only three hours were left until sunset. My visit with Zhen had taken longer than expected.

I thought it strange for her to help me the way she did, but I wasn't going to dismiss her advice. If she chose to help me, great. It was what she'd said that had me worried. What rumors were circulating about me? That a newborn had killed its would-be master? That I was different from all the other vampires? Whatever these tales were, I had no idea; but then again, I was always the last one to find out, like when I was given cryptic messages by angels or by vampires.

Whatever the rumors were, the most important thing was getting to Miranda. I didn't really know what would happen, and I wasn't too sure if I should believe the wonderful advice from the ancient vampire that had come exactly when I needed it.

A few birds flew in my path, most of them deflected around the shield I had in place, but one flew in my face, stunning the both of us and making me lose my concentration. I plummeted, but when I picked a few of the feathers off my face, I regained control and saw an old, abandoned building that was deserted, run down, and large enough to have been a nursing home. And, after searching three others like it already, I hoped this was the right one.

I landed on top of an old shed behind the facility and scanned the place, hearing dozens of heartbeats. Most were barely audible, slower than any mortal ones could ever be. Above the others were six rapid drummings, scattered throughout the building. They were human, but I had no clue which one belonged to Miranda.

I willed my wings into my back; they sunk under my skin and I was able to pull on a T-shirt I'd carried in the waistband of my jeans. That was the only thing I hated about flying—every time my wings emerged, they tore my shirt, leaving me feeling like the Incredible Hulk. I hated going through tons of clothes—it was easy to shield myself from human eyes, but it was cumbersome to always have to remember extra shirts. Luckily, my corset from the other night had been saved. I don't know how, probably because the vamp I killed unhooked it instead of shredding it, so at least the three hundred dollars hadn't been wasted.

Taking one last assessment of the place, I saw it was easier to start from the third floor, since the largest concentration of heartbeats came from the basement. Even though I still had daylight, I didn't want to walk into a nest and have them wake up on me. I was damn lucky with Zhen's brood, but then again, I had some inkling she'd assumed I was coming and had power over her children. I figured I'd be taking the ones here by surprise, and with the fifty plus undead creatures in the basement, I would provide an early start to their night.

So I jumped off the shed and jogged to the fire escape, rapidly climbing up the rusted bars that practically broke in my grip. Then again, with the bats in my stomach, I guess I underestimated my own strength. At the top, a large plywood board covered a window. I smirked. After my encounter with the steel door, this was cheesecake. I grabbed the edge and pulled, and the nails screamed out of their wooden frame. Moving the board aside, I stepped through the window and landed on broken glass. The stench from the dungeon was overwhelming as it assaulted my senses; human shit and decay was the only way to describe it.

With the lowering sun, I had plenty of light to see by, considering there were no lights inside, even though I heard the crackling of electricity in the building. That was strange, but hell, never put it past a vampire to get what it wanted. Patches of blue and puke-green tile had come up off the floor from water damage, or perhaps they'd been pulled up by a random punk kid who wanted a souvenir. I wondered how many had been dared and were never heard from again, meeting their fate at the hands of the monsters that dwelled below.

As I surveyed the room, I saw that windows that were not boarded up had been pelted by stone missiles, which lay scattered around. I drew in a deep breath on instinct, immediately regretting it, tasting the musty dankness and everything else on my tongue as though I was eating a mouthful of dirt. Willing myself not to breathe to try and get rid of the taste, I remembered I didn't have to anyway. Breathing was just part of my lingering human instinct.

The passage was a long corridor with doors on either side. At one end of the hallway was a set of double swinging doors, and at the other was a window that had long ago had the glass assaulted from it. The whole corridor was littered with pieces of fallen plaster, pigeon shit, and records of old patients. I crept slowly, but each step was amplified, echoing throughout the place.

The eruption of pigeon's wings made me jump. I told myself there was nothing to be afraid of, but it didn't seem to matter. I was on edge, knowing there was a nest below me. The bats in my stomach had turned to giants and were not nesting in the belfry as they were supposed to be, but rather going berserk. This place had an energy of its own. Something dark hung over it, and no matter what kind of creature I was, it scared the shit out of me.

I shook my head as an overwhelming sense of warmth flooded me, a reassurance from my guides that I wasn't going crazy. They helped me to focus and remember why I was here. Centering in on the nearest heartbeat, I made my way down to the other end of the hall, almost tripping on exposed piping and beer left by midnight visitors. When I gazed into the room, I saw a half-naked man chained to the radiator. He glanced up at me, but his eyes were glazed.

Dead.

There was no soul left to claim as his own. He was fodder for the undead. I couldn't save him, and that broke my heart because no creature deserved to be kept as he was. This thing in front of me might have been classified as a human, but it was no longer even an animal; it was just a warm body for vampires to feed on.

As I stepped closer, he noticed I was there and automatically craned his neck, scarred from so many feedings, for me to taste him. He made a grunting sound akin to a lost animal, and I nearly lost it and dashed out of the room, stopping on a stairwell. I leaned against the wall, trying to erase the image from my head. The junkies I encountered had never been so forlorn. Many had been near death, yet they'd always had a spark of life as they got a high from being drained. This man was empty, dull.

I took a few breaths, forgetting I hadn't breathed for several minutes because of the smells, and I noticed the air tasted worse in the stairwell. It wasn't the stench of pigeon shit that painted the stairs. It was human fear that made the aroma so wretched. Usually, fear excited me, but this didn't. I jumped the stairs, realizing the stink came from the nest itself, from the gathering of so many vampires.

Not even Zhen's nest was this bad. I landed on a patch of ground that the pigeons hadn't gotten a chance to have target practice on, then I jumped down one more short flight to the second floor.

The second floor corridor was much like the third floor's, but had more papers strewn about. Wheelchairs and gurneys lined the way as the suspended ceiling sagged from water damage, and the scorched concrete blocks had been victims of fire. Along the walls were various tags from graffiti artists, reminding me of the victims I had taken earlier. Broken bottles littered the floor, but here the tiles were even more warped. Listening for more heartbeats, I found a cluster as I searched and came into what used to be a cafeteria.

Here, the whole place was lined with windows. During the day, the sun must have streamed through and made this a wonderful place to sit and look out into the woods behind the hospital. I could almost see the old folks in wheelchairs staring, dreaming of their lost childhoods, but now this place had become a prison. All the glass was broken either by birds, target-happy kids, or a very large monster that burst through the window. I went with the large monster.

The room was half the size of a football field. The floor was once nicely polished hardwood, maple by the lingering smell of it, but now many of the boards were pulled up along the seams or splintered. The middle sagged, making me wonder what truly supported this nursing home so that it didn't collapse, but what impressed me the most was that the floor was covered with dried blood. It was everywhere, enough to paint the cafeteria several times over. This was obviously where the vampires feasted.

I stayed on the outside edges of the floor, trying to find the heartbeats, when I noticed a large pile of rags in the far corner near a small stage.

On the stage was a large, wooden chair displayed like a throne. All that was needed to complete the scene was a haphazard crown.

Perfect.

This was the great hall where the vampire subjects feasted while the Master looked on. As I climbed on the stage, the rags stirred to life. I touched one and it moved. Underneath were four starved females who didn't know where or who they were. Quickly, I scanned their minds and found them to be vacuums. The vampires had taken their identities, using them as drinking tubes. All had lank red hair that was falling out. Their skin was sunken, and I could see their skulls underneath. Their eyes weren't even crazed. They were just blank. I curled my nose at the sight. All were soulless corpses. I prayed that the same fate hadn't befallen Miranda.

I walked through the other entrance of the cafeteria and into a hallway much like the other. The last fluttering heartbeat had to be Miranda's. Rage built in me as I thought about the wasted human life in the other room. I began to heat up, and energy coursed through me, settling in my heart as it had done earlier in the day. I was going to destroy the monster that had done this, for all the innocence he had stolen.

First, I had to get to Miranda, had to find my way down to the basement, hopefully one the pigeons didn't like as much. I walked the hallway, darting underneath spider webs and over pieces of fallen sheetrock and plaster. As I stopped to hop over an obstacle, something in one of the rooms caught my eye.

There was a lone wheelchair, but as I looked, a chill swept through me and I felt as if someone were watching me. I blinked, stepped out of the room and went to move on, ignoring the feeling, but I heard the screeching of wheels on the tile floor. When I glanced back, there was an old woman sitting in the chair, staring at me. She appeared like any other grandmother in a blue robe, wearing pink slippers with her wrinkled hands crossed over one another. I knew she wasn't alive because there was no heartbeat echoing in the tiny room, and she was semi-transparent, a spirit trapped between the worlds who decided to speak to me.

I stepped in, keeping my senses locked on the ghost, wondering why she hadn't moved on. The more I thought about it, the more I realized she must have been caught in some kind of time warp and not known she was dead. Seeing phantoms wasn't new to me, but the look on her face was so serene it surprised me.

You can see me? the woman asked.

Her voice was wispy, like a breeze through wind chimes as it echoed in my mind.

"Yes."

The others don't notice me. Sometimes I wonder if I'm the only one left.

I glanced around. The sun would be setting in an hour or so. The nest might awaken sooner, and I didn't want them to find me wandering about. I only wanted to deal with the Master and not the other heartbeats I heard. I might be strong, but I couldn't take on the fifty in the basement. Even as I gazed on the old woman, a need to save her, to release her from her years of suffering, stirred in me. The idea lingered, and the heat in my heart surged through me and almost made me shiver, as it seemed to be tinged with ice. I should have been able to help her, but I didn't know how, so for now, she was dead and Miranda was my priority.

"I'd love to stay and chat, but someone I know is in trouble. But I promise I'll come back when I can."

I turned to leave, but her fingers wrapped around my arm. She shouldn't have been able to do that since she was a spirit, but the sheer force of her will had made it possible, and that stunned me.

Wait.

"Yes."

You aren't like the others that wander the halls, especially the one who oversees them. Whenever he comes, he peers in. Over the years, my friends have grown quiet. They don't come down for bridge anymore. We used to have a game every Thursday, but he can't see us like you can. He only hears us. He's mean. I don't know where your friend is, but she's lucky to have someone like you. You're a sweet girl, coming to visit an old lady.

She began to fade out, evaporating like early morning fog. A part of me yearned to release her. Something in me knew how to give her soul some respite from the purgatory she lingered in, but the only being I knew who could complete the task was Azrael. I'd have to get him to come here and do me a favor. He owed me one, considering all the trouble he'd caused with his cryptic messages.

"Wait."

The woman stopped and returned to semi-solidity so I could see the back of the graying wheelchair through her.

"I'll send someone to visit you if I can't come back right away. He'll be able to help you. You'll know that I sent him."

A large smile appeared on her face, and she motioned me down and patted my cheek. I felt the wrinkles on her skin and the cold metal of her gold wedding band.

You are a good girl. Go help your friend.

Then, she totally disappeared, leaving an empty wheelchair. I closed my eyes, saying a silent prayer for her. Azrael was the only one who could free her soul.

For now, I bolted out of the room and down the hallways, trying to beat the setting sun as I came to another stairwell, which I jumped. That landed me in the basement, which was freezing. The corridor was strewn with more papers, books, and file folders of patients' records. It stretched in both directions and was pitch black on both ends. Lights sparked here and there, though most were broken. The cellar seemed more like a dank dungeon with winding hallways, a maze, and if I didn't have Miranda's heartbeat to follow, I would have gotten lost.

I found myself in a large room with two huge brick ovens in it, piled high with pigeon shit. The room had four doors, and as I listened, I realized I'd taken a right instead of a left and had to double back. As I did, the hair rose on the back of my neck. I was either being watched or followed, but I couldn't sense anything, hear it or even smell it. There was something else, something not right about the bowels of the nursing home, and as I looked down, I noticed the grates and then remembered all the heartbeats.

For curiosity's sake, I pulled up one of the grilles. It was awkward to move and scraped across the concrete, and as it did, I was afraid it might wake the dead. If no one had known I was here before, they sure did now. I pushed the grille aside and dropped down into the hole.

I landed in a large tunnel with an inch of water in it. The walls were streaked with blood, as if it had leaked down from above. I wondered how long the nest had occupied this space. I moved a few steps, and my eyes picked up shadows and certain light red and brown colors, but that was all I could see. When I stepped, I heard the crunching of something underneath my feet. It was big enough that it was probably bones, and knowing my luck, it was a skull. I could only imagine what it looked like, grinning at nothing while it rotted away into oblivion.

Opening my senses, I looked around again. Dark blue auras of vampires jumped out as they slept huddled together along the floor. There were more than I thought—their heartbeats were on top of one another's, and I saw that there must have been a hundred or so.

Without waiting, as I felt the sun setting in my bones, I jumped and grabbed hold of the grate and pulled myself up. Replacing it, I knew there was some kind of outside access to the tunnels, but there was no way in fucking hell I was going to be searching for that right now. I would need an army of fifty just to exterminate the nest, but I wanted the head honcho.

Before I could think of anything else, Miranda's heartbeat called to me from one of the cells. Opening the door, I found her on an old, filthy mattress, her shirt stained with blood. I looked her over as I took her in my arms. There were fresh wounds on her neck, along with the purples and yellows of oncoming bruises. Checking her pulse, I had to make sure. Her heartbeat was a little slow, but steady, but there was something different in her energy. I sighed. Julien had given her some of his blood. The color of her skin hadn't begun to lose its pigment and bleach out yet, and when I pulled her eyelids, her eyes were as they were before, not yet tainted black with the beast. He might have given her blood, but it hadn't taken root yet. I thanked God for that.

I heard something outside in the hallway; it could have been the stirring of pigeon wings, or the vampires getting ready to rise. So I wrapped my arms around her and, as I did, my charge stirred and opened her eyes, but she didn't see me. Immediately, she started flailing and worked her way out of my grasp.

"No more. I won't let you." She ran into the corner and curled into a ball.

"Miranda, it's Brenna," I whispered, trying to get close to her. I approached slowly with my arms open, showing I wasn't a threat, but she still didn't see me. She was lost in her mind, reliving the trauma he'd inflicted on her. I knew he'd raped her, since the scent of sex clung to her like a bad air freshener. Bruises adorned her wrists where she'd been held down, and some were even on her face. It was obvious her attack had been recent, and my heart leapt out for her. I'd never been forced. Devon had wanted me, and I'd almost fallen under his spell. I knew how rough vampires could be because it was in their nature—they wanted to be fucked or dominated. But Miranda was still human.

I was close enough to her to get a grip, but the look of fear was still plastered on her face. Her eyes widened while the door slowly creaked open.

Wonderful. I assumed that the vampires had awoken, but instead, the smell of a wet dog immediately filled the room, and the hot breath of another beast radiated on my neck. Miranda's eyes darted to it and back to me. I turned, expecting to find a vampire in hellhound or beastly form looming over me.

"Fuck."

It was worse than that. Much worse.

16

CHAPTER SIXTEEN

My name is Miranda.

Brenna stared at the monster with no fear. At first, I couldn't believe she was here, staring at the thing that stood in the doorway as she came to rescue me from Julien. Somehow, she'd found out where I'd been taken, and my whole being jumped at the thought that I was going to be rescued. But as she looked at the monster, I knew she had no chance against whatever it was.

This was the brute that had taken me, but as I examined it, I noticed something different. It was bigger, bulkier, standing on all fours. It had a more pointed muzzle with silver fur instead of brown, and a long, bushy tail that looked like it should have belonged to a German Shepherd. Its claws were shorter, thicker, more curled. It all reminded me of a wolf on steroids. Its teeth were longer, and as it looked on Brenna, its eyes were not black, but hazel, reflecting the flickering light in the hallway.

I retreated to the corner. Brenna saw the wolf move and dodged it so that it crashed head-on into the concrete wall next to me. I looked on as it got up, shaking its head as if stunned. Slowly, it turned its face to me and sniffed and growled a minute; as I looked in its eyes, I knew I was next. Then, it turned to Brenna, and for a few minutes they circled, assessing each other. Then, without warning, the beast seemed to grow taller, and it leapt and tackled her. She landed hard on her back as the creature's gigantic paws held down her shoulders, its claws digging into her skin, ripping it to shreds. Blood darkened the floor and held me transfixed. My savior tried wrapping her hands around the thing's throat to get it off of her, but it was too heavy.

Gasping, I tried to get up to help her, but my body wasn't responding. She heard me and looked over, and when she did, I couldn't believe what I saw. Her eyes were black as ink, and her canine teeth rested on her bottom lip like Julien's had the other night.

She can't be one of them. Oh God! What if she never truly wanted to help me, but just wanted to use me as Julien had?

Of course it's possible. Why do you think she found us? She wants us just for herself. But what does she matter? You and I both know who really cares for us. Who desires us! Let Julien's pet have her, she's nothing, the thing in my mind whispered.

Go away!

Brenna fought, and I knew trying to save me was her bottom line. The other inside my head was only trying to get me to lose faith. Slowly, I began to get up, knowing I had to try and help her no matter what. But as I did, she locked her gaze with mine and sympathy crossed her face along with fear as she realized I knew what she was.

A scream pierced the room. The wolf wrapped its jaws around her throat and bit down. She scratched and clawed at her captor, but her cry was silenced as her head lolled to the side and her hands fell limp to the floor. The beast jerked its head and pulled out the section of flesh that had been in its teeth. Blood poured from the wound as color drained from her eyes and her skin. I watched the life leave her eyes and her teeth retract as she appeared to return to human form once again. A large pool of blood grew under her as the wolf swallowed the meat he'd just taken. And then it turned its gaze to me.

I shrieked as it stepped over Brenna's lifeless body and held its muzzle inches from me. I hid my face under my hands, looking through my fingers at the blood on its silver fur. It sniffed me and then let out a puff of air, curling its lips into a sneer or maybe even a smile. As it did, I saw the flesh stuck between its teeth. Brenna's blood and skin.

How could I have been so stupid? Brenna hadn't come here to claim me. She only wanted to save me! The other inside my head was wrong. My savior might have been a vampire, but she was nothing like Julien. Now she was dead. Tears pooled in my eyes, and I was able to take my hands away, as the wolf wasn't going to strike. It dawned on me that he guarded me like any good watchdog would.

Slowly, I got the courage to stand and move a little as the thing gave me room, but not much. I got to Brenna's body, trying to ignore the open wound where her spine had clearly been severed. Part of it peeking through the gaping wound. I really didn't know this woman who'd tried to help me.

It seemed I was cursed, that everyone I was involved with ended up dead. First my mother, then my father, then Gina and Jeremy, and now Brenna. This all had to stop. It all had to. I glanced at the wolf and then at the open door. Maybe I could make it. Maybe I could escape.

With one last look at Brenna, I leapt for the door and tried to dodge the wolf, but the monster jumped in my path and sat on its haunches with its tongue hanging out. There was no way I was going to get by it. There was no way I was going to escape.

I slid down into the corner and kept my eyes locked to the door that could have meant my freedom, and as I did, Julien appeared, patting the head of his pet, scratching it behind the ear. His pet closed its eyes, enjoying its master's touch. Julien glanced at Brenna's body, and a smirk appeared on his face as his eyes trailed over to me, a look of rage passing over his features.

"You didn't think you could get away from me that easily?"

I just stared at him and shook my head. It was a foolish thing for me to hope. Hope was no longer a part of my vocabulary. Every time it came to me, it was squelched. No matter how far I ran, I'd never be rid of him. He was part of me, part of it.

"Hush now, Mira. Your friend was no match for Lupe." The wolf nudged Julien for more attention.

"She's yours."

The wolf grabbed onto Brenna's leg. Its teeth crunched down to the bone as it dragged her back to its lair. I stretched my hand out before I could think and tried grabbing hold of her, not wanting the beast to shred her body.

"He really is a wonderful watchdog." Julien stopped, closing his eyes as he sensed something. "I'll be back."

He staggered out of the room, but I didn't hear his footsteps, only the horrible sound the werewolf made as he dragged Brenna's body down the hall. I glanced over and saw the trail of blood that had been left behind. The scent was intoxicating, the red smeared as if by a crazy painter. I didn't know if it was the color that grabbed me, or that it was just wet and fresh. I licked my lips, and before I could think, I crawled over. The thing in my mind surged forward and we looked on the blood. The pressure on my gums tightened as my teeth grew.

This is what we need, what will make us feel better. You know that, don't you? the thing whispered.

"Yes."

It was right. The blood would make my heart stop racing and my fear evaporate, driving all thoughts of Brenna away. My other half was right. Brenna had come to take me back to her world where she would be the Master, so being with Julien wouldn't be that bad.

I stuck my finger in the blood, inhaling the warm aroma. My other sighed and knew the blood was rich with human blood. Brenna must have fed recently. I stared at the cooling liquid, and everything in me yearned for it. My eyes rolled back in my head as I just imagined the ecstasy of drinking it. The other smiled and we licked our lips, extending our tongue, about to taste the drop when someone grabbed our wrist. Our eyes snapped open and we hissed, but when we saw Julien, we lowered our eyes immediately. We had to make him happy, had to break his gaze and let him be pleased with us, as he was our Master.

"Interesting," he said, lifting our head so that we met his eyes.

His power rolled into our mind, assessing us as we kept our eyes on the blood. "You want more, pet?"

"Yes."

He bit into his wrist and held it out as blood slowly welled to the surface. Time slowed as gravity drew the liquid down, expanding it, making it more appetizing. Then time accelerated as the drop made contact with the concrete floor. Everything in us wanted to reach out and snatch his wrist. Even I wanted it as the other did. Only I hesitated with the thought of everything that had happened, of what he had done to me, but the other surged forward, wrapping our fingers around his flesh. Our tongue lapped at the blood, drinking a few swallows so it eased our hunger. With each swallow, the thing inside of me wove itself more tightly into my bones, fusing itself into my psyche. I'd been denying something that was part of me since I was born, even before my roommate dragged a razor across her wrists. We drank a few more sips and then let go, sensing our system couldn't take any more of the thick liquid, not until his blood molded our body into something more like his.

Julien leaned in and kissed me on the lips, licking away the rest of the blood. "Come, Mira. I think it's time you meet the rest of the family."

We smiled, eager to meet those like us. It was good to know we had a new family, because all my friends were dead. Brenna was dead, and Julien's children were all we had left.

17

CHAPTER SEVENTEEN

My name is Brenna.

Everything about me hurt like hell. I tried swallowing, but my throat felt cracked and dry. Pain filled my neck, and then there was my leg. It felt like I'd been pummeled by a steamroller, but the rest of me was just sore from overused muscles. The connections in my brain weren't working. I tried to open my eyes, but even as I thought about movement, everything in me grew fuzzy, like I'd had too much to drink, and my body began losing sensation.

When my eyes did flutter open, light surrounded me. A sense of warmth infused the spots where pain had been, and in the distance, a sense of serenity and peace like I'd never known filled my heart. I desperately wanted to move beyond, to let the current of the wind blow me to a place without pain or anguish. The closer I got to my destination, the more my responsibilities floated away. My thoughts of Miranda left me, my love for Veronica lingered, but it was so easy to give up. All my pain disappeared, and I was about to be encompassed when my journey ended abruptly as liquid silver passed through me.

I was hurled backwards, tumbling away from the light where it was so warm, sailing across space, through universes, forgetting time as everything about me grew heavier. The dimensions pressed down upon me, and I was back in my body. The cold made me aware of the miles of veins in my flesh as blood shot through my organs and muscles. It made me remember my responsibilities to Miranda, Veronica, and those I gave advice to.

Itching started in my neck, traveling along my spine and moving into my leg as I realized my skin was knitting back together. The healing forced my heart to throttle forward and my lungs to take in a huge breath, and I was able to slowly open my eyes.

Everything flashed in my mind: the werewolf's attack, how its fangs closed around my neck, how it tore away my windpipe and snapped my spinal cord. My hands grasped my throat, desperately looking for the wound, but the skin was whole. Looking down at my leg, the jeans were torn, but the skin had no blemish. I was totally healed. But that was impossible. I should have died. I *had* died.

I tried to remember the sensations from before, from where I was, but they dwindled like a dying wind. All I knew was, I'd been at peace, and then cold had infused my body.

As I did a quick scan of myself, I noticed something defined about my energy field. It vibrated higher for some reason, and the color was murky, but other than that, I had no idea what was going on. Whatever had brought me back had altered me somehow, but it was too early to tell how, as it was just settling in my system. I was definitely stronger and felt like I'd gotten a good day's sleep, but as much as I wanted to dodder on what had happened to me, I had to get back to Miranda.

I glanced around. Piles of bones lay scattered about—whoever these victims were, nothing was left but shreds. Then it dawned on me. A werewolf had killed Zach and that girl. Zhen had been right about that, so at least that was one mystery solved. But could it be this werewolf? I didn't know how many were in the city, but I wondered. Now I just had to get out of here before it decided to come back and make me its lunch again.

I listened closely and heard those six heartbeats I'd heard before. All of them were above me, and so were all the others. Slow and methodical, each contributed to the symphony. Half the nest was above me and it was better than the entire hundred or so, but Miranda was there, and I had to go to her. Besides, she and her Master thought I was dead, so at least I could surprise them there.

Wrapping my shields around me, I ran out of the basement and went upstairs to where I saw all the vampires on all fours, waiting. Many of them crawled toward Julien as he sat on his throne, enjoying the groveling as they waited to be told they could have their food. I entered silently. The four in the corner had been released, but they stayed huddled in the corner—they were hopeless junkies, waiting for the vampires to pounce on them or fuck them. The brood salivated. They seemed almost too obedient, but with the wave of their Master's hand, they pounced on the four. Fifty or so vampires with only four humans—that was not a pretty sight as they all clawed and tried to get something out of the meat. Those four girls were only the appetizers.

As soon as they saw the beasts coming, the four women screamed. Something stirred in me. My teeth grew, and my wings pressed against my back. Clenching my fists together, I banked my own desires. I wanted to join in the feast, but I didn't need blood. The vampire in me craved it, wanting to see blood squirted, tearing the mortals apart. But no. I was not like them. I turned from the scene and looked to the stage.

"You see, Mira, this is what happens when they are obedient. Humans want us to ravage them. They are our food. Only meat. Do you understand?"

Miranda nodded. My heart shrank. She was becoming his even as I watched. The beast crawled under her skin as her muscles rolled. Her aura was darker as it tried to latch on, but there was also some of her left underneath the surface, fighting. And that meant there was still something worth saving. I dropped my mental shields, making my presence known. The mayhem ended abruptly as vampires looked up from the pig-pile, some with blood smeared on their faces, others with globs of flesh in their hands, others with it caught in their pointed teeth. I doubted there was much left of those four redheads.

Julien looked up to see what had stopped the carnage. Astonishment painted his features long enough for me to see beneath his cool exterior. "So, Lupe didn't devour you."

He blasted his mind at me, trying to hack into my thoughts and take control, but I held fast under the barrage. Hatred and wonder coursed through him as he realized that I wasn't going to bend to his will, that I was going to take Miranda no matter what.

"You can't have her. She's mine by right."

I gritted my teeth. This was the typical way vampires behaved, thinking they owned mortals. I swore the male ego was inflated tenfold when men were turned. All undead were chauvinistic and arrogant, but Julien was over the top.

"She's coming with me whether you like it or not, asshole."

I stepped forward, working my way through the nest, waiting for a signal, wondering why we were talking. I had a flashback to Malachi's lair when I humiliated him and could have taken control of it because I'd defeated the Master. Of course, I didn't want the brood. What I'd wanted was more valuable.

"Do you think I'll just let you have her? After all the years I've searched? After all that I've been through to find her?"

"Oh, cut the shit! I've heard the sanctimonious vampire bullshit before, and I'm fucking tired of it. I'm taking Miranda, and you won't stop me. You have no right to treat mortals the way you do. At least other vampires I've encountered let humans live, but you—you lock them up and steal their souls."

A look of surprise crossed his face as I spoke, and then he smiled. I didn't like that smile because it said he knew something I didn't. It said that something was about to happen.

I got up to the stage and stared him down as he tried using his power again, but I didn't flinch. It was impossible for most vampires to enter my thoughts. Standing next to him, I was taller by a good three inches, and he wasn't that muscular, but that didn't mean jack when it came to strength. He might have had ten times the physical strength I did, as this was different for each vampire. I was strong, yes, but my mental abilities were my prowess. Next to him, I realized he truly was the one who'd been following me. The energy was the same as it rubbed against mine and stuck to me like oil.

The tension between us mounted. I waited for him to do something and extended my hand to Miranda. My eyes never left his, and I couldn't help but smirk as he glared at me. His charge looked from my hand and then to her captor, and her inner battle between sanity and devotion raged. Before she was able to take my hand, something hit me from behind and I was thrown forward onto the stage, knocking over the throne.

A shitload of vampires pig-piled on top of me. Their talons dug into my back, tearing away my shirt and my already ragged jeans. Trying to get at the better meat, they turned me over to get a good biting spot somewhere on my body. I was just another appetizer. Not having much time to think, I covered my face, threw my shields open, and called on all the power in me.

The heat exploded in my heart like a huge bonfire that was about to rage out of control. Power immersed me, bursting out of all my chakras like a broken dam, encompassing me in a blazing, white-hot bubble. For a split moment of infinity, everything around me was perfect and I got a sense of the place I'd been in before, warm and peaceful. The things trying to eat me had all stopped, as time itself seemed to cease. I saw frozen particles of air, and the grotesque expressions plastered on the undead looming above me, reminding me that they were real and this wasn't some bad horror movie I'd put myself into. Then, time sped up.

All the undead around me spontaneously combusted. The flames were white and blue, only burning for a split second as their bodies turned to ash, leaving a thin film all over me. It seemed the sun had exploded in on them, or a mini nuclear bomb had gone off and left nothing but devastation.

Slowly, I got up and saw that all the monsters in the cafeteria had been vaporized. All of my energy points sang, vibrating as the cosmos filtered through me, then reduced to a trickle. I should have been weakened by the discharge, but in contrast, I was ready to take on the other half of the nest if they showed up. With them out of the way, I could focus on my charge.

Dusting off the ashes, I looked on Julien, and the expression on his face was priceless. The astonishment was worth it. Then came his fear as he realized he was no match for me. In truth, I had no idea how

I'd pulled off that display, and I prayed that when I needed the ability, it would come back. I stepped toward Julien, my hand held out, but he looked back to me and then Miranda. He bolted, crashing through the window, taking out the rest of the glass left in the cafeteria.

Miranda stared at me from under the scum's spell. I pushed my mind into hers to see how much of the beast had gained control. She was standing in the very middle of oblivion, half-human and half-vampire, both parts vying for dominance.

I shook my head and guided her off the stage. As I did, I saw darkness swirling one way in her eyes, then they cleared instantly as her system, her very soul, was fighting the invasion. I smiled and wondered how she dealt with this. Her circumstances were so very different from mine. I was turned, and Julien had been after her for decades when it seemed that I was just the victim of circumstance. But I knew that wasn't true because I had *decided* to become a vampire. It was my destiny, but who knew I was also signing on for this too, for becoming the avenging angel type.

Honestly, I really didn't know if I could help Miranda any more, except by killing Julien. Maybe Veronica could help. Maybe she could reverse the effects of the vampire. But until then, I willed Miranda to sleep, gathered her in my arms and took off to the refuge of my house. At least she'd be safe for a little while, but then again, I was never going to be safe from the tongue lashing my lover would give me. By now I was sure she'd figured out I'd gone to the nest, and she might be thinking the worst.

Well, that mystery would be solved in a while, and I'd tell her what had happened. It was better for me to leave out the small detail that I'd somehow been brought back from the dead. I didn't think Veronica would really want to hear that.

18

CHAPTER EIGHTEEN

My name is Miranda.

When I opened my eyes, Brenna stared down at me.

That's impossible. The werewolf tore her throat out. She shouldn't have survived. If she were human, she'd have been devoured.

Her smile was warm, and her eyes filled with concern. Her hand pressed against my forehead and then my neck, checking my pulse. Her touch was cool, helping to calm my racing heart. Something about her soothed me. A part of her was made to help others, something ingrained in her, part of her legacy, I realized. I smiled, glad to see she was all right, dismissing my earlier thoughts.

"It's good to have you back."

Her teeth were even and white. Her skin was slightly clammy, though not marred with any imperfection, and something sparkled in her eyes, but it could have been the light. Then, as I stared at her, I remembered. Brenna's canines shifted in my mind, growing long just as Julien's had when he attacked me. Her eyes had been black, not brown. Talons had replaced her nails as she'd wrapped them around the throat of the werewolf. I recalled everything, all the way back to Julien having sex with me, forcing me to drink his blood. My other half had welcomed him. Panic grabbed hold of me. She was one of them.

"Get away from me." I snarled, backing up against the back of the bed. "You're just like him."

Brenna glanced at Veronica as I tried to get further away from the both of them. I stared between the two of them, wondering if I could make it to the door, but if they were like Julien, they'd get there before me. I checked the window to my right, but there was no fire escape, just a two-story drop. If I jumped, it would be better than ending up their slaves. I glanced back, and they were both staring at each other.

A look of understanding crossed Brenna's face as she glanced from Veronica to me. I assumed they were having some sort of silent conversation. Brenna knelt down next to me.

"Miranda, I—we—won't hurt you. You've been through enough. I—"

"No. I saw you. You only rescued me because you want me for yourself."

She clamped down on my shoulder. I tried moving, but her hand felt like a vice, and it only proved my point that she wanted me for herself. I wiggled under her until she backed away, but the distance didn't help my racing pulse. I swallowed hard, trying to keep my stomach in check as it threatened to spill, but the more I fought for control, the more my other half awakened.

She took you away from our Master. Why do you still trust her?

"Miranda, if I was like him, then you'd be dead, or you'd be a sniveling bitch trying to please me. All I've done is help you. If you want, I'll take you back so he can fuck you all over again. Is that what you want?"

The coldness in her voice scared me. She wasn't lying. She would take me back if I wanted. She didn't want my soul. She just wanted to help me. The thing in my mind screamed for retribution, yelling that Brenna lied, but I shoved it back into my consciousness. I squeezed my eyes shut at the effort. When I opened them, Brenna was smiling before me. Calmness settled over me as I saw something like stars and small universes being born in her eyes, but when I blinked, they were gone.

"What *are* you?"

The woman in front of me was not all she seemed to be. She might have been a vampire, but she was something else as well Maybe she could tell me why my other was trying to take over? Ever since Julien had taken me, my sleep had been blank. I would have been grateful if I hadn't traded one nightmare for another.

"What are you? What am I?" I asked, trying to answer the questions I wanted to pose to her.

Brenna sighed, gazed lovingly at Veronica and ran her finger along her lover's cheek. I grinned internally, sensing how much they cared for one another. There was an understanding between them that went deeper than I could fathom. It made me wonder if Veronica was the one who created Brenna, but if that were the case, why wasn't Brenna being subservient?

"When you first came into my shop, I thought you were like me. But you're something else. That's why you've had dreams. Why there were two personalities vying for dominance over your flesh. Julien must have sensed that you're unique, and that's why he's enamored with you. His blood awakened the beast inside, or at least brought it out of holding, and now it wants total control. Does this sound right to you?"

"How did you know?"

"I read minds, silly. I flip through thoughts like pages in a photo album, but I leave all the private ones alone." Brenna giggled.

I laughed along with her and began to relax. They might be vampires, but they were not going to kill me. My trust in Brenna slowly returned, and I needed to believe everything she said.

"How did you become like you are?" I asked, wondering how she could read minds, how she'd become a psychic and a vampire.

"It's a long story, but first, I want to know about you. You once told me about one of your family members being attacked by a vampire."

"So?"

"If my hunch is right, the vampire must have infected your ancestor with its blood. Somehow, the process was interrupted, and through the generations, each human born drove the beast into the mind until it was awoken by a traumatic event in your life. It sees Julien as its Master and will do anything for him, even pushing your personality out of the way. But you're strong-willed and, for now, you're winning the battle. If you remain as you are, you should be fine. If not, then—" She trailed off.

I understood now. The stories about my ancestor Marie being attacked by a vampire were true. Through generations of her bloodline, something of the vampire had been passed down. It made sense that there'd been a history of mental instability in the family. I understood why my mother had committed suicide, why my grandmother had been committed when she was thirty, both raving about the evil inside of them. The dreams must have been a way for the beast to present itself in my psyche. When I'd been in the hospital and my roommate had committed suicide, the sight of all her blood had stirred it up.

What happens now? I can't go back to the life I had before. Claire'll be wondering what has happened to Gina and me. God! Has she found the bodies?

Claire would keep Crimson Liquids going. The only way she could cope with losing Gina was to work. That was the way Claire dealt with everything.

"So ,what happens now?"

I waited for Brenna, but Veronica answered. "You'll learn to survive. It's hard to live with the beast, but it can be done."

Staring at the both of them, I wondered what she meant, but before I could ask, the door burst open, landing on the bed next to me. The thing on the panel looked something like the werewolf, but it was bigger, bulkier, and covered with brown fur. Its talons were longer and sharper than the wolf's. It had a short tail that didn't cover its balls or black dick. It sniffed the air and turned its head in my direction.

Brenna pushed me off the bed and jumped in front of me. Veronica leaped in front of her, forming a line of defense. The thing looked at all three of us and snarled, and a gargle came out of its mouth, more like it was laughing, as its eyes settled on Veronica. Its muscles bunched and it pounced on her. She landed hard on the bed I'd originally been lying on. The monster jumped on top of her, trying to swipe her throat with its claws, but she held it and kicked, hitting the monster in the balls, but that still didn't dislodge him.

They wrestled as Brenna hopped out of the way and tried to pull the beast from Veronica, but the animal was propelled across the room, and Veronica got up. Her jeans were torn, and blood ran down her leg. I saw bone underneath. Scratches adorned her neck and cheeks. Brenna went to her aid and said something I couldn't hear. Veronica shoved Brenna off to the side and faced the monster that now stood on two legs, looking like the beast-vampire Julien had been. Brenna wanted to go to her lover, but instead, she protected me.

Then, something strange happened. Veronica and the monster locked eyes. She took on a tackling stance. Her nails grew, and she invited it to come at her. It leaped, but instead of letting it take her down, she opened her arms and caught it. The beast latched onto her throat. The crack of bone was evident as it pulled out the tender flesh of her neck. Blood and tissue splattered across the room. Some landed on my cheek, but I had no desire to lick it off my face. Veronica's body crumpled to the floor.

I didn't see what happened next, but Brenna fell to her knees, crawling over to her lover's body and taking it in her arms as the thing backed off. It stood up, running its tongue over uneven, pointed teeth. I glanced over, noticing it had a paw missing, or hand, whatever. Its stump was a mass of twisted and scarred skin. I wondered why, if this thing was a vampire, the limb hadn't grown back.

It looked on me and then smiled at Brenna. "Payment in full," it said with a snarl.

She looked up for a second through tear-filled eyes. Confusion and then understanding crossed her face as all the color drained away. Her sadness filled me, even though I had no idea what this message meant. I understood what it meant for her to lose the one she loved.

Brenna sat as Veronica's blood seeped onto her clothes and the floor around her, letting the shock of what had transpired sink in. Her demeanor changed. Hatred decorated her features as they danced and twisted. Her wings burst out of her back, ripping her clothing, and I noticed they were feathered like an angel's. The skin stretched as if it were wax, and her chin lengthened. Her face had distended with two sets of canines.

She charged after the beast, dashing down the stairs. I heard the rustle of plastic tarps falling and the scaffolding being knocked down. Slowly, I was drawn over to Veronica's body. Her life formed a pool around her head like a halo; her eyes were closed and her look, serene. I glanced down at her throat, seeing how the skin tried to piece itself back together, how her severed bones tried to heal. Silvery transparent tissue formed over the wound, and small ropes grew in the membrane, veins, I assumed. As the injury sealed, the thin flesh broke down, trying to reform again.

This reminded me of Gina. Holding Veronica, I cried for everything I'd lost, for my friends and parents, and for Brenna. Because of me, everything she cherished was gone.

I glanced up when I heard the creaking on the stair and saw Brenna back in human form, but there was no expression on her face. It was as bleak as the desert, vacant as the moon's surface. She knelt down and took Veronica in her arms. I backed away, knowing there was nothing I could do except sit on the bed and watch as Brenna rocked with silent tears streaming down her face. In that moment, all of my problems seemed miniscule in comparison. Deep down, I forgot about everything else, and only thought of my savior and what she'd lost to save me.

19

CHAPTER NINETEEN

My name is Brenna.

As I took Veronica in my arms, her life was leaving her. Our connection was dying, passing out of my thoughts like a fading wind. What would I do without her? She was everything to me. Pushing my mind into hers, I wrapped it around her soul, trying to anchor it. There was a spark in her dying flesh, and for an instant, it seemed like she was holding me once again. Even as I wanted to talk to her, her spirit was somewhere beyond words, drifting to the place I'd been the day before. I should have been able to go to this place again, but I didn't know how to.

You can't leave me alone. You can't die. I'm not ready to be on my own. You promised me an eternity. I'm not ready to face that alone. I don't know what I am, and you were going to help me figure that out. I need you here to show me just how to be. You can't leave me alone, not yet.

Please, not yet, I whispered to her soul, but she didn't hear me.

I touched her hair briefly and gathered more of my power, opening myself to the universe, letting it filter through me and into her. I'd done this once before, using my own aura to heal her, recharging her immune system when Devon had locked her in a closet and denied her food so her wounds weren't healing. In the astral realm, I found her through the bond we shared.

Energy moved through me and into her. Now, as my aura expanded and filled the room, I was about to burst. At the climax of the power high, I willed the power into her, pushing it all into her body. Her soul soaked up some of the energy, growing like a candle flame drinking in air, but it only lasted a moment. The excess streamed over her body, doing nothing. Blood still leaked from her wound, and the skin had stopped trying to heal. Worst of all, I couldn't feel her in the back of my mind.

"Come on, Veronica. You can't leave me alone. Not now."

The ember in her filled with sympathy, but even as I tried to embrace it, it began to unwind from my psyche, slipping through a spider-webbed veil. Even as I tried holding on, she just drifted away. But I couldn't let her go. I just couldn't.

Power drowned me until I choked on it. I drew it together into one raging burst. It seared my insides, causing my organs to boil. If I couldn't save her, then I'd go with her. Internally, I screamed, hearing my voice echoing into a dark abyss, not feeling the shards of glass as the windows exploded in the house. All I knew was that I was losing the woman I loved. The more the heat raged, the more I began to sweat, and being engulfed in this cleansing power was a wonderful feeling.

The heat scorched my soul, and I knew if I continued, I'd join her. This was what the vampires must have felt in the nursing home, what it felt like to have the sun eat away at skin and turn them to ash. It was a wonderful feeling, and now, at its peak, there was nothing I could do except ride the wave. All I had to do was let go and go with her.

Peace started to come over me, but a hand clamped down on my shoulder, filling me with cold. I dropped Veronica and growled at whoever had grabbed me. My fingers hardened to bone and came to slash at whatever had stopped me. It would die with me.

As I spun around, I couldn't see anything except white dots on a black background. My instincts guided me. At first, I thought it was the thing come back to finish me off, so I sliced and met empty air. Before I could do any damage, my wrists were caught.

Instantly, my vision cleared, and I saw who had grabbed me.

The Angel of Death's power washed over me like a silent tsunami. Liquid silver filled my being, extinguishing the heat once and for all. I felt like I'd been dowsed with a bucket of ice water. His eyes were bottomless, like the empty sockets of a skull. There was nothing of the being I'd seen before. My heart ached for Veronica, and it also whispered of the moment Azrael and I had shared on the beach. Nail-biting cold drowned me, chilling the marrow of my soul. Then, there was a sudden tingling as the frigid touch wore off because he wasn't trying to hurt me, just get my attention.

"Why are you here?" I half-growled, half-whispered.

I have come for your beloved. It is my duty and her time. Will you deny me my obligation?

There was nothing I could do with him standing over me. I couldn't fight Death. Veronica was lost to me forever. But if he was going to embrace her, then he was going to take me as well. "You can't, please— take me, too. I can't—please."

Azrael passed his hand over my face, brushing my skin as lightly as a cobweb. *I'm sorry.* The ache in his voice mirrored the one in my heart.

Soundlessly, he was gone, taking with him the one thing that held me to life.

Veronica's expression was peaceful and very human. Her face had filled out, but the serene look only lasted a few seconds as her body melted away. First, her hair fell out and her face caved in, along with her chest and legs. Her skin turned from pale to gray, and then it cracked, forming tiny hairline fractures much like veins. The tracks splintered and then flaked off, revealing nothing more than white bone. Even that turned gray, and then her whole body seemed locked in dust, like a mold in Pompeii, but even that disintegrated into a pile of clothes and fine ash.

I collapsed next to the remains, wondering what to do. Without her, I had no purpose. She'd been my anchor. Now everything I was had been squashed in one instant. Images of the things we'd been through flashed in my mind. She'd given me life, helped me understand what kind of a creature I was. She loved me for everything, and even though I'd killed her Master, she'd forgiven me in her own way. She'd even forgiven me for running off the other night. Of course, I hadn't told her about my brush with death, but that didn't seem to matter now because even though I'd tried not to endanger her, in truth, I had. What would I do without her?

A whimper drew my attention.

Miranda was huddled in the corner. Fear over what had happened looped in her mind as I looked on her. Veronica would have wanted me to guard Miranda, just as my lover had protected me from Devon. I would have to be the guardian. Yes, Veronica would have wanted me to do that.

Miranda felt my gaze and smiled. The look in her eyes told me she understood how I felt, since she'd recently lost her friend. In her own way, she would see me through this. I wiped away my tears, and in the back of my mind, I felt beings around me. Energy pressed on my back as my guides comforted me the only way they knew how. Silently, I thanked them, but pushed them aside. They'd done nothing to warn me. No tingling on the back of my mind, no flashing lights or whistles. What good were they to me if they hadn't warned me?

Politely, I thanked them and shut the door on my psychic connection. The lock turned in my mind and, mentally, I threw away the key. Now I had to worry about Miranda. My sorrow turned to anger. The anger simmered to rage and then burned to revenge.

Julien would trace my charge through his blood, coming to claim her and to reap vengeance. He'd be out for my blood since I'd killed his brood. I didn't care. I'd beat him, and if I didn't, then I'd be able to join my lover. That was my goal now, after Miranda was safe.

For now, I had to get Miranda out of here. I opened my arms and gave her a big hug. She returned it with force, and I sensed the trust in her now that she knew I wasn't going to hurt her. I released her and then knelt over my Master's remains. Veronica was happier in whatever place Azrael had taken her to. For one moment, I touched her soul and knew she was beyond this world of pain.

"So, what happens now?"

Rage built in me, and the coldness Azrael left behind with his touch leaked into my eyes. Liquid steel seeped into my bones and hardened them. The heat from before turned to ice, remaking my entire being. In the back of my mind, I saw my white-gold aura turn blue-black. It felt like the universe had opened up and poured itself into me, like a new part of me had been unlocked from Death's touch. Just like it had with Devon's touch. I flexed my fingers, hearing them crack at the knuckles like breaking twigs, and I remembered what the vampire had said after it killed Veronica.

Payment.

Zhen had taken the one thing I loved for compensation. It wasn't enough that I was supposed to kill Julien for her help. She had to have Veronica also, probably to show her dominance. Probably to make good on the teasing she'd done with me. The Elder had tasted my blood and admitted she wanted me. She might be ancient, but soon, she was going to wish she'd never invited me to her lair.

20

CHAPTER TWENTY

My name is Miranda.

After three days, life reverted back to normal while I stayed with Brenna. We both agreed it wasn't safe for me back at my house, since she didn't know how long it would take Julien to come after us. He'd seemed pretty shaken up when she destroyed his vampires, so for now, I lived with her.

On the second day, I ventured to Crimson Liquids. Claire dropped her café latté on the floor and just stared, not sure if I was a ghost or some figment of her imagination. The other staffers gathered around me and gave me a huge hug, asking questions about what had happened. I didn't know what to say except that I'd been staying with a friend; I pretended to know nothing about Gina's or Jeremy's deaths. My instinct told me it seemed safer that way, and I agreed.

Claire told me the police had stopped in, asking where I was. She'd gotten me a cup of tea, waiting to hear my version of what I knew and calling the cops an hour later, thinking it might be better to speak to them so they wouldn't think anything about my involvement. Of course, I wouldn't kill my own friends, but the staff knew I had issues, so then again, they might just think that. While I waited, I flip-flopped between tears and stunned silence.

The police arrived, settling next to me at my usual table and telling me that my friends were dead. They asked me what had happened, since they said people had seen me at the house that night. Did we have any enemies? Had anyone been harassing us? I answered no and told them I'd gone over to a friend's house, which was why they couldn't find me or reach me. Gina had promised to pick up my shifts, and I'd told her I'd be back today since I was staying with a friend. The police wanted to know what happened when I went back to get my things.

Had I seen anything? Heard anything? Maybe something was amiss? I told them I'd gone home and seen that the door was slightly open, which nothing new because it always swung open unless it was slammed shut and locked. Gina and Jeremy's cars were in the driveway and music blared from the basement, so I assumed they were busy. I grabbed a few things and then headed to the T to stay with a friend. I was only in the house for about ten minutes.

The cops asked me what time that was, and I lied and said around ten. They asked if I saw Gina dead in the basement. I blanched at that detail and started sniveling and moaning as the image came to me again, and I remembered discovering the bodies. I carried on, but said nothing, crying. My nose was dripping; my eyes stung from the whole ordeal. The detectives looked at one another as one grabbed me a napkin to blow my nose. Everyone hugged me again, knowing how hard this was for me. They asked for my friend's address, which I admitted I didn't know, but I gave them Brenna's business card, which I still had on me, and said I'd be with her if they wanted to ask me any more questions. After a while, they seemed satisfied and left.

I thanked God when the police interview was over and, being at work for a full day after that, every time the bell rang, I expected Gina to walk in. Slowly, I was getting used to the fact that she wasn't coming back, which weighed on my heart. If it hadn't been for me, she'd still be alive. That knowledge hurt worse than anything else.

I sighed and went back downstairs to wipe off the tables. As I began, I glanced over at the bookshelf and noticed all the vampire novels sprawled in no particular order. Humanity didn't know what a real vampire looked like. They weren't creatures with capes and deep, sexy, hypnotic voices. No, they were much more than that. I plucked a book off the shelf, leafing through it, discovering it was one of the many spinoffs of Dracula that kept being released. For so long, these books had been my solace in the night, but now they did nothing for me. Now I knew what true vampires were.

Time to change the décor. I gathered a few books in my arms. The macabre theme was way overdone. Gina'd been right when she mentioned that the horror motif got old, but I had never listened. Something bright and cheery might give Crimson Liquids a new feel. It would definitely be a shock to the customers. I took the handful of books and threw them in the trash. A few amazed expressions appeared on the patrons' faces. I smiled and took another armload, and as I was about to throw them in the bin, it spoke to me.

If you think by throwing away your books you'll be rid of me, then you're fooling yourself.

At first, I thought it was a customer talking to me. It took me a few minutes to realize the voice was in my mind. It had more validity than before, more personality, and was distinctly female. I tried to ignore it, but when I did, it worked under my skin, sending piercing talons of pain through me. Books scattered all over the floor as I fell to my knees.

Someone's arms guided me to a table, and I heard them run upstairs, but the thing demanded attention.

Let me out, Miranda. You can't keep denying I'm here. We're part of each other. We bonded the other day. You saw the blood and wanted it as well. So don't think I don't know that you want me here.

"What are you?" I asked the thing speaking in my mind. Claire and the others crowded around me, trying to figure out what was wrong with me. I knew they were there because I could smell them. Claire always had a buttery smell, and the others—well, I could just sense them, something I'd never been able to do before.

I'm just another part of you that has lurked in the shadows since I was denied a Master ages ago.

"Where did you come from?" I wanted to know how it had gotten inside of me. I figured it was something I was born with. Even though Brenna had told me how it matured in my mind, I wanted to hear it from the vampire's mouth.

The beast smiled. I didn't move, but my face twitched, as my flesh had become a mask, and underneath was the monster.

From the blood of my Master passed down through human inbreeding.

"Why me? Why didn't you awake in the others before me?"

They've all felt my presence as I lingered in their minds like a second self, waiting to be born. But you, I took root in your soul, yawning from my centuries of sleep when you saw blood spill for the first time. Each year since, I've gotten stronger. Then, one of my kind freed me. And here I am. Soon we'll be one and I'll be the dominant force inside this bag of flesh.

The beast surged forward, catching me off guard. My eyes rolled in the back of my head; my veins seemed to be running dry while my heart pounded mercilessly in my chest. Panting, I squirmed around, trying to regain control, but the thing took its claws and sunk them inside of my brain. I rode out the pain, clawing my fingers into whatever I could hold onto while my body convulsed. It was not going to have me. Not yet. I was the one in control. If I ended up like the other vampires, then I'd lose my identity, my humanity. I wouldn't let that happen!

For a moment, my teeth grew, and the skin on my hands itched incessantly. The bones in my fingers were pulled out of their sockets, as if I'd been thrown on the rack. Flesh on my back stretched, and I heard large cracks as my shoulder blades started to shift. Pain seared me, but I forced the thing into the recess of my mind, pushing against it like an anchored concrete truck, but in the end, it began to budge.

"I'm the strong one. You're nothing. Go back to the hell you came from," I screamed, ramming with all my might, forcing it back until I thought my brain would hemorrhage.

It retreated unable to overcome my will. The pain vanished as abruptly as it had come, and everything in me returned to normal. Opening my eyes, I saw everyone that surrounded me. I glanced at Claire and saw the red marks where I'd grabbed her. She looked at me, assuming I'd lost it because of Gina's death. That was the best thing for her to think.

After placating everyone, I withdrew into the office and tried working on the finances. It seemed to be the only thing to make time pass. I had to meet Brenna about eight. Claire would close. I promised her the day off tomorrow, but she wouldn't hear of it after what had happened, and she said that she and Linda would work as long as they needed to. Both of them were happy, considering overtime would kick in by the next day. It wasn't like I was worried, since business was almost out of control.

Numbers blurred as I stared at them. Fighting the thing inside me had sapped my strength. Every day, it took more and more effort to stay awake during the day. Light bothered me, and I had the urge to wear sunglasses all the time, but everyone thought I was freaky enough so I decided against it. The good thing was, at least I knew where the beast had come from, but I didn't know if I could live with it always vying for dominance. When I saw blood, I wanted to drink it. Even the thought of it made my stomach gurgle and the other stir.

The rest was crap, and as I stared at the numbers, all I could think of was Gina and how she'd died, how her head had rolled underneath the chair. The dead stare in her eyes. I'd watched Veronica die too, and now Brenna suffered more than I. Nothing seemed to be going right in my life, but that was nothing new.

I shook my head, trying to rid my mind of every-thing.

When will it all end?

21

CHAPTER TWENTY-ONE

My name is Brenna.

Two days passed in a blur. I called Peter and told him something had happened to Veronica, so I wasn't coming in. He didn't ask any questions, which I was happy about, and I considered he could probably tell by my voice that something awful had occurred. When I could deal with it, I'd tell him everything. His relationship with Veronica had been good, considering she'd been there for such a short time. Everyone had been surprised when I showed up with a female lover, since in college, I'd been straighter than an arrow, the only heterosexual in the Tearoom. When everyone found out my partner was female, they all cheered, saying one day they knew I would turn. But in truth, sex didn't matter. I enjoyed both men and women, and now, as a vampire, sex wasn't as important as it had been before. It fell to the back burner, and blood became the more important aphrodisiac. Of course, that wasn't the case with other vampires and their Masters, for whom sex and blood went hand in hand.

Peter canceled all my appointments, and even though I told him I'd be out, I found myself back in the Tearoom trying to keep busy. So, when I walked in on the third day, Peter glanced at me and didn't say a word—he was probably reading my emotions, which where erratic. If I stayed at home, I'd be apt to eviscerate the carpenters, and that wouldn't be a good thing.

I told Miranda to try and go back to work because the cops would be wondering what the hell had happened at her house. Besides, I didn't want to take my rage out on her either. Her employees might be thinking the worst. I didn't think Julien would come after us this soon, not after my display of power had put the fear of God in him. He knew I was a force to be reckoned with.

Veronica was the only thing on my mind. I pictured the serene expression on her face when Azrael had taken her. He was doing his duty, but a seed of something had been planted in me because of it. And it was hatred. *Why couldn't he have spared her? Done me one favor?*

All I had left of her were ashes I'd gathered into a jar. For now, they waited on my bureau to be scattered, so she could be released once and for all.

The first day after her death, I stayed home, staring out the broken windows. The workers asked me how the glass had been blown out. I shrugged, suggesting a very loud sonic boom. They just looked at me for a second, but I sighed and told them to order new windows. Money didn't matter.

On the third day, Peter rescheduled my readings, almost knowing I would be back early. I told him that was fine. I had to get back into the swing of things sooner or later. So, I did the readings, stealing the clients' secrets from their minds. I couldn't bear opening up to the universe and feeling my guides. Their loving presence was too much to handle, ever present, and truthfully, I didn't know if I ever wanted to be part of it again. It wasn't like I would miss the ghosts whispering to me, or the feelings of humans pressing on my mind. Clients didn't know the difference anyway. I astonished them by using basic psychology and pulling on their memories.

Even while I did the readings, I was in a daze, replaying the last moment over and over again as Veronica stood before the vampire. She told me to protect Miranda. As the vampire struck, she whispered that she loved me. When I saw the smug smile on the beast's face, rage tore through me. Zhen would pay. It was her fledgling, the drag queen, who'd attacked us. But I wasn't exactly ready to face the ancient vampire. Not yet.

Everything in me was dead, and even hunting had no appeal. Miranda was the only reason I kept going, and the faint candle of revenge, or else starvation was looking pretty fucking good. I'd brave the pain of my body eating away at itself, or of insanity, as long as my efforts would reunite me with the only person I loved. Besides, I didn't want to face Azrael in any form. He was on my shit list too, and if I chose suicide, I'd fight him with all my resources, even if he was an angel and nothing I did worked on him anyway. But, hell, I'd try. He would take me.

I sighed and gave one quick smile to my client before sending him off. I glanced at the clock—it was ten minutes to closing. Peter would lock up, and Miranda was waiting. The arrangement was that she'd call if Julien appeared. But that hadn't happened yet, and I hoped it never would, since I had no idea if I had the strength to face him again.

I left the Tearoom and met Miranda downstairs, and we walked back to the house in silence, each of us struggling with our own inner demons. Veronica stayed on my mind. Would I ever be able to feel her spirit on the other side? It was hard for psychics to call upon the ones we loved. I'd have to wait a full year to even speak with my lover, since it took that long for spirits to pass on to some higher plane, leaving the burden of their mortal lives behind.

Miranda and I came to the house. The windows had been either boarded up or covered with plastic. The house looked like it was abandoned, resembling how I felt. Veronica had had other remodeling planned, but I'd canceled the work. I wanted nothing more to change. New windows and whatever the contractors were doing now was all I wanted. Nothing else could be altered.

My charge went up the stairs ahead of me, and as she did, an overwhelming sense of dread descended over me. Julien would be coming soon. To protect her, I pushed all my other agendas aside. It seemed a far cry from when I'd been out looking for Zach's killer.

Maybe I'd never find the beast. That was why I'd gone to Zhen in the first place, but Veronica had warned me about the Black Rose. I should have waited for her to go with me. But like always, I had acted on impulse and blew off steam. If I'd listened, then she'd still be alive. *What if...? Why did I...? Why not...?* All these questions and their consequences were haunting me. Here I was, longing for my lover to hold me in her arms once again, but sadly, that would never be. I wrapped my arms around myself and shivered as a chill danced down my back. A prickling feeling drummed over my neck. Someone watched me. It didn't feel like a person or an angel, but something akin to a shadow. It wasn't a ghost, but a more ominous sensation got my attention, so I turned around. There, leaning against an oak tree, was Azrael.

I glanced back at Miranda, who stared at me curiously, wondering what I looked at. She couldn't see the angel.

Miranda. I reached into her mind, not wanting to frighten her, but she knew what I was, and I was tired of hiding it. *Go inside. I'll be back in a while.*

She stiffened as my thoughts brushed hers and tried to fight me until she understood it was my voice and not the beast inside her mind. She nodded, placing the key inside the lock. Scanning the house, I knew there was nothing inside. For now, I could leave her alone, but whatever Azrael wanted, he'd better make it short.

"What do you want, Azrael?" I growled, making it easy for him to see my fangs.

"You are in danger."

The expression on his face was cold and hard as stone, and uncaring as ever. He strolled down the street, moving by people who didn't notice him. One even walked through him, which didn't stop his stride. But I stopped and stared, as he had become a phantom. It was how he existed in this dimension, showing himself to those he wanted. It didn't faze him as someone passed through him. I doubted he even cared.

He stopped in the garden and sat on one of the benches overlooking the duck pond. Most of the ducks were asleep on the island in the middle of the pond. I heard them quacking in their sleep, thinking they'd be cute under better circumstances. The wind whipped around me, cutting to the core. I started to shiver, but my movement was cut off. With my mind's eye, I saw the outline of Azrael's wings, blue-black against the night. As I focused on them, I saw every feather, more delicate than the finest bird's. At first glance, they seemed like mine, but they were more fragile, and that made me envious. Something about being around Azrael made me feel like I should know what I was, where my destiny lay. My fate revolved around this creature, but whenever I asked him anything, he evaded me. It was frustrating as hell, and I was tired of his games.

"All the times you've appeared, you've given me nothing but riddles. Why? Why do you care so much about me? I'm nothing more than a vampire, and I'm surprised a creature like you would even talk to me, being all high and mighty as you are."

He reached out and took my hand. His skin was silky and cool against my own. He traced my finger, studying my flesh and wrinkles. This display was something he'd never done before, showing his humanity. Slowly, he wound his fingers through mine. I stared at him quizzically, wondering what he was trying to prove. Did he really have feelings anything close to a human's? Did he even know what emotions were? He had to, since he was Death. Being with mortals all the time, some of their emotions must have rubbed off on him, but I assumed pity wasn't one of them, since he wouldn't even spare me that.

I glanced at him. Strangely, his eyes were normal. I saw my reflection in them as I would in any mortal's, but only for an instant, and then his flesh grew warm under mine, sending bolts of energy up my arm. The feeling wasn't unpleasant, just odd. Time slowed again, and my heart sped up. Words stuck in my throat. What could I say to him? My heart was in my mouth, bleeding, wounded, and he had done it. My eyes broke his gaze, and I pulled my hand away as his spell broke. I saw hurt in his eyes, but he was an angel and couldn't possibly feel pain.

"I care. More than you fathom. Because of you, I have broken many sacred vows spoken long ago. But you don't want to hear that. You wish me to speak of Veronica, or of whether I know of your destiny or your origins."

"Do you?" I asked, hating the fact he could read my mind, but intrigued he even brought it up when I knew I'd never hear the answer.

Azrael smiled, showing his canines. They were more noticeable than they'd been in a while with the moon accentuating them, making them sharper. His features were detailed. Veins ran under his skin like the lines of a map; his flesh was opalescent in the silvery rays. Something about him sparked a faded memory, of warm light and floating until I was immersed in cold and thrown backwards, and then there was pain.

Then I made the connection. It made perfect sense. He'd been the one who'd brought me back when the werewolf snapped my neck. He was Death, with the power to spare or destroy. The liquid silver wasn't his power, but his blood.

"Why did you bring me back from death the other night?"

"I had my reasons." He placed his hands in the pockets of his trench coat and stared at the trees, reading them as they blew together. "For now, know this. You and Miranda are not safe. You should leave Boston."

I flung myself off the bench and pounded my hand into one of the old oak trees. He was telling me to flee after he was the one who'd suggested I go to the Black Rose and the nursing home. Now he wanted me to abandon everything I'd discovered.

"I won't run. It would go against everything Veronica taught me. Besides, they all deserve to die for killing her. They will pay. It's my duty to—"

"Is it your duty to die?" His voice didn't rise. Its deathly calmness made my skin crawl as his eyes darkened and fell away, again becoming the empty eye sockets of a skull. "Next time, I shall not heal you. There are only so many souls that can take your place. Will you sacrifice Miranda next?"

My mouth dropped. *Take my place? I was the target! Veronica wasn't supposed to die. That was why Veronica had pushed me out of the way—she'd been protecting me as she always did, somehow knowing it was my time. But how had she known?*

"If it was my time, then why not take me when you saved me the night before? Why not let her come back? I felt her life in my hands like a strand of silk, and then it blew away. When you took her, everything in me died. Why?" I peered into his eyes as sorrow overwhelmed me. Tears rushed over my cheeks as he gazed into the star-studded sky, denying me the knowledge I sought.

Azrael sighed. "Because I told Veronica part of your destiny. She could not have you lose your path to another lifetime. She loved you too much to see anything happen to you. As hard as it is for you to hear this, she deeply craved the peace only I could bring; she yearned for my embrace. She was tired of struggling with her other half. Three hundred years of life was too much. In you, she discovered true love and found a brief sanctuary in that."

"Why? How— She wouldn't give up on her life! We had just begun." I tried brushing away the tears, but it didn't seem to be any help.

Azrael grabbed my wrist, forcing my attention. "She was exhausted. Do you not understand? You gave meaning to her life for a brief, joyous moment. Your selflessness gave her a reason to see existence as it should have been for her. Devon made her life unbearable, and with you, she flourished. That was one of the reasons she called upon me. She—"

"How could Veronica have gotten your attention? She never knew your kind existed."

I waited for the seraph to answer, but he dropped my wrist and listened to the breeze. His eyes closed, and his face went lax. His wings flapped silently in the light wind. Tension rose. I tasted it as the air thickened around me. His eyes snapped open, and he stared past me.

"Miranda is in peril."

I didn't wait to hear anymore. A lot of things hadn't been said, but they would be discussed later; I would see to that. Racing down the street, I feared the worst and cursed myself for leaving her. Somehow, it seemed the angel always caught me off guard and got the better of me. That was something that would have to change as well. I was getting tired of being influenced by celestial forces, be them angels, demons, or Fate. My life was mine to lead.

22

CHAPTER TWENTY-TWO

My name is Miranda.

Entering the house, I searched the wall for a light switch. With the windows boarded up, it was impenetrably dark, and as soon as I flipped the switch, the bulb blew. Swearing under my breath, I stumbled my way into the kitchen, banging my knee at least three times on the framing, each time in the same damn spot. All the while, I wondered who Brenna was talking to. I hadn't seen anyone, but the streetlight was out, so with the heavy shadows, she could have been speaking to something I couldn't see, considering her unusual abilities. If that was the case, then I didn't want to know what, or who, she spoke with, unless it was Gina.

Since she was psychic, Brenna might be able to talk to the dead. During the past three days, she'd only mentioned her job and her abilities in passing.

When she'd brought them up, there was a longing in her voice that made me want to hold her and soothe the vampire, but I sensed she wouldn't go for that. It was clear she wanted an exit out of life and was only hanging out to protect me.

Still, I was grateful to her for rescuing me. I couldn't imagine what would have happened if I had stayed in the concrete cell. I doubted I'd be anything like I was today.

My stomach growled and I opened the cabinets, looking for something to eat. But as I pondered food, the thought of it wasn't appetizing. I desired something else, something red and warm.

I swallowed hard.

I wanted blood.

It wasn't a question of desire. It was a must, something I needed to keep me going. If that was the fact, then I was only becoming more like the vampires. That only made me more scared, considering I now knew what was inside of me.

I didn't want it. I wanted to send it all back to hell, to hope it was all a dream. My body called for sustenance, and the nourishment it needed wasn't solid. I swallowed hard and tried to push the craving down. Life had returned to some semblance of normalcy. Brenna had encouraged me to eat, to see if that would ease the other inside of me or slow down the blood changing me. I tried munching on chocolate cake at the café, and later on some rare steak. I ate only a little of each. As it was, Brenna only picked at her food when she cooked. I assumed that, as a vampire, she couldn't eat anymore. *Hey, no more thoughts of gaining weight.*

Thinking about it, I giggled, and it felt good to laugh. Closing my eyes, I got a hold of myself. Whatever my body needed, I wasn't going to give in; I wanted to hang onto every bit of humanity I had left. So, I had to eat.

I sighed and looked around. For the first time in a while, things felt good. If Julien came back, Brenna would protect me, and even though her house was old and dusty and full of ghosts, it was comfortable. The place was big enough, and I was getting settled, but I missed Gina and Jeremy, still mourning their losses. I had to stop blaming myself for what had happened. I could never go back to my house. The police said it was a crime scene, and with all the bad memories associated with it, returning seemed out of the question, especially since Julien might appear.

The thought of him made me quiver. I didn't want to end up back in his arms after he'd already raped me once. At least I had healed from his assault. Even the bite marks had disappeared and, come to think of it, so had all my other scars. The color of my skin had evened out and seemed lighter. There was less hair on my legs. I hated the beast inside, but the side effects of what it was doing to my body were interesting. I liked the changes—or some of them, anyway. I wasn't too happy that my skin rolled or my bones creaked because my other was trying to get out.

The door opened, which meant Brenna was back. I had to ask her about what had happened at the coffee shop. That was something I hated about my changing personality. How could I fight with it all the time and live? I had to ask her how she dealt with this other vying for her body.

As I listened for my savior's footsteps, I heard nothing. The hairs on the back of my neck stood up immediately. I checked the hallway, but it was so dark that all I could see was a foot stepping into the corridor. I took a step forward. One of the tarps rustled as it fell to the floor. My breath caught in my throat. The temperature plummeted. I glanced around. The back door wasn't open, but the pantry door was. Slowly, I made my way over, squeezing myself into the small space and closing the door a crack.

The floorboards creaked. My heartbeat picked up, frantically beating in my ears. I tried swallowing, but was sure that whatever was in the house heard me. The wood on the kitchen floor moaned again. Something was there, and it wasn't a ghost.

"I know you're hiding, Mira. I can smell your fear. Don't think you can hide from me. Come out, please. I know you didn't want to leave. It was the other, the human-loving bitch, who took you away from me. I promise I won't hurt you; we share something, you and I. Now, be a good girl and come out."

Julien's voice was cool and hypnotic, tempting me. The other knew he could offer a solace I'd never known. All I had to do was go into his arms, but I knew better. If I went with him, then I'd be giving up everything I believed in. Everything Brenna had fought for. Veronica would have been lost for nothing, as would Gina.

Julien knew I was hiding. I swallowed and felt something in my mind. It was a tickle, almost like Brenna's voice had been before, but this sensation wasn't her. It was a hum, worming around in my thoughts, and I didn't know how to keep him out, how to erect barriers and push him away. He moved until he connected with the beast, and that was all the leeway it needed.

The beast surged forward. Its cold otherness filled my senses, its thoughts penetrated my brain, and I melded with it. Just as it said it would, it pushed me out while part of us was joined, so instead of it being me, I became we.

We opened the pantry door and sniffed. This was the man who had set us free. It was his blood that allowed us to be as we were now. He had given us blood, enabling us to break free from the prison of the human mind. There was something oddly familiar about him, something else that we should have recognized. But we weren't strong enough to know what exactly it was, as centuries of humanity had driven many of our instincts down. Now it didn't matter, and we would soon figure the mystery out.

We smiled, our teeth stretching, still just baby fangs, but soon that, too, would be rectified. Soon, the we would become just an I again and the I would be me while the human self, Miranda, would be destroyed. Soon. But first, we had to have enough blood to complete the transformation.

We ran our tongue over our fangs. We stared into Julien's face. He assumed he would be our Master, but we had no Master. The ancestor's husband had destroyed our true Master centuries ago, as we'd been buried underneath the rubble of human thoughts and petty emotions for far too long.

We stared deeply into Julien's dark eyes. He did not expect this from us, and his expression turned to anger. We were the fledgling and weren't supposed to challenge the Master, but it didn't matter. We knew how to push his buttons.

"I'll make you a deal," we purred.

The anger dissipated from Julien's eyes, turning to intrigue. He was interested as he sensed our mind, still monitoring our thoughts. We didn't kick him out because we weren't strong enough, nor did we have to hide what we wanted. We wrapped an arm around his neck, fingering the vein that ran up and down his throat. Blood rushed deep and hot beneath the skin. This was the sustenance we required to become an I, as this had to be achieved before the bitch took us away from him.

The human part of us stirred when Brenna was referred to as a bitch. It didn't matter. I, the vampire, wanted her dead, even if the human half didn't. We could manipulate Brenna so Julien would be proud, for she had destroyed his nest and he wanted her dead. We could be the bait. Once she was dead, I would rise, the true being in this flesh, the true vampire that was meant to awaken centuries ago.

Our tongue tasted the sweetness of his skin and the blood running hot like lava underneath. We nipped at the flesh, showing our intentions, and pleasure rolled off our would-be Master in waves. He was fascinated, but then again, males were always eager to please when it came to sex or the promise of it.

"What kind of deal?"

"You want the bitch dead for destroying your children. I want a foothold in this body. I'm tired of passing down through generations of human blood-lines, losing a piece of myself with each new child. It wasn't until you came and gave me the strength to take over that I realized how much I'd lost, but my power never lasts. The human persona is strong and has control when you're not around. Finish what was started eons ago, and I'll bring you her heart. What do you say?"

Julien looked at us skeptically. He wasn't sure if what we said was believable, but there was something else lingering in his eyes, something that seemed all too familiar, that we should have known. It brought back vague memories of years past, when blood had first been introduced to the original human host.

"Tell me, why do you like vampires so much? Answer me truthfully, and then I'll consider your offer."

We sighed, both the human and I. It was the same thing we'd heard from him since the beginning, but this time, the answer would be different, as I was the one replying. The human side's answers always displeased him. I knew the right one. We met his eyes.

"Because I am one."

Julien smiled. "Welcome to the world, child. You will have your wish, but first, you have to remember one thing."

Before we had time to react, he forced his mind into ours, pushing out even my thoughts, working his way back to where memories were stored in the subconscious. There, he dragged them into the front of our mind. Images flashed. We saw through hazy eyes just beginning to wake up, felt the struggling human heartbeat, the caress of the human soul that struggled against the demon taking root.

As our vision started to clear, we stared into the face of the Master. The very one who was before us now. Then, he had been different. His blond hair was long with wisps hanging in his face. His blue eyes were gray, turning black. His seemed to hold less stature, and he was younger, a little unsure of himself. And then, as we were about to reach out and take him into ourselves, the blood-bond was broken. Our contact eliminated as we felt him die. With him gone and our lack of blood, we were stuck in a darkened void. We lamented for his passing in the human body, and over the years, struggled to take control, but the human host always seemed stronger—until now.

Julien pulled himself out of our mind and we were left in awe, but remembered that he was Master, and lowered our eyes. He put his hand under our chin and let us gaze upon him.

"It's been a long time, Mira."

Tears sprang to our eyes. It was glorious to look upon the face that had given life to me. After so many centuries, he had found me. He'd never given up hope, and now, he'd resurrected me. I struggled not to cry, a human emotion for sure, but after living so long with humans, I understood sorrow.

"But you died, Master. I felt it."

Julien caressed our face. "You only felt the bond between us extinguish because you weren't given enough of my blood. It was enough to awaken you, but not to let you have control. The wolf that attacked me paid for it with a lifetime of service. Now, he's my broken pet. You met him the other night when that bitch took you from me. It took me almost a century to track down the hound, and by that time, he had distanced himself from his progeny. When I tortured him, he revealed the fact that my child did, indeed, live, but in a different form. It has only been in this generation that I've found you, my Mira. Your dreams were messages that I was coming. I've sent them since I found out you were alive. It was only when I saw you that I realized you were my lost child from ages ago. I was surprised to discover you here. It was unexpected to say the least, but Fate has been kind and has led me here to find the one thing I loved, as well as the other. Do you hate me for taking so long to find you?"

Astonishment crossed our face. *He was asking if we hated him? How could he think that? He was our blessed father, the giver of life.*

"No, Master. I've waited centuries for you to find me, hoping it wouldn't be too late, that I'd still be able to recognize you. And here you are. I've lost much of my strength over the years. Can you help me regain it so I can be the child you wanted from the beginning?"

Julien laughed. His laughter touched our heart and made it sore, but in the back of our mind, the human side was getting stronger, ready to surge forth. I didn't know when I'd be able to reemerge and see the Master.

"You're stronger than you think, child, if you survived almost three centuries passing down through human bloodlines. But, I promise I shall finish what was started years ago. Come, let us do that so you shall eternally be mine."

The Master brought us to his lips. Teeth grazed over the flesh of our neck and sent chills down our spine. He pressed his fangs in, breaking the surface.

"Let her go!"

It was the bitch. She'd come to take us away from the Master again. Julien looked over to her and snarled. Hatred twisted his features as he pushed us away.

"Not again," he swore under his breath. "She's mine. Go get a human of your own to corrupt. Stop trying to save mine."

We looked on the both of them as they stood studying each other. Master was old and she was young, but she was something other than what we were, and Master knew this. In some part of me, I felt his fear, but it was only a small part. The bitch had none for us. There was only hatred, malice at what he was doing to the human side, to Miranda. I grew angry with this. Skin tingled on the back of our hand as the flesh stretched and the fingers hardened. I would help my Master.

We stepped forward. Julien glanced at us, feeling the change, and smiled. He was going to let us help. An honor. We envisioned her decapitated with her insides on the outside, her limbs strewn on the floor and her blood covering the blue tarps. Yes, that was what we wanted. We lowered ourselves and got ready to spring, but without warning, everything went black.

Things were hazy, but my body was in motion, and there wasn't much I could do. My other half wanted Brenna dead, but I wasn't going to take out my friend, so at the last moment, I willed my body to the side. Julien was expecting his child to come out and destroy Brenna, but when I connected with him instead and sent him flying, I knew he wasn't going to react well. My hit sent him into the scaffolding in the hallway. The whole structure crashed down around him, and one of the tarps covered him like a morgue sheet.

Brenna looked back at him and then at me, a little stunned that I'd actually helped her instead of jumping her. I shrugged.

"Come on. We have to get out of here."

I didn't hesitate as she made for the back door and offered me her hand. I took it. She grabbed me, holding me close as her wings burst out and we took to the air, running from the demon who had haunted my dreams.

23

CHAPTER TWENTY-THREE

My name is Brenna.

The roof of the Tearoom was the only place I could think of where we could get a chance to breathe and regroup. I didn't know where else to go. My house wasn't safe, and neither were the places Miranda inhabited. Besides, I wasn't going to lead Julien into the Tearoom. The place had seen enough carnage and death. It had been bad enough last year when Veronica had found me with Devon as I lay dying on the blood-soaked floor with the back door busted open. That same night, Edmund passed away unexpectedly. Peter told me the police thought some Satanic cult had broken in and used the place for a ritual sacrifice. It was the only thing they could think of, considering the blood on the floor wasn't human, but more akin to canine, which was odd considering I was still mortal, but fuck, I wasn't knocking Fate.

Now that I was on the roof, looking at Miranda, I knew Julien would be coming soon. He would keep coming in an endless pursuit until he finally captured her, so my only options were to keep running or destroy him. The second was my plan. I didn't want to be like my former Master, who'd kept running. I would face the one who came after us.

When I'd walked in on Miranda and Julien, I thought I had lost her. The expression on her face had been alien, but suddenly, she'd become herself again and had driven the beast away. It wasn't hopeless for me to try and save her from Julien's clutches. Watching her now, I wondered if her other half still lingered near the surface, waiting for me to leave. I pushed my way into her psyche and found the thing struggling to take over. When it sensed my presence, it snarled and thrashed around in her mind, trying to find a dark corner to hide from me, but it was too big, with all the shadowed places taken.

I've had claim to the body, the thing said. *It's my birthright.*

You're nothing more than a parasite. Miranda will remain as she is, and when she dies, so will you.

She may die, but if she breeds, I'll continue. The blood in her will pass down to the next generation. I may not be strong, but I'll be there. One day, I'll awaken again and gain control. It may take my Master another three centuries to find me, but I'll survive.

Go back to the hell where you were spawned.

The beast laughed. *At least I have a Master that cares for me. You just sat and watched yours die. Poor thing, you don't even have a grave to put her in. Who's pathetic now?*

I couldn't stand to hear any more, so I blasted Miranda's mind. The beast screamed and retreated so it could lick its psychic wounds. Miranda winced.

"What just happened?"

What I'd done had a noticeable effect on Miranda. Her flesh was flushed, her heartbeat accelerated. I sighed. The vampire was more ingrained than I suspected.

"I drove your other half away for a while. I doubt it'll come out while I'm around." I paused, feeling the night around me as humans in the building talked beneath us. Music blared, and a homeless man peed in the alley. There had to be somewhere safe I could take her, somewhere full of people. But even that wouldn't be safe, as Julien could shield himself like me. I had to find a place where he couldn't hurt either of us. The Black Rose. It was the only location, and during most nights, it was open for human and vampire business, neutral ground for both species. No harm could be done to either while it was open. I knew this because I'd been there a year ago when Veronica was still alive and Devon searched for the both of us.

It was there he'd tried to pick a fight, but he couldn't. I'd decked him, but now I realized even that had been a set up, since it led me to Aria, Devon's child. Both Devon and Aria were dead. Now all I had to do was find Zhen. Maybe that was a good thing, as at least then I could flush her out, but there was always a risk—Miranda might find the influence of the undead overwhelming, and the beast might be able to burst out. I sighed. Maybe it wasn't a very good idea letting my two problem-worlds collide.

What do you think? I sent up to my guides, but honestly doubted they'd answer, considering I had brushed them off. Still, I waited a moment, and sure enough, there was nothing.

"Don't blame yourself for leaving me alone," Miranda whispered, mistaking my silence for guilt. "I've been thinking. Maybe he isn't so bad. I mean, this other part of me, the vampire, is getting stronger. Even if I wanted to remain as I was, it wouldn't happen. Eventually, it'll control me. You should just let him take me. He'll find us and kill you. Besides, the next time he comes, I don't know if I'll be strong enough to fight her."

No way was she giving up, not after everything she'd been through. Not after everything I'd been through. I wasn't going to let that happen.

"Don't say that. The beast, the vampire, isn't stronger than you. You fought it. If you let it, it'll consume you. You can't give up. Veronica didn't sacrifice herself for me to lose you. He may come for us, and granted, you may have to live the rest of your life fighting against the demon in your head, but shit, Miranda, he's not going to have you. They're all evil fucks. Trust me. I know."

She looked at me quizzically. "Then why did you get involved with Veronica?"

I stared into the night, feeling the moon shining down as it slowly shrank, leaving the sky darker now that it had passed its full point. Neither the whispers of the wind nor the feel of a slight chill of magic in the air could ease me. Somewhere far away, I heard the tinkling laughter of fairies like the chiming of glasses, and even that meant nothing to me.

I tried drawing in some of the cool essence of the silver orb, but nothing about the darkness held any pleasure for me. A year ago, living in New Orleans, thinking about readings for my psychic business, I hadn't even known Veronica as I strolled down Bourbon Street. I'd only thought about tomorrow and how I'd better fit into the Goth culture. How I could be a better pretend beast.

Then, my life had become something like Miranda's, constantly running from a vampire. Those days had been horrible, and when Veronica had revealed herself to be a true undead creature, I'd freaked. I'd assumed I was the fiend and she was human, but I'd also believed vampires were creatures out of fairy tales. Nevertheless, her revelation had broken all of my beliefs. She was real. Moreover, there I was, a human pretending to be undead, just like all the other good Goth children.

"It's funny, really. I thought she was human, and she thought I was a vampire. Somehow, I'd learned to manipulate my aura and deceived vampires for years. I moved among the vampires at the Black Rose, and they never bothered me. Sometimes I wish I was still there, pretending, but there's no way to turn back the clock. Then we both learned the truth. Veronica had been running from her Master. He'd been following her for a decade, and just as she'd settle into a place, he'd find her and drive her out. It was all a game. He used her to find me—or at least that was what he said. He used me to get her back. It almost worked, but in the end…well, let's just say he's fish food. It was only these past few months—"

The image of Veronica's corpse flashed in my mind, the way it had decomposed, nothing like Devon's body, or Aria's. Maybe the difference was that Azrael took Veronica's soul—I figured the others didn't have souls, since they were demons. Now there were only ashes for me to scatter to the wind. I had to give Veronica peace.

Rage bubbled over in me. I'd find the fucker who killed my lover, and then I'd get my revenge on the one who ordered her demise. But tonight wasn't the night to seek retribution—tonight, I needed sanctuary.

The friend of my enemy is my friend. Or some shit like that, I thought smugly. Energy in me rose as my muscles tightened, and I pulled off the remnants of my shirt, leaving me with only my bra.

"We have to go; he's coming." Miranda tugged on my arm.

"How do you know?" I wondered how deep their connection was. I watched Miranda's eyes mist over for a second as she focused on something in the distance, and then she shrugged her shoulders and looked at me.

"I have no fucking clue. I just feel him in my body, resonating like a hammer on a piano string. The beast is alert, but afraid. Come on. Look, who gives a shit? We have to go. Please!"

I stroked her hair for a slight moment and kissed the top of her head. She was my charge, and I'd do anything to protect her; I'd even go into the belly of the literal beast. My arms enfolded around Miranda, and I wished my embrace could be the only thing she needed to protect her from the bogeyman. My wings folded out of my back, the night air took hold, and I flew into the unknowing darkness.

We landed outside the club, and Miranda settled on the ground next to me with sheer exhilaration coursing through her. She loved flying. I think if she didn't know the consequences of being a vampire, then she'd choose to be like them. I hoped she wouldn't make the transition unless she was forced into it.

Outside, the stench of vampires was heavy, and their presences weighed on my brain. There were many in the club and as I listened, I heard the distinct flapping of wings as they hovered above the Rose. Miranda felt them too, and being in such close proximity to so many made her shiver.

"Do we have to go in there?"

I nodded. It was the only way either of us would be safe until I could figure out how to get rid of her would-be Master.

"Isn't there a dress code or something?" Miranda chuckled half-heartedly.

My bra top would fit in. This club wasn't Miranda's style, but even her outfit wouldn't be noticed. A line of Goth kids waited anxiously for admittance. Miranda stared at them, not used to this crowd, but I didn't care how I looked. I was so used to showing skin, it wasn't bad at all. I shrugged.

"We'll be fine. This is the only place where he won't be able to touch us. Besides, I've gone in with worse."

She only glanced at me. "You have?"

I smiled.

"The Black Rose is a human/vampire club. When it's open to the public, no vampire can take you against your will. It's safe; trust me. I've gone in here numerous times, and nothing's happened to me."

The bouncers glared at me as I pushed through the crowd with Miranda in tow. One of them stopped me. He was short and stocky. I saw the lines of his green contacts. His head needed shaving, and his pants were two sizes too small. Two healing puncture wounds on his neck were covered up with makeup. *Vampire junkie.* I stared him down. He looked away, but still wouldn't let me pass.

"You can't go in dressed like that."

I growled. "I don't care what the fucking dress code is, you're going to let us in, and that's final. Understand?" As my teeth lengthened, he got the message. It also helped that I gave him a mental nudge, but I think my winning smile worked best.

I motioned for Miranda to pass in front of me, and as we did, the happy little Goth children all hissed—they'd been waiting for a while to get inside. We trotted past the cashier, who started protesting, but I glared at her and she stopped in her tracks. I hated mortals who tried to intimidate me. As soon as we got in, I knew there had to be at least five other vampires there. Their presences stuck out like neon signs, and more were coming; I'd heard them hovering moments ago. Tonight was going to be busy with both breeds of clientele, and I planned on staying as long as I could.

I ushered Miranda past the first room on the right, mostly filled with ravers; the other, off to our left, was a sitting room with old settees scattered around the floor and a pool table in the far corner. A staircase led downstairs to the liquor room, but who knew what else was there besides that and the bathrooms?

Miranda wound her hand through mine as I scanned the room. Her unease crawled up her skin like a spider. She wanted to bolt and face the dangers outside—this was too much for her. I squeezed her hand, reassuring her, and led her through a small door that brought us onto the main dance floor. The bar on the left sported a large mirror covered with pictures of the macabre and postcards of fairies. There was even a plastic rat in the center of the mirror, blood dripping over its mouth. I assumed Miranda would like the décor, considering her café was decorated in the same fashion, but she wasn't interested with all the other vampires close by. The bartender glared over at me. Her power brushed over my mind, but I deflected it easily, letting her know I wanted to be left alone.

Humans lingered on the dance floor, moving and grinding. Another set of stairs led down to the coatroom and the bathrooms. I smirked, remember-

ing the last time I had been here. I still had the coat
check ticket sitting on the top of my bureau. If I'd
known I was coming, I'd have gotten my jacket, but
it had probably been claimed by one of the employees or whomever, thinking it was just another forgotten accessory.

"Sit at the bar until I get back. If anything happens,
get the bartender's attention. She won't let him take
you."

I sat her down, and then leaned over, catching
the bartender's eye. "Watch her."

"Why should I?" she asked. She flipped her dark
hair over her shoulder and then walked away.

Without thinking, I reached out and grabbed a
handful of her hair. She spun around, her flesh a
mass of swirling tissue, but she calmed herself quickly before anyone saw. Her human face, deeply set,
had wrinkled around her eyes and mouth. A hawk
nose accentuated her features while long, red nails
were attached to her fingers. She'd been in her forties
when she had been turned and was by no means a
looker. I smirked. She was weak and almost a century old. I wondered why Zhen employed her.

"Look, bitch, you'll watch her. If not, Zhen might
not be too happy. Get it?"

At the sound of her Mistress' name, her eyes
widened and she shrunk back. The darkness in me
smiled, wanting her to shiver. Fear did wonders

when used in the right manner, but I could tell this woman would be terrified for her life if she angered the one who had sired her.

"If anyone comes near my companion, you come get me. Understand? No matter who or what."

She nodded as I let go of her hair, though I really wanted to rip it all out. "Stay here. She'll watch you. I have to find the owner. If anyone looks at you the wrong way, just get her." I began to walk away when an idea popped in my head. I settled real close to Miranda and put my arm around her. "Just play along," I whispered close to her ear. She cringed, as she thought I was going to bite her.

I traced her cheek, feeling the heat of her flesh. Part of her was still so human, but as I stared into her eyes, the faint hint of darkness peeked out at me. Her heart sped up, as she wasn't sure what the hell I was doing, but possession was nine-tenths of everything. I smiled slyly.

The sweet perfume of her fear warmed her flesh even more; even her other persona stood up at my caress, sensing something. Then again, it would be aroused, considering it was driven by blood, sex, and violence. Slowly, I pressed my lips against hers. Miranda almost pulled away, but I held her in place and, after the initial shock, she fell into my embrace, melting like softened wax.

Her tongue wiggled against my mouth with the curiosity to explore. Her hands rested lightly on my cheeks, enough so I felt the indentation of her fingerprints against my own flesh. I parted my mouth as she traced her tongue over my teeth. We stayed locked in the kiss for a minute or so, long enough that most eyes were on us, as they would be when two chicks made out. Already, the buzz about the kiss was moving through the patrons' minds, and that was enough. *Hands off.* I pushed Miranda away and let her recover.

"Wow."

"What?" I asked, as she gazed on me with astonishment.

Her fingers traced her lips as she thought about what had just happened. "I never thought it could be that good."

I laughed. "Don't sound so surprised. I've had lots of practice. Now stay here. I'll be back." I caught her chin for a second, just to enhance the idea, and Miranda nodded. Miranda was attractive, but not my type. I wanted Veronica, as my heart called out to her. Sorrow threatened to overwhelm me, but I pushed it down and embraced the rage instead.

I wove in between people and vampires, heading down the stairs I'd jumped days before. At the bottom was the coat check, and in it was the same boy. I smiled.

"Where's Zhen? And don't tell me you don't know."

He looked at me blankly. "I don't know who you're talking about."

"Look, I don't want to play games with you. It's important I talk to her. Now, where is she?"

"I told you. I don't know. Now, if you don't mind, I have people to wait on."

Vaulting over the counter, I growled and pressed him up against the shelves behind him. He groaned as I cracked a few of his ribs. I wrapped my hand around his throat and squeezed. His eyes bulged, and his face went from red to purple, his lips tingeing blue.

"I'm tired of all this vampire bullshit. Now, where is she?" My temper flared as the muscles in my face started twitching, weaving around, and my features began to change. I didn't care who saw me or that the bouncers were coming, as I heard the rumbling of feet on the wooden stairs.

"Where is she?" I hissed as my chin elongated.

"Right here, little one."

24

CHAPTER TWENTY-FOUR

My name is Miranda.

My fingers passed over the spot where Brenna had kissed me. Even though it was just her way of showing the others I wasn't for sale, I'd never expected that a kiss from another woman could be so good. It wasn't much different than a guy's, just softer, as if she knew how to use her mouth better. I blushed thinking about what it'd be like to sleep with her. Her hands all over me. The thought made me tingly inside.

Glancing around the club, I saw everyone dancing. Many were dressed in simple black outfits, but others had more elaborate costumes. They were all Goth, wearing corsets over leather dresses and stiletto boots. It seemed fitting that vampires would want to hang out in this type of atmosphere, but I wondered how many of the humans actually knew about the beasts that hid behind other faces. Observing many of them, I found that I could tell which ones weren't mortal. Or I thought I could. They didn't move right. Some flopped like puppets. Each simple movement was controlled—where a human would lose balance and fall at a misstep, these creatures never missed a beat.

What category did I fall into? I didn't think I qualified as human anymore, and I certainly wasn't one of the vampires. Honestly, I didn't think I'd ever really been mortal, or at least that was what the beast had said.

I remembered the whole conversation even though I'd been just an observer. The beast confirmed that Julien had been the vampire who attacked my ancestor, passing his vampiric heritage down through generations. It made sense, I guess. None of my predecessors had more than one child. And those who did had had very difficult births. My mother had died because she thought it was her fault my sister was stillborn. Two days after the funeral, she'd put a gun to her head. I had been ten. After that, my father had raised me until I went off to school, and then he'd perished in a car crash. He'd left me his estate, and it was enough to open the coffee shop with Gina's help.

Now, I lived in my old house, but I didn't think I'd be residing there anymore, not after everything that had happened. With this thing living inside of me like some parasite, I'd never be normal. My life would never be the same. I hoped I could tame it, but every time I thought about it, it squirmed around in my mind.

"Would you like to dance?"

I looked over and saw Julien leaning on a metal pole, showing nothing of any injuries he'd gotten from the scaffolding. I hadn't sensed him like I had before. My breath caught in my throat. I glanced back at the bartender and caught her eye. She observed me anyway, keeping an eye out so she wouldn't get in trouble.

Julien's hand wrapped around my wrist as he pulled me toward the dance floor. My other hand wound around the stool and I forced myself to stay where I was as I felt myself tugged toward him by some invisible leash.

"No."

His features hardened and twisted. He yanked me off the stool, sending it, and me, flying across the floor. My head hit the back of the bar. Pain and stars erupted in my vision.

"I've played games long enough, Mira. My patience is worn thin. Now, you will come with me. Screw the bitch who brought you here."

Fingers enclosed my wrist again and pulled me up. I struggled at first, and then someone slapped me across the face. It was the bartender I saw as my vision cleared. Two security guys held my would-be Master. He glared at me, but didn't say anything. He fought at first, but calmed when one of them punched him in the stomach.

"You all right?" I noticed the hint of an Irish accent, which didn't surprise me, since Boston was the most Irish city in the country.

I nodded as she led me back to the bar. I sat on another stool and waited for the dizziness to subside. The bartender poured me a drink. I drank it in a couple of swallows, not knowing what the hell it was, but it went down fine and helped heal my head.

I sighed. Julien had found me like I'd suspected he would. At least Brenna had been right. He couldn't take me in this place, but that only delayed the inevitable. I knew he'd be waiting outside for me. Already, I felt him pacing, walking along the vertebra of my back, plotting what to do with me. His presence only endangered Brenna more, and I couldn't have that. She'd risked her life to save mine more than once, and now I could return the favor. Julien would keep coming wherever I went, forever. If I went back with him on my own, maybe he'd leave Brenna alone. After all, it was me that he wanted, not her.

Well, he might be pissed about her killing his other vampires, but I was the main goal. It was the only logical thing to do to save her and spare myself from of years of running. There was no way I was having children and passing this thing on to them. So, I took one more swallow, knowing it would be my last. The beast inside me stirred as it heard my thoughts and smiled.

I closed my eyes and gave one last thought to Brenna. With all she'd done for me, I'd always be grateful, but this was where it ended. In my mind, the beast and I stood face-to-face, judging one another. It growled, hating that it was locked away, but I stepped aside and let it take control. I didn't feel any pain as it settled into my body, and I was moved aside to share its perceptions.

We left the club, venturing beyond the bouncers, who didn't look twice. As we walked down the street, Julien appeared out of a dark alley, grabbed our wrist, snarled, and pulled us into the darkness. His hand came up to slap, but we caught it in mid-air. This shocked him even more.

"Good evening, Master."

His power sliced through our mind as he sensed the change. Triumph plastered his features as he looked on his child and brought his lips to kiss her. His tongue snaked between our lips and then, for the last time, the beast surged forward, fully embracing its Master, extinguishing everything I was.

25

CHAPTER TWENTY-FIVE

My name is Brenna.

Zhen leaned against the wall behind the group of people who'd gathered at my spectacle. They automatically parted for her when she spoke, on command, I was sure. Her teeth glowed in the black light, giving her skin an eerie sheen and making her look like something from another dimension. She wore a skintight vinyl top with a large oval in the center so her tits pushed out. A black mesh mini-skirt showed off peeks of her red garter belt. Six-inch dominatrix boots laced up to her knees, making her almost even with my height. It took practice to parade in them. I only dealt with the three-inch ones.

I dropped the coat check boy and hopped back over the counter, landing softly on the other side, not taking my eyes off of her. She waited patiently, not fazed by those who had gathered. They waited for a catfight, but they weren't going to get it.

Amusement painted her features as she anticipated my next move, but before I could act, I was thrown off my feet as if I'd been hit with a wrecking ball in the stomach, just from the impact of her power. Stars appeared in front of my eyes and then cleared as my breath returned.

As I hung there, the crowd began to dissipate with dazed looks as if nothing had happened. That told me she'd hypnotized all of them. But I didn't have time to worry about that because the pressure of her power threatened to crush my lungs, and it would take me a while to heal from so severe a wound.

"How dare you come here thinking I shall come at your beck and call? This is my domain." Zhen snarled.

I tried to speak, but choked as her mind pressed against my throat. As vampires, we had the ability to move things with a thought, small objects mostly, and we could even unlock doors and pull bolts off, but Zhen was pretty fucking powerful and old. That didn't mean shit to how much power she actually possessed, or even where she'd originally come from.

Her fingers grew, the nails turning black and becoming talons. She stuck one of them under my chin, lifting my head even further up until it felt like she would pop my head off like a soda can tab. She cut into my skin, drawing blood, and her eyes closed as her tongue snapped out and lapped at the liquid. Her expression changed as she savored the liquid, rolling it around in her mouth as though she were tasting wine. There was nothing to do but wait for her to release me or kill me. Either way, I was screwed. She was powerful enough to rip down my mental walls if she wanted, and there were few who could accomplish this; but after a moment, she stared at me with a puzzled expression, like she couldn't exactly figure something out about me. Something in my blood had gotten her attention like it had before. Almost as if she hadn't expected it again.

Her fingers shrunk to normal, now covered in flesh instead of the bone-hard talons that the skin and nail had fused into. Gently, she stroked my cheek, running her hand down over my neck and my bra to cup my breast. The nipple hardened through the satin in response to her cold hands, but my expression remained impassive. I was cold and dead inside. Nothing could open me up now that Veronica was gone. This bitch was the reason Veronica was dead.

Next, she started rubbing me through my jeans as she searched for some response. After she realized her manipulations were doing nothing, she withdrew her hand, but still held my chin.

"Why did you come here, unless it was to tell me your debt to me is paid?"

Ahh yes, I had almost forgotten about that. I had to kill Julien to be free of her obligations. Oh well, that hadn't happened yet, even though it was on the top of my to-do list.

"Nope, sorry. Haven't gotten that far. I came here for sanctuary for the one I protect. She's upstairs at the bar," I croaked out as the pressure was released from my throat.

Her power rushed into my brain like a cool breeze, reaching every part of my mind. I could hide nothing from her. She knew all my secrets, fears, desires, and everything that I was and wasn't. Even though I wanted to kill her, a part of me gave her respect, considering she'd survived this long without fucking up somewhere along the way. I wondered what she'd been like as a human and how she'd gotten this far. If I'd been one of them, I might have asked her advice on the matter. But I wasn't, and as soon as I killed Julien, she was next.

She withdrew her mental tether so I fell to the floor. I got up and looked over at the stairs and the unblocked hallway to my right. Either one would get me back upstairs, but before I could reach them, she'd stop me.

"Look, Brenna. I know you want to kill me. So forget about escaping. I can kill you with a thought. If you think what I just did was interesting, you haven't seen anything yet. Now, why do you want me dead?"

I bore my gaze into hers, which I knew she would hate. All vampires thought they were dominant, and when one acted like an equal, it rubbed them the wrong. By looking straight at Zhen, I showed her exactly what I thought of her

"One of your lackeys killed the only thing I loved just because I wasn't quick enough to fulfill your payment. Because of that, you're dead. My not acting quick enough to suit your ancient ass was not worth killing my lover over."

I stepped forward, and to my surprise, she moved backwards as a look of puzzlement crossed her face. Like a quick ripple, her face melted away, revealing bone and muscle before beginning to re-form human features once again. It all happened in slow motion. I saw every piece of tissue and tendon. It was quite disheartening to think she had such control over her own body, but then again, after five thousand years, I figured she would know every nuance of her body chemistry.

She shook her head and just walked down the hall, then opened the door to the hallway and motioned for me to follow. Rage built in my stomach, boiling over into my veins. Sweat started to bead on my forehead as my heart chakra opened. Energy bubbled into my aura, surrounding me like a sphere. I came closer to a meltdown with each step.

Zhen stopped at the door and let me go before her. I watched as she went in front of me and walked through the wall at the end of the coat check. It was another illusion, like the concrete wall in the subway tunnel. I passed through it as though venturing through a membrane and it vanished, bursting like a bubble. Zhen spun around and stared, waving her hand as she sent a small amount of energy to the opening to hide it again, but she couldn't.

"Remarkable," she whispered.

We walked down a short hallway and then through another illusion-wall. At this point, Zhen sat in an oversized plush chair. I sat across from her and scanned the room. In the other corner was a mini-fridge with plastic glasses on top, but I doubted it held soft drinks. I glanced at the walls and saw a golden Chinese dragon wrapped around the room. The longer I looked at it, the more it undulated, and then it winked at me. This was all another part of her power, but it was still cool. Of course, I wasn't going to admit it.

The wall we faced was painted the color of dried blood. It didn't match the rest of the décor, but it faded out, becoming transparent like the ghosts I saw, until it revealed the other half of the room. I sighed, and some of the energy in me calmed a bit. Then, I realized this was a viewing area, and the other half was a dungeon.

In the center stood a rack, and an iron maiden sat in the corner. It was rusted, but the carving of the women was intact. It was definitely authentic. There were four sets of manacles on the wall, and one of them was occupied. Off to the side were a variety of whips I was sure had been used over time.

The occupant was naked, his skin a mass of twisted flesh that made his face horrifying. He had fresh welts all over, probably from the bloody bullwhip on the rack. He was also castrated, and blood seeped from his wounds over his stomach and arms. He came to life as he sensed someone in the room and lifted his head. His eyes had been cut out, but strangely, the sight didn't disgust me. What made me gasp was that he only had one hand, and the other was freshly burned. This was the monster who'd attacked me and killed Veronica.

Zhen ran her finger over his chest above his heart, where he'd been left untouched. I watched as she grew one talon, piercing his flesh centimeters from the beating organ. The vampire gave off a sound like a moan, but when his mouth opened, I saw that his tongue had been cut out. Zhen offered her talon, but I turned my nose at it. She shrugged and licked it clean. I glanced back at the wound and saw that it spurted black blood. She had pierced his heart, the one place where a vampire could scar, since if our hearts were ripped out, we died.

Veronica had four pucker wounds from Devon's talons when she'd once disobeyed him. Except for heart wounds, severe brain injury, severing of the spinal column, and damage caused by sunlight and fire, we were durable creatures. At least that was what I'd seen and been told, but the vampires I'd been around had surprised me more and more lately, just as I was surprising myself.

The more time went on, the more I didn't know what was happening to me. Even now, as this heat formed in me, all of it was triggered by rage and sorrow, and the thought of not having Veronica was all too much. I'd lashed out in self-defense and burned this vampire's arm to the point where he couldn't even heal. Really, I wondered how I'd accomplished that. It would've been nice to know how to raise energy at will, but then again, with my emotions heightened, it was hard for me to deal with everything. Veronica had said that she could help me with them, and now that she was gone, I flew off the handle at anything. She'd said it was all part of adjusting to the new lifestyle, that my human emotions were becoming erratic and would dull over time, but we'd never made it to that point.

"I didn't kill Veronica. Nor did I order anyone to." She glared when she saw the shock in my eyes at

Veronica's name. "Yes, I know all about your Master, as well as the others you've killed. Malachi was a friend of mine. A stuck-up asshole, but a friend. News travels when old ones are destroyed. It's felt when they are killed, vibrating down the web of the blood that binds us. But I don't hold grudges. Besides, Malachi was a dick, thinking that because he was male he could do whatever he wanted. I'm not as bad as you think I am. Not all of us are. There are many that, well, care. Not all of us kill for sport."

I didn't believe a word she said. All vampires were monsters. There were only a few exceptions, and the vampire community considered these meat-lovers because they doted on humanity. Veronica had been one of them. Even when Devon forced her to kill the way he wanted, in her heart she defied him. That was one of the reasons I hated all the undead. I'd seen what they truly were. And Zhen hadn't convinced me otherwise.

"Why should I believe you?"

"Because I could explode your heart with a thought, but I've given you the benefit of the doubt. I keep my word. I do business honorably. How do you think I survived so long? Why do you think Robyn is shackled in my dungeon? I like to play with my food, I admit, but not my children. He killed the one you mourn for. Unless they disobey me, I do nothing to my children. I agree I was rash the other night and wanted to have you, but I told them not to hurt you. Robyn and Greg had no right to try to rape you. They might be gay, but that doesn't mean testosterone didn't get the better of them. You had every right to defend yourself. Robyn was pissed you maimed him and took away his lover. He was impulsive. My payment was Julien's death at your hands. That asshole betrayed me. He was here the first night you came in. My other half might have mentioned him."

I looked at her and then back at the vampire shackled to the wall. Everything came up in me at once. Why was this happening to me? Maybe she was right. Maybe my anger toward Zhen had been misguided. Maybe she told me the truth. But what if she only wanted to trick me? Now I could have my retribution on the one who killed Veronica. I'd taken his lover, so he had to kill mine. An eye for an eye. Vampire retaliation. Well, here was my vengeance.

I screamed, not caring, releasing what had built up in me. I aimed for the beast on the wall. In an instant, he was reduced to white ash. The area behind him was scorched black. The energy moved around Zhen as the burst of heat evaporated into the room, seemingly absorbed by the dragon.

I backed up and collapsed on the chair, drained. My eyes caught the cups on the mini-fridge, which had all melted into one mass of plastic. All my feelings, everything, had gone into that burst. I stared at the shackles. Veronica's killer had been consumed. What else was there for me to do?

I realized Zhen had told the truth. She hadn't been the one who'd ordered Robyn to kill Veronica. It'd all been for revenge, and now there was nothing. Revenge was not sweet. His death had felt good at the moment, but the satisfaction was short-lived as emptiness replaced my vengeance.

I felt Zhen's hand on my arm and I saw her kneeling in front to me. As she did, I saw something in her face that reminded me of Veronica. It seemed Zhen cared for me, like she was relating that at one point she'd also lost her lover, her Master. She opened her arms and, without thinking, I let her hold me.

Her arms were strong, warm, and comforting in the way I needed them to be. She tapped into my psyche, and before I knew it, I was crying, releasing some of the void I held at bay. I pulled away, exhausted. She smiled and went to the fridge, tried to grab a glass and then frowned. Instead, she grabbed a small, plastic bottle of water and gave it to me. I sipped it slowly and almost spit it out.

This was not water. It tasted like blood. It seemed distilled, sharper, and stronger. It was cold going down, but warmed me as it hit my stomach like liquor and gave me some strength.

"Good, isn't it?"

"It's different. What is it exactly?"

Zhen smiled "It's an ancient secret. It's blood, of course, but I put it through a process that makes it stronger. It's wonderful when you need a pick-me-up."

I wondered why she'd shared this information with me. "Why are you being so nice? One minute you want to kill me, and now this." It didn't make any sense; she wasn't acting like all the other vampires I'd encountered. All of them had only wanted things for their own benefit. I had to be wary of her and try not to get too involved.

"You're powerful, and you know that. I wish you could show me how to do what you just did."

I laughed. Of course, she wanted my power. "I wish I knew how to do what I just did."

Zhen chuckled as well, settling further into her chair. "Brenna, you are right to be mindful of me. And your powers are remarkable. I have a feeling there is more underneath the surface. I understand you haven't had any good experiences with others of your own kind. Or not your kind, as you would put it. Let's just say I have my reasons, and we are more alike than you can imagine. We have more in common than you know. I want nothing from you that you might suspect. All I want is, just maybe, a friend. I get lonely with no one to talk to, and you intrigue me. Let's just say I have a feeling you and I are walking the same path."

It was my turn to laugh. *Friends? That was interesting. Why would she want to be my friend?* "You want nothing from me—that I find hard to believe. And yet, I still have to kill Julien for you."

"Yes. You do owe me payment. Besides, you were going to do that anyway. It is—"

"Vampire code and all that bullshit."

She smiled, and then her expression turned serious. "It's not bullshit. It's how I live. Besides, Julien is a nuisance among our kind. And an oddity to say the least. He thinks he can take this club away from me because of something said centuries ago. I want him out of the way. If you think you have problems now, you really don't want to see me mad. But, honestly, I think you and I could be good for one another. There is so much I can tell you, show you. No strings attached, outside of Julien. What do you—"

Zhen stood up as the bartender burst into the room. The younger vampiress dropped to her knees, glanced up at her Mistress once, and then stared at the floor.

"Please, ma'am, forgive me. She told me to tell her if anything happened to her human. She said you'd be angry. You aren't, are you, Mistress?"

Zhen looked back over at me and then ran her hand over the head of the bartender and patted her like she would any good pet. I tried to hold a look of disgust from crossing my face, but it didn't work. Zhen saw it, but I didn't stay to see her reaction.

Instead, I bolted and ran upstairs. Miranda wasn't on her stool. I scanned the now-full dance floor, and she was nowhere to be found. I ran into the sitting room and, again, nothing. I turned around to jump over the rope that separated the two doors, and Zhen was standing at the top of the stairs.

"Do you know where she is?" Zhen asked.

Miranda was gone. I'd lost her, failing in everything I'd told her I would do. I would get her back, fulfill my promise to Zhen, and then seek a reunion.

"I don't know. Miranda and I weren't bonded. She could be anywhere."

"And you say you know so much about us." She shook her head. "Hon, from what I've tasted in your blood, did it ever occur to you that maybe Julien wants you all to himself? I think Miranda just happened to show up. He's been searching for his child for centuries. Whenever I saw him, it was his child this and his child that and how he would find her and make her into his own image. Now he has found her, but you took her away from him. He's going back to his nest to finish the transformation, and then he'll deal with you. I'm not sure what he wants with you, but I guess you have to figure that out for yourself.

"Sometimes we are creatures of habit—some of us don't change. Besides that, some vampires are just stupid. If you go to his lair, you'll be able to catch him. I know that you can kill him. I realize you want to save your friend, but he has a right to his child. I want him dead though, so I won't stand in your way. Just be careful. He's got a few tricks up his undead sleeve. Now, go on. In the future, if you need anything, come here. If not, I know where you live." She spoke her final words in a creepy-horror-movie voice that was cheesier than anything else.

I let what she'd said sink in. If her words were true, then Julien had been the one following me since the beginning. Maybe he'd even killed Zach, or had him killed? If that was the case, then I was in over my head, but with these new powers, maybe I could take him. I had already killed half his nest. Zhen had faith in me, and I had to get Miranda. She was what kept me going. I couldn't crack now.

Zhen might be able to find me, but I wasn't asking for anything else from her. I didn't need to become her personal assassin. This was a one-time-only deal, but her information had been useful, and now, I ducked under the rope and ran out into the night.

26

CHAPTER TWENTY-SIX

My name is Miranda.

It's all mine, just as it should have been ages ago when I opened my eyes in Marie. After centuries, the night is finally mine to glorify in.

Julien held me in his arms as we flew. Wind raced around us, winding its fingers in my hair, and every molecule enthralled me. The grit of the city stuck to my skin; the atmosphere was thick with smog. I heard every vibration of the stars and absorbed the silky song of the moon. Aromas of blood and shit blew on the breeze. For the first time, I was truly alive. Julien whisked me away from Cambridge and back to his nest, where only half of the vampires survived, but he was powerful enough to rebuild it. His power wasn't instantaneous, but soon others would join us, renewing his family.

The warmth of his arms encompassed me. His fingers traced my shoulder blades where soon I'd have wings of my own to carry me through the starlit sky.

We landed in the cafeteria where I'd been stolen from him before. The smell of old blood lingered from the feasting of a few days ago, igniting my senses. The hairs stood up on the back of my neck while my veins burned, shivering from the inside. Pain ran through me and my teeth emerged from the gums, still baby points. I tried willing them longer, but they couldn't grow because I needed to complete the turning process, which Master would do soon.

The bones in my fingers fused together at the knuckles and joints. The skin itched and twitched as muscles stretched and grew together. My nails and fingers extended. I clenched my fists, surprised to find I could bend my fingers at my knuckles. Slowly, I turned, feeling Julien, and found him on stage. I glanced up once and saw that he was naked. I smiled as he offered me his hand.

"After so many years, at last you're mine."

His hand caressed the side of my cheek and ran down my neck. I looked into his eyes and knew there was no humanity in him. Nothing of the weakness that remained in me. He was all-powerful, and he wanted me. His other hand snuck under my shirt and palmed my tit. I pressed against him, wanting him to take me even as I was so unworthy of his attention. He squeezed my breast until it hurt. His other hand tilted my chin so I could meet his eyes. I looked into them for a second and then away, as it was customary to do.

"Mira, never look down again. You are my equal, my bride. Do you understand?"

I nodded. I wasn't going to question his authority. He was my Master. Anything he said was true. I smiled up at him and tentatively stared into his dark eyes, which were all black now as he let the hunger into them. He grinned, showing me his fangs as they grew, resting on his bottom lip. He pecked me on the nose and then moved down to my lips. His tongue, black and forked, flicked between my lips and moved along my teeth, catching on my baby fangs. I sucked in his tongue, marveling at its smoothness, like a snake's, at how slender it had become, only half an inch wide, and I returned his kiss. His hard nails shredded my shirt, but he was careful not to graze my skin.

He flung the remains of my top into a pile of rags and bones from the other night. I stepped out of my pants gingerly as his hand found my clit. He rubbed slowly as I pressed myself into him, feeling his hard cock against my leg. With each touch, I grew wetter as his hand slid into my pussy, and I began mewing. His joy at seeing me yearning to be fucked entwined around my mind, as he knew my devotion was genuine.

My hands ran up and down his back, feeling his spine as it stretched like a string of beads. The skin swirled and danced, preparing for fur and wings to burst forth as he took on his true form. I held onto him as his hands wrapped around my waist, digging into my ass, piercing the flesh like spikes. My finger-talons ran furrows in his back. He felt no pain because he lifted me onto his dick and plunged me down onto it. The friction between us mounted.

His tongue flicked along my neck, and he nipped my skin. Master's other hand settled under my ass to give him a better hold, but my weight was nothing to him. I screamed because I wanted him to fuck me, to ravage and tear my insides as he had the other night. The human-self didn't appreciate his affections, rather called it rape. This was what our kind did, this fornication. This was what I wanted, to be dominated by my Master. Each time he pounded into me, he made me understand who the conquered one was.

My breaths came in short pants as the pressure mounted, and I knew not to hold my feelings in. Everything in me wanted to change into my true form, but I couldn't. The body wasn't completely mine, not yet. My blood-hunger overwhelmed me and, without thinking, I bit into Julien's shoulder, swallowing a piece of flesh, latching onto the wound.

I looked up guiltily into his eyes, but he just smiled, showing me his fantastic maw. He pushed his mouth into mine, shredding my lips, but his kiss was wonderful despite the pain. Our lips met and his form changed underneath me, taking on our wonderful appearance.

Wings like brown leather burst from his back, and fine black fur sprouted all over his body. His muzzle grew, as did his rows of teeth. Moreover and best of all, his dick fattened and grew another inch, and that was just what he wanted as he rammed into me, mounting me like the bitch I was. Then, he wrapped his teeth around my throat like a mother would to her cub and bit down. I came at that moment while he sucked. My breathing became labored, but he still pumped into me as he drank.

Blood left my body. Master knew he had to bleed me dry to get rid of the human taint. He unfastened his grip and took me in his arms, morphing back to human shape. He smiled down at me and bit into his wrist. He held it over my lips, and his blood dripped onto my tongue like hot lava. Before I could think, I latched on and pulled. One swallow after another came into my body, remaking it, reforming it, so I could regain my true strength and real self. With each mouthful, I felt my human self dying. My body was changing to fit what I truly was, going through the process that should have been completed centuries ago. My heart sped up and slowed down. Pain passed through me as his blood bombarded my cells. I writhed in the ecstasy of it all, knowing my Master was going to be with me for eternity, knowing I was the dominant force in this bag of flesh.

"Get away from her," the bitch's voice echoed in my ears, coming through a long tunnel.

The fountain of blood halted. What was left of my humanity latched onto my consciousness and took hold, pushing me back into the cage I'd been in for so long.

27

CHAPTER TWENTY-SEVEN

My name is Brenna.

Julien looked up from Miranda; both were naked. Obviously, they'd just finished, as Julien's dick was slick and purple. I shrank back at the sight and wondered what Miranda saw in him, but then again, vampires were known for their talents of mesmerism. He had fed her blood, trying to change her. I ran my senses over her, sensing the fight for her soul. Her mortality and the beast were going head to head, and I wasn't sure who was going to win. Her aura was a swirling mass of black and red because of the beast, and underneath that, I saw the mortal side surging at times, yellow and purple.

I glanced at Julien as he jumped down, snarling at me. I took a few steps toward him, letting my fingers grow into claws. The skin on his face twisted, bubbling as he began transforming, but before I could tackle him, I heard a growl behind me. Slowly, I turned, spying a huge werewolf standing on two feet, half-human and half-wolf. It was the same beast that had killed me before.

"Nice wolf. Good werewolf." Its beady yellow eyes only saw me as a dog treat.

The muscles bunched under his fur and then he sprang, but I anticipated this and moved out of the way. Julien laughed, knowing I was no match for his pet. I turned to see him gather up Miranda, claiming her. However, looking away from the beast was my mistake because the wolf pounced on my back, his claws raking my flesh. I got up enough momentum to throw him off, sending him sailing across the stage.

I rose slowly, jumping up on the stage and finishing my transformation with wings unfurled and my double set of fangs. I was going to take care of the werewolf once and for all. I lengthened my talons as far as they would go. The wolf looked up at me and grinned.

While I was distracted by him, I didn't feel the other pressure on the back of my neck, the sensation of someone watching me, until it was too late. Twenty other snarling vampires were staring at me, all of them in their true demonic form, part of the leftover nest I hadn't destroyed.

"Fuck."

* * * *

The stench of death permeated the room along with old blood, decay, and mold lingering underneath, adding to the noxious aroma. The moans of victims surrounded me, and their fading warmth caressed my body, but it did no good. They were barely alive. Their heartbeats echoed faintly in the room, and with each beat, my hunger vibrated to the surface.

When I opened my eyes, I assumed I passed into the other reality where Azrael took his souls, but this place was cold, and pain raged in my body. It was not the other world I vaguely remembered from when I'd died before. This world was hazy as my eyes tried to focus. I tried to move my arms, but couldn't, and I heard the rattling of chains. I figured I wasn't dead, but in deep shit.

Closing my eyes again, I tried to refocus, but again, my vision cleared only a little, and I was able to make out that I was in some kind of cell. Summoning my strength, I tried to break free of the shackles, but the vampires had drained all my blood. I sensed I had over sixty bites on me. My bra was gone and my jeans hopelessly shredded, but the worst were my dry veins. Yet, somehow, I'd still survived, maybe because of the strength of Azrael's blood. Its coldness still lingered in my aura, chilling my core, but it wouldn't sustain me for long. Hunger thrived in me as spasms of pain racked my helpless body. My veins shriveled from the lack of nourishment and started to eat away at my body. My fangs burst from my gums and cut into my lips. I felt the coldness of my hunger enter my eyes. Anyone who saw me would know they were black, staring into the eyes of monster from the bowels of hell.

Human heartbeats called to me, begging the remnants of what was the vampire to ravage them. The symphony of blood was wondrous. Once I was free, I'd rip them all apart, feeling my talons dig open their chests and encompass their warm, beating hearts. I imagined the slickness of the organ against my teeth as I drank in all its fluid like a juice box. Then I'd take the rest of the victims, tearing them limb from limb just to see blood dripping from the ceiling. It would all make me strong again.

A seizure racked my body. I bit on my tongue, splitting it in two. No blood emerged from the wound. It was just dry. I screamed in frustration and then stopped as a wave of fatigue washed over me. My heart had stopped beating, and it was hard to feel my fingers.

I need blood. I don't need to take a heart to satisfy my hunger. That isn't me. I swallowed hard and my head cleared a little, but that was a mistake.

As I inhaled, I tasted the humans' salty skin along with their essence. I felt the vibrations of their pulses through my fangs. It pounded through me, and I imagined slowly sinking my teeth in, feeling the pressure of the flesh as I separated it, pushing through muscle and tissue. And then I'd reach the vein, or better yet, an artery where a river awaited instead. Then, as my mouth fastened on the wound, I could draw life into me, taking swallow after swallow as my body soaked it all up. It would fulfill me, and my heart would beat. I would be whole. It would renew me. Yes, that was what I wanted, what I needed.

The tingling in my tongue continued as it tried to heal.

Why am I thinking this way? It has to be the hunger.

I tried pushing it aside, conjuring up images of Veronica to help tame my mind. I remembered the first time I'd seen her, as she frantically ran down Bourbon Street to get away from Devon. I'd thought she was human and had made me lose a man who was going to be my meal for the evening. Of course, I was going to fuck Devon and nothing more, since I was human at that point. Something about Veronica had intrigued me, so I'd followed her down the street into a bar, and there, I handed the waitress a napkin I'd written on and asked her to meet me the next night.

Then I remembered the first time Veronica had fucked me. It was the last night I'd been human. By that time, I was in love with her, and we'd spent the night making love, holding one another until we both fell asleep. Devon had kidnapped me that next morning. Her Master had drained the life out of me, elated that he'd gotten me away from Veronica. He was rubbing in the fact that I'd be his child, and Veronica would return to him. How easy it'd been to fool me, as he'd pretended to be human and made me believe I was in love with him, until I'd discovered he was an undead creature. Then, my lover had rescued me and turned me into what I was.

Another spasm of pain ripped through me. The fear of the other victims was an elixir I craved. Desired. It would make my day to swallow them whole. My eyes tried refocusing again, but nothing worked. I pulled against the chains, trying to break free, but they held. A hollow echo formed in the pit of my stomach as a death rattle stirred in my mind. The nearest heartbeat was inches from me. I needed it, had to consume it, had to feel the meat's life-liquid coursing through me. Yes, the human meat would make me whole again.

I smiled, finding renewed strength enough to yank against my chains. They gave some in the mortar. I tried pulling, but my reserves gave out. As I lay against the bricks, waiting, I sensed another presence invading my territory. It was bestial, feral. I hissed. A growl grew in my throat. I couldn't see what it was, only making out its auric field. It was yellow and fuzzy, with brown dashed through it.

Something snapped and crunched, the sound of bones breaking underfoot. The thing got closer. I swung at it, but it laughed as the chains held me. It grabbed my throat, pulling my mouth open. I tried biting, but all my strength was used just in trying to stay conscious and keep the hunger from consuming my sanity.

The thing held me fast and forced scorching liquid down my throat, filling my stomach, and the liquid was instantly absorbed into my system. I coughed at first and then realized the liquid was blood. My eyesight cleared, and I saw what was in front of me.

The liquid kept coming, and I didn't care that it came from the wrist of the werewolf who'd attacked me. I kept swallowing, trying to draw life out of him, but he pulled away. His blood was stronger, thicker than human, and restored my broken flesh. My tongue healed, as did all the bite marks—they were only skin deep. I still felt half-full, half-alive, but at least I was sane again.

The werewolf grabbed my chains and pulled. They snapped. His furry, claw-studded hand seized the cuffs, breaking the pins that held them, and I was free. I glanced around the cell and saw the things I'd smelled, barely alive, clinging to life, chained and starving. The stench of death was unbearable, and an uncontrollable shiver overtook me. Their eyes were as blank as those of the other victims I'd seen, but it seemed hunger could turn even me into an unimaginable beast when I'd thought I was beyond that.

Slowly, my eyes swept the dungeon, resting on the werewolf in front of me, half-human, half-wolf, standing on two legs, fur covering his whole body. His hands were those of a wolf, with short, stubby claws at the end, but still deadly enough to rip my head off. Bulbous muscles stretched from his neck and out from his arms. The creature was stronger than any vampire I'd seen. This more than explained how he'd overpowered me, but then again, physically, I wasn't the strongest among the vampire kind.

The wolf's muzzle showed off his teeth, but it didn't seem as long as it had been. When I looked into his eyes they were hazel, reflecting the light.

The werewolf blocked the door, and I had to get to my charge. I didn't know how long I had been out, but it had probably been long enough for Miranda to have lost her battle with the thing inside her. This beast might have freed me, but he still barred the doorway. I was sure he was another obstacle for me to pass. Another one of Julien's games. Revive me, and then let his pet have me for a play toy. My talons grew, and I sprang without thinking. The werewolf caught me in his arms easily, and we both went down, landing in a roll in the hallway. I began slashing at his face and chest, but he caught both my wrists before I could do major damage.

"Enough, enough. I'm not going to hurt you."

I stopped struggling as his voice came out garbled. "Stop."

As I looked closely, his eyes turned deep green. His form shrank some under me. His muzzle retreated and reformed into a human mouth and ears. Bones snapped and fused back together into a human skeleton. His head shrunk and all the fur receded, leaving the pale-pink-flushed skin of a man underneath me. All this occurred while he still held me in his iron embrace. Even through the transformation, he never let me go as his claws blunted and became human fingernails.

I stopped moving, and he released me. I got up slowly, as did he. He was almost as tall as me with broad shoulders and skin riddled with scars. Four parallel claw marks stood out over his left nipple. He was naked before me, but hell, I was half-naked already. His brown hair was tousled and greasy, but he wasn't hairy. There was some gray in the brown hair, but it wasn't noticeable. His dick stood at attention while he took me in. As we inspected one another, I sensed a quiet calmness around him. Whenever he walked into a room, his presence demanded attention.

"What do you want?"

"I'm here to help." His voice held the faint trace of a French accent.

I laughed. That was funny. "What kind of a trick is this? You're his pet."

His hand clamped around my throat as his teeth filled his mouth and he growled. "I'm not an animal. *They* are the animals. I just saved you. Do you want my help or not?"

I grabbed his wrist and pulled it off. His snarl lessened as he calmed, regaining self-control. It seemed to take a little effort, but it was interesting and made me wonder if he was being held captive, as I had been, taking orders to survive. I didn't know much about werewolves, but I'd met two of them, and both had tried to eat me. Well, this one had technically killed me, but maybe he really wanted to help.

"Why do you want to help me?"

He sighed. "Look, we don't have much time. You and Miranda are in danger. We have to get her out of here. He's going to complete her transformation, and he has some twisted interest in you. I thought I was doing you a favor, but maybe I was too impulsive." He turned to walk out the door.

He was right. Miranda was my first concern, but I still didn't trust him. "Why do you care so much about Miranda? You should be happy your Master has a new pet."

The werewolf stopped and turned. Rage rippled through his muscles, but he held it in check.

"He is *not* my Master. I only serve him because I wanted to make sure he never finished what was started with my beloved Marie. After all these centuries, he found Miranda. I'd hoped the vampire in her had died, or been beaten down by the humanity in her soul, but I was wrong. Then, when I saw you with her, I thought you were going to corrupt Miranda too. That was the only reason I attacked you before. I thought I'd killed you, but obviously I didn't, and when I found out what you were trying to do, I regretted my action. I realized you were only trying to keep Miranda safe, not turn her into a vampire. So, here I am. Does that satisfy your curiosity?"

I looked on him, stunned. Was he really telling the truth? Was he only with Julien to watch out for Miranda? My instincts told me he spoke the truth, vibrating the psychic chord in me, but I still didn't trust him. How could I? He had killed me.

"Who are you?"

"My name's Xavier. I'm Miranda's great-great-great...grandfather. Julien attacked my Marie in France centuries ago. He'd already given her too much blood by the time I arrived. I almost grabbed his heart to destroy him, but he came back a century later. Marie and I ran. I raised our child after Marie died, but she had the taint of the vampires. I'd hoped to bring Marie into the night, but as a werewolf, not a bloodsucker. When the child was old enough, I went to find Julien, but he found me first. Good enough?"

He was the husband of Miranda's ancestor who'd been attacked by Julien. Xavier had stopped Marie's transformation and now watched his great-great-whatever turning into exactly the same kind of monster. Okay, so he'd proved I could trust him, but time was running out for Miranda. My worn senses caught her heart beating erratically. Her mind was being torn in half. Both sides were in battle with the beast being slightly stronger. I wasn't sure who was totally in control, as my own senses were shot.

While I probed her mind, Miranda came to life. Her attention turned to me as she sensed my thoughts against her. For a second, I touched her soul, and her humanity called out for help, but the beast surged forward, aware of my presence. It pushed me out with one slash of its claws. My psychic tether rebounded, leaving me dizzy from returning to my body too quickly.

My eyes snapped open. I almost lost my balance, but Xavier steadied me, his hand catching my falling manacles so they rattled against the wall. I smiled weakly at him.

"Let's go."

28

CHAPTER TWENTY-EIGHT

My name is Miranda.

The bitch was awake. She'd been probing my mind to see who was in control. In the cafeteria, the human half had gained power, but I'd clamped down and pushed it out. There was no reason for me to lose the glory of the night. The only reason my mortality had surged forth was that it had felt the bitch come and thought it was going to be saved. That wasn't happening.

The bitch was powerful—she'd broken out of the shackles where Master kept the meat. Even as she scanned our mind, she wasn't as strong as she had been. My brothers and sisters had stolen most of her blood, but to my dismay, Master had intervened before they killed her. He'd said she was special. I hoped he would give me the privilege of draining her. I licked my lips at that thought. Her blood would make me powerful and kill off my remaining humanity.

Master wrapped his arms around me, pulling me back from my thoughts.

"What is it, Mira?"

"Brenna has escaped. She's coming to free me from your evil clutches. Do you think I need rescuing, Master?" I purred as I ran my hand over his chest.

His hand wrapped around my shoulder as he hugged me, kissing the top of my head and running his hand over the spot where he'd taken out a portion of my throat. The skin was sensitive, the tissue still reforming since he'd removed muscle and flesh. I held no malice towards him; I understood why he'd done it. His blood had given me the strength to blossom. Now, he held me in his arms like a porcelain doll human children played with. Nothing was going to keep me from him.

"Yes, child. Let her come. It's all part of my plan."

"But Master—"

"Shh."

29

CHAPTER TWENTY-NINE

My name is Brenna.

I followed Xavier down a dark hallway, trudging through an inch of water. As quiet as I tried to be, silence was impossible, as I splashed with each step. All I knew was that it was pitch dark, and I was following a werewolf I hoped I could trust. I was somewhere underneath the nursing home, deep within the heart of the nest. Mostly, I followed the werewolf's aura, which trailed behind him like a slimy slug's tail. Everyone had an aura, but his blared out against the darkness.

I cursed myself for not having complete night vision. It would have been great. In total darkness, all I saw were certain colors within my visual spectrum, but if I looked with my psychic sight, I saw the aura. This was funny since I'd switched off my psychic powers, but this one lingered, so maybe it was part of my vampiric powers as well. I even got a peek at my own aura, a faint line of silver around myself, which had grown smaller as I'd used some of its energy to stay alive. This silver had been left over from Azrael's blood. My body hadn't processed it all yet. The Angel of Death survived by rules I didn't have any experience with; I had no idea what it was like in his universe.

The end of the hallway forked. To the left, a cool breeze came from the end, and I made out points of light in the distance. This was where the vampires got in and out. Yup, we were in the grated-off section I'd looked into on my first visit to this horrid place. And to the right, the air was dead. Of course, this was where we were going. *Wonderful.*

It seemed the darkness was even thicker than it had been in the main tunnel. Each step was like cutting through cloth. It was even hard to breathe — not that I had to, but I did out of habit. As we went further into the abyss, I heard heartbeats at the other end. Julien's thumped very slowly, and the other was Miranda's, alternating between a rapid human beat and the slow, almost non-existent one of the vampire. She was in the midst of losing what she was.

I ran the rest of the way, praying I wouldn't fall, and came to a curtain that hid a room. It was some kind of storage room and contained the only light in the whole place, but it was also a dead end. Broken pieces of furniture sat stacked all around. Wheel-chairs with bent wheels were toppled over on rusted gurneys. Filing cabinets that looked like they'd been in a train wreck were nestled in another corner. Papers spilled out of the drawers, littering the floor, stained and soaking up rusty water. In the middle of it all stood Julien, waiting for me with Miranda at his side, smiling.

The air grew hot, thick, and even denser.

"Master, I have brought her as you commanded," Xavier said in a garbled voice as his vocal chords shifted.

I turned and saw the werewolf transformed again. I was an idiot for believing such a sob story. My intuition hadn't warned me, but then again, I hadn't been too friendly with the universe lately. With Veronica dead, I wanted nothing to do with that world. My only reason for living was to save Miranda, and I'd even failed at that.

I'd lost two lives just to please my own whims. Just as Azrael had predicted. But he'd also mentioned that Veronica knew what I would become, whatever that was supposed to be. I'd been searching for that answer for the past eight months, but on my own, I'd found nothing. When I wanted to talk to an angel about what I was, one appeared, but wouldn't give me a straight answer. Go figure!

With the werewolf behind me and the two of them in front of me, I wasn't going to survive. This time, the Angel of Death would have to take me. Even with the thought of death, I had to fight with all my might and save Miranda if it was the last thing I did. Julien had a good hold on her, but there was still something worth fighting for. I had to drive the beast away and let Miranda out.

"You assume that Mira is yours, don't you?"

I cringed. Why did vampires always give their children annoying pet nicknames? It was so irritating. Devon had called Veronica Ronnie, and when I was under his spell, he'd called me Raven. I'd thought about giving the name up after a while, but I'd kept it since it represented who I was, a bird of prophecy, and now a harbinger of death.

"Her name is Miranda, asshole. And, yes, I've come to rescue her. Not everything you touch automatically becomes yours."

Julien stepped forward, baring his fangs. Xavier seized my arms. His grip was far too ironclad for me to break away. Julien came closer, caressing the side of my face, trying to gain my attention. His touch was clammy, but I didn't flinch as his finger trailed down my cheek and throat, then came to rest on my chest. He stopped a minute and weighed my tits as he admired them. Being exposed didn't bother me, but this guy was a slime ball anyway, so this made me want to rip his head off even more.

I moved my gaze to Miranda, but she kept her eyes obediently downcast. Her expression remained impassive as he caressed my breast. She didn't want to anger her Master, and I was just another plaything, something she didn't have to worry about.

"If you'd been mine in the first place, then you'd never have denied me. Devon was a fool to think he could possess you, even after you were bled. But he was short-sighted, assuming he could use your power to see into the future and rule our world," Julien said while stretching my nipple until it almost tore off.

Pain was nothing. I was used to pain. But the surprise that he knew about Devon ran rampant in my mind. How was that possible? How connected were these creatures? Zhen had mentioned that most knew when old ones were killed, but Julien was young compared to Devon. I presumed he was around seven centuries old, which, from a vampire's perspective, meant he was still a child. Then again, I assumed the ancient ones I'd encountered were flukes. How old was the average vampire?

But what Julien said was true. Devon had wanted me to be his next Oracle so he could manipulate my psychic abilities to learn where others of his kind were, the same way he'd used Aria. She'd once been a Delphic Oracle, but then, after seeing her own destiny, she'd dug out her eyes. When Devon found her and turned her, they'd grown back. He'd used her until her psychic energy was sapped and she had no more connections to the universe. In the end, I felt bad for her. The vampires had even tried to control Marie Laveau, the Voodoo Queen of New Orleans, but she'd gone crazy after becoming one of the undead. Hell, who wouldn't? I had been there. I could attest to that.

"I sense the astonishment in your mind. I'm not as old as Devon, but I'm quite powerful. You see, I've been tracking you for months since I heard about the deaths of Devon and Malachi. It was quite the talk among our kind when a fledgling humiliated one of the oldest and most respected among the undead. When you were hardly out of swaddling clothes. You were given credit for his death, even though his pet did him in. It's quite an honor.

"Do you think it was a mistake that one of your employees was killed, or that you just happened to overhear a conversation about a human being butchered in a hallway at your business? I knew the murders would get your attention. Yours and your bleeding-heart Master's. By the way, how is she? I heard Robyn sliced her to ribbons. It's unfortunate you took his hand. He was a good recruit. Too bad. Zhen never used him for the right purposes. But, then again, she might be the oldest among us, but she's such a humanitarian. It's disgusting. It has something to do with her bloodline, her Master or something. I forget the rumors about her."

Julien had been the one who'd ordered Veronica killed. Zhen hadn't known. Then again, maybe she had. She'd sent me here, knowing Julien was going to be waiting for me. In her best interest, I owed her a debt, so maybe that was the reason. He'd ordered my lover's death. I thought I'd taken care of the problem. Now he admitted to killing Zach and Veronica. It made sense—Robyn wasn't clever enough to plan Veronica's murder. There must have been a mastermind behind the whole thing. And here he was. How much of this had been a trap? How much was Miranda really involved in? Had she lured me from the beginning? Had she befriended me just to trick me?

No. She's been an innocent through the whole thing. No one would struggle as much as she has just to get me. She has to be mixed up in it as Zhen mentioned. I've been Julien's goal all along. Miranda got mixed up in the middle of it.

"Why kill Veronica?" I whispered, choking back tears.

Julien smiled at my reaction, which was exactly what he wanted. I hated when the undead got their rocks off by glorifying in the pain of others, even their own kind.

Well, technically, I wasn't anything like him. I was something different. And that was why he wanted me. If he had heard about the other deaths, then I wondered what was flying around the vampire community about the being that had killed Devon and Malachi. What were they saying about me, about how different I truly was? All of this made me want to kill Julien even more.

"Ahh, pet. Veronica was the only thing holding you back from realizing your true potential. Your true gifts. Besides, she was a meat-lover and had to be put out of her misery. Now you are free to be mine."

He kissed my neck as tears I couldn't hold back streamed down my cheeks. All because of me, Veronica was dead. All because of what I was, because I was different. It seemed everyone knew. I'd thought I could fit in, thought I could pass as one of them, but that wasn't the case, and it would never be that way. As it was, there might be others like Julien who would try to come and claim me. Well, hell. He would be the last. Azrael had been right. All my friends had been sacrificed for my whims, and now, Miranda was next.

Julien's mouth enclosed my tit, redoubling my hatred. *He's dead,* I thought. He'd never possess me like that. I'd kill him first. When he glanced up at me and saw no reaction, his grey eyes turned black.

"You taste good. You're sweeter than any others I've had. I can tell the difference in your skin. The rumors were true—you're something special. I've been tracking you for months, and you led me right to my child. Fate brought the two of you together. I should have known you'd try to rescue her; it's in your nature, it seems, since you were infected with that meat-lover of a Master. So what do you say, will you serve me?"

He bent down to my stomach and licked with his forked tongue from my belly button to between my breasts. "Serve me, and I'll let you live. You'd lose your sanity, of course, as I would feed on your soul like I do with all my humans. You'd be ever so much tastier. Vampires that retain even half of their souls are such rare delicacies, but you. Mmm."

He stared into my face and expected me to take his offer willingly. He was quite serious. Had he said he fed on souls? I'd never heard of a vampire who could do that. I only knew of the ones who existed on blood. Nothing was going to make me want to serve Julien.

Xavier still grasped my arms as his Master wrapped his hand around my ass. His teeth bit lightly on the flesh of my stomach. He took my silence as a sign I was thinking about his offer.

"I almost killed Lupe when I saw you wounded on the floor. Then, you rose, and now here you are again. So what do you say; are you going to join me?" He looked up at me.

I grinned slowly and stared at Miranda. She had raised her eyes and now stared at her Master. She was getting pissed because she thought I was going to be taking her place. Why not play along, at least for a little bit? If she got angry enough, she might charge him, and that might give me some advantage.

"I've never heard of a vampire who can eat souls. How do you do that?" I asked, and moved my body into him a little more. I sensed the change in him. He smiled, thinking he'd won me over.

"Oh, Brenna. You're going to make such a fine servant."

He smiled at me, moved a piece of hair out of my eyes and caressed my cheek slowly. He seemed satisfied. I glared at Miranda and gave her a smirk as Julien kept his eyes locked to mine, the swirling black reminding me of a hypnotist's wheel.

His hand trailed down my tits, undoing my zipper, slipping my jeans off. A curved talon slid into my pussy as his human thumb rubbed my clit. I leaned against him and began grinding my hips toward his talon. His tongue caressed my neck, and his hot breath whispered into my ear.

"You like this, don't you, Brenna? You know how to please your Master, don't you?"

"Yes," I breathed against him, grinding my hips even more.

"You know something?"

"Wha...at?"

"It's a shame you're fucking faking the whole thing. You should have been an actress."

His other hand yanked my head back far enough that I thought he would rip it off, but he looked me in the eyes, and I found my will crumbling.

"You want to know how a vampire eats souls. Well then, I'll show you, bitch."

His talon impaled me, and I felt a gush of blood between my legs. I tried not to moan as he massaged me, but there was nothing I could do as he made me wetter and my body rocked with orgasms. My bottom lip quivered as I bit down, trying to hold on. His power pushed into my mind, into every part of me, and I tried erecting walls, but he'd gotten too strong.

Miranda's expression darkened as her eyes became slits. She was waiting for her Master to throw me away, but she hated my expression. She knew she would be replaced if Julien got his claws on me, but decorum held her in place, and she used all her will just to keep from clawing Julien. A faint flush had even appeared on her cheeks. There was still something of the human in her.

His eyes kept going deeper into mine, and they were almost like Azrael's, endless. My eyes closed to half-slits, and his thoughts wove around my brain, coiling about the many folds and taking hold like a leech. His talon shoved into me more, and all his teeth elongated, becoming uneven fangs as his tongue flicked against my lips. My body responded to his power, and I felt like I had with Devon, like I was a puppet. Everything in me wanted to destroy him, but I didn't even know if I could fight him anymore; he was so wrapped around my mind that it almost didn't matter what he did to me.

His lips pressed against mine, his teeth catching the inside of my gums as he kissed me. I returned the kiss furiously, as I wanted to be fucked. Every manipulation felt wonderful as I bucked under him, soaring on the orgasmic high that he kept giving me until it was so much I didn't know what the hell was going on. Then, the pain started.

The tether in my brain tightened, as did his grip. He kept finger-fucking me, and I kept kissing him, unable to stop. My body writhed in his arms, and Xavier held my wrists. Pleasure from my orgasms rippled through me, taking all of my attention, but the pain in my head felt like something being yanked out of me.

First, it seemed like my energy field was collapsing, that all my chakras were being extracted, running up my spine. I lost feeling in my feet first, until not even pins and needles remained. The strange thing was that, even though my very personality, my soul was being devoured, something else still lingered inside of me. It was alien, but basic. I surmised it was the demonic influence left in me, making my body function on automatic. It was this part that got the better of me sometimes. This very thing was part of my hunger, and it was the beast, if I had one.

If I gave up, I'd be a bag of flesh, a mindless vacuum Julien could manipulate. Frantically, I caught Miranda's eyes again. Her expression was seething. Just what I needed. The prized child knew she was being pushed aside.

You heard what he said. I'm going to be his new paramour. You're nothing to him, bitch. He's put you aside for me. I'm what he wants—you heard him say that for yourself.

At first, she did nothing but eye Julien as my body moved under his control. Of course, she didn't know that. Xavier's dick bumped into my ass; he was getting a good ride out of the whole display. I gazed back at Miranda. Everything began to take on a tunnel-vision look. I thought I saw her move, but I wasn't so sure. Everything was cold and getting colder, and that wasn't a good sign.

30

CHAPTER THIRTY

My name is Miranda.

I looked on my Master with pride while he chatted with the bitch. He wasn't going to give me up, but with each word he uttered, I sensed something. Then he began touching her, kissing her, fucking her. The bitch loved it as her lips quivered, and she tried not to show her pleasure. My human half surfaced after I thought she'd given up to the Master. She was still there even after I'd consumed all the blood.

You waited all this time, and he doesn't want you. Doesn't it mean anything that he's casting you aside?

I pushed her off, but I knew she was right. For once, the human self actually had words of wisdom for me. The bitch bucked under Julien, coming against him as if she were riding a mechanical bull. She'd been playing hard to get all the times she came to find me. He'd even said he wanted her for his own, knowing about her power, her strange abilities, how different and special she was. But I was the long lost child he'd searched for, and now that I was free, no one was going to have him except me.

My jaw tightened. He'd promised me an eternity of wonderful nights.

I stopped watching the show and stepped forward, going against everything I knew. One never acted against the creator. The Master was always in charge. You never looked at him more than once. You never raised your voice or questioned him. It was an honor to hunt with him, to be with him.

I wrapped my taloned fingers around my Master's waist, prying him off, trying to entice him with me as his main choice. He stopped when he felt the coolness of my hand. He threw me aside so I landed in a pile of old wheelchairs, which toppled around me. I glanced up as he descended on me to leave Brenna collapsing to the floor, pale and blue. I smiled. She was no more, or at least out of the way for now, and Master was mine again.

The wolf prodded her with his foot. I heard him whimper, but Master gathered me in his arms.

"You must never disturb me when I'm feeding. Don't believe anything she said, Mira. I just want her abilities. She's unique, but she means nothing to me.

As a vampire, she is very special, and if I can gain her power, then I'll take what she was."

His eyes were so deep. I knew he was sincere.

"Forgive me, Master. I only thought she—"

He kissed the top of my head. "It's okay, young one. I understand."

I sighed as he held me, his lips connecting with mine, and I was in heaven again.

31

CHAPTER THIRTY-ONE

My name is Brenna.

Warmth returned slightly to my body as I swallowed the blood that came in my mouth. I was aware that Julien had dropped me, but I couldn't do anything until the liquid came into my system, which seemed to be happening a lot lately. The taste of blood told me it was Xavier's. I thought that odd, since he was the enemy. Slowly, he helped me up, as I wasn't steady on my feet. Julien was an outline leaning over Miranda. Their voices came filtered to me through a long tunnel.

"Yes, Master," Miranda answered.

I blinked again. That seemed to help, but if Julien got a hold of me again, I was toast. He was the first vampire I'd heard of who survived on souls. Then again, I'd heard of humans who considered themselves energy vampires, which basically meant their auric fields were low and they constantly had to replenish themselves with energy.

I guess the principal would be the same for vampires. They could take in souls. If I could manipulate energy, then so could vampires. And I was sure a soul held a lot of energy, one just had to tap into it. If Julien survived on souls, then maybe he'd been an energy vampire when he was human. He and Zhen were right. I knew little about the species I'd been born into, considering I really wasn't one of them. Then again, maybe I was just a different breed, another branch of the family tree.

Xavier held me up as some of his blood returned minimal feeling to my feet, but my vision was still tunneled. I swallowed and wondered if I would ever recover what I'd lost. It would suck to go through eternity with half a soul, but then again, after I smoked this guy, I was going to see Veronica. But who knew? This was my last chance to get Julien as he consoled Miranda.

Are you going to help me, or are you going to alert your Master like you did before? I asked Xavier mentally.

He was my only chance, so I put my hopes on him. This was the moment. Friend or foe. I backed up against the wall, closing my eyes. Things around me rattled and fell, furniture crashed, but I didn't bother to open my eyes. Xavier growled.

"Lupe, what are you doing?" Julien asked, surprised that his beloved pet was attacking him.

With whatever energy I had in me, I tried opening my chakras. If there was anything in me that could connect with the cosmos, then this was the time I needed it. I needed to reopen the psychic door.

Slowly, my chakras sputtered to life, spinning like pinwheels, faster and faster the longer I concentrated. Energy started moving from the bottom of my spine to the top of my head, flooding me slowly, building, trying to infuse itself in the areas of my body that needed to be replenished. Yet as much as it raced through me, little of it stuck where Julien had sucked me dry. I reached with all my senses, trying to draw more in, trying to build up the impending heat that had annihilated Julien's nest, but it was no use. All that remained was the frigidness left behind with Azrael's blood. Maybe that was the key. Maybe I could tap into that, but I didn't have much time since Xavier was losing the battle.

The wolf had been thrown against the wall and wasn't getting up. I could sense that. At least he was on my side, but now it was my turn to take care of the asshole who thought he was all-powerful and could rule my world. At least he was out of my mind. I'd have to shower when I was done with the whole ordeal to get rid of his stench.

Slowly, I rose, gathering whatever remaining power I could, but my body couldn't absorb any more. My soul had to heal, replenish, and hopefully, it would regrow like the rest of my body did. I stood up and found Julien by the still form of his pet werewolf. Pure hatred was embedded in his features. He kicked the body as it slowly returned to human shape.

"That will teach you to defy me."

Miranda hovered over the body, watching the blood spread into a small lake. She licked her lips. Her body hungered for it, yearned for the stuff that would help stop the burning pain in her veins. A fire could be quenched with one sip of the crimson liquid. Boy, I knew how she felt. It would have been great to have even one sip of Zhen's special brew.

"Don't think you can get rid of me that easily," I said sarcastically, sounding more sure of myself than I really was.

Julien turned and stared, and then he laughed. "Do you really think you're a match for me? You can hardly stand. I fed on half of your soul. Such power. Your heat burns in me, settling over the heart as it does. You really are an interesting individual, Brenna—or should I call you Raven, as you call yourself? As Devon called you, since that is your true name. It's a shame you shut down your abilities, as your connection to the other side is remarkable. I've felt things before, like the spirits in this place. They sustain me when I need them to, but you actually see the dead and predict the future. But it's your other abilities I desire. Devon really didn't know what he was getting himself involved in when he thought he could control you."

I was amazed that Julien knew about my psychic powers, even felt them, knowing my connection to the universe. Even when I'd shut the door, it appeared that he'd opened it. Then again, it made sense that if he stole my soul, he'd acquire my powers. That didn't mean he knew how to use what he'd taken. As he laughed, I started to get mad. Laughter wouldn't appease my rage over Veronica's death. He wasn't going to win. My teeth pushed through my gums, grazing the top of my tongue. He was dead.

I closed my eyes, gathering my energy, projecting it directly at Julien in the form of a big fireball. Whatever was left formed itself into an orb and left me, leaving me drained. I didn't see the energy depart, but it hit the mark, and the center of Julien's shirt exploded in flame. The fire spread quicker than he could pull his clothes off and caught his skin.

Miranda screamed and ran to help him, but he pushed her into a pile of old gurneys. She lay dazed, but not dead. Her Master wouldn't allow that. Julien dropped to the floor, screaming, rolling around until the fire was extinguished. He acted quickly enough that his skin blackened, but his body worked to repair the damage faster than normal, since he'd just fed. He'd said my energy was stronger, more potent than humans', but I didn't know how long it would take to process the energy. To process my soul, which must have been a mass of some sort of texture.

If Julien could take souls, then he could reach into other dimensions—at least, I assumed another dimension was where the soul resided, but honestly, I had no clue as to how his power worked. It did explain why his children were mindless sacks, pure animal instinct walking around in human flesh, which was how he wanted me to end up. I didn't agree.

He stood up, his fingers stretching into darkened claws. I tried to change my form, but it was getting hard to concentrate, as my energy stores had been used up. He stepped forward, slowly, edging me back against the wall. Pure evil shone in his eyes. With each step he took, the charred skin flaked off, showing new pink flesh underneath.

"For that, you'll pay. I'll suck the rest of you slowly, taking just enough so you feel yourself slipping away until there's only an empty shell. It seems a more fitting end. At least when I drink other vampires into me, I know the beast survives, ready to do my will to the end. But you, you'll just be a zombie with no soul that stays around. Of course, I'll have your powers, so they won't be lost. But that was the whole idea anyway. I wonder how it will feel to predict the future. Maybe I'll even take over your business. Wouldn't that be interesting? No, wait, I know. I'll let Mira have what's left of your body so she can suck you dry, taking in the enjoyment of vampire blood, and once she's strong enough, I'll let her drink in souls, gaining power until she's my equal. What do you think of that? Oh, I know, you think her humanity will suffer, but soon there won't be any left."

I didn't give a shit what he said. I didn't care what happened to me anymore. I knew where I was going when I died. It was what he said about Miranda that bothered me. I couldn't let that happen. She couldn't be corrupted any more than she already had been. I closed my eyes, calling on my powers, but nothing came. The only chance left was the silver line from Azrael. It was the only thing I had left to utilize, the only energy source that could fuel my body.

In my mind, I pictured myself tapping into a maple tree for syrup, but instead of the slow flow I expected, power flooded into me like nothing I'd prepared for. The power was frigid, cold as the moon's surface and frozen like a glacier. It rushed into every part of me, filling my capillaries, my muscles, and my bones, even the places where Julien's power had touched me.

Even though it was cold, it made me feel light and expanded, like I could disappear from this dimension and blend into the shadows. The world around me became two-dimensional, and everything appeared to be a hologram, although I remained solid and occupied the same space.

Julien wrapped his talons around my throat. I assumed he felt the cold my body gave off. It should have frozen him like liquid nitrogen. His hand pressed against my larynx so I couldn't breathe, but it didn't stop the way I felt. His eyes bore into mine; his mind wrapped around my thoughts as it had before, but his movements were slow compared to how I experienced things. Quick flashes kept zooming in the room like small passing lights speeding by, reminding me of flickering fairies. His lips locked to mine while his tongue worked inside my mouth. My body began to respond, but my mind was beyond him while my body desired to be dominated.

Not knowing how or why I was doing what I did, my hand plunged automatically into his chest. It didn't occur to me that I shouldn't have been able to do this, considering I had no talons. His flesh was resistant at first, but I kept going through muscle and bone, feeling the warmth of his heart in my hand. It beat slowly and methodically. The slick mucous sack covering it was like tissue paper. The chambers opened and closed, pushing the blood to his body.

Naturally, the remnants of the beast in me should have wanted to pull it out and drink the blood. My hunger should have ignited at the thought, but in truth, I didn't care. It seemed that, for that instant, I was beyond the call of blood; I was something else.

Instinctually, I knew the heart was the seat of Julien's power. So I pulled, plucked it out as if it were nothing. Julien's expression froze. His body locked for a split second, as though I had paused him. Then, he pulled away, going from shock to pain all in a moment. His hand wrapped around my wrist, trying to stop me, but he couldn't get a hold of it. Pure panic crossed his face. His flesh grew red and then purple. His eyes swirled from blue to black when my hand came out of his chest. He staggered backward, clutching his chest like he was having a heart attack. His mouth distended in pain as if I'd ripped his heart out, but as my hand emerged, I wasn't holding his heart.

I held a glowing silver orb, with tiny thin extensions embedded in his body like puppet strings. As he backed away, the little threads broke free and blew in the breeze like a broken web. His face became a twisted mass of flesh morphing into something like the drawing of a preschooler. The thing I held was warm, and its glow filled the room, blue-silver and light as air, though it still weighed my hand down. Julien fell to the floor and began twitching like he was having a seizure. His form stopped changing, and he lay still.

I glanced at the thing in my hand and squeezed. The orb was liquid silver, squishing between my fingers with all the threads dangling like broken fishing line. After a moment, the strands retracted into the silver sphere, snapping back like a vacuum chord. In amazement, I realized I held Julien's very soul. An impossible feat for me, but here it was nonetheless.

The only being who could take a soul was Azrael. I glanced over at Miranda and saw her coming to. She stood up slowly and blinked. Her eyes were clear and unhindered by the beast, and I thought for a second that maybe it had been taken along with Julien. As she looked at me, puzzlement turned to anger. Her expression darkened. Her eyes swirled black, and the beast reemerged.

"Master!"

A glass-shattering scream echoed through the darkened hallways, piercing my eardrums and causing them to bleed. Miranda collapsed next to Julien's body and lifted him up as she would a child. For a moment, she reminded me of how I'd mourned Veronica—I knew how she felt, even if it was the beast that was crying. Miranda even felt his pulse and along his temple, but when she realized nothing was there, she dropped the body and lunged at me.

I tried to move, but I couldn't. Before I could manage anything, I saw a blur out of the corner of my eye. Then Miranda was on the ground with Xavier on top of her in some twisted werewolf/human form, looking the worse for wear. He glanced over at me, grinning dumbly with his tongue hanging out of his mouth and two rows of sharp teeth. He would hold her while I figured out what to do with this thing in my hand.

As I concentrated, the raw essence of Julien seeped into me, sending warmth tingling up my arm. It was tempting to absorb the whole thing into my own system, but then again, I didn't want to think what it would do to me. I assumed I'd take in everything Julien was on top of my own energy. If I did let his soul fill me, what kind of side effects would I have? Tempting as it was, it was a bad idea.

The coldness I'd tapped into was leaving me, seeping away into the marrow of my bones and draining out my toes. As it left me, I lost feeling in my legs, and my eyesight became blurry again as the tunnel vision returned. I backed up against the wall to steady myself, considering that it was the only upright thing in the room. I tried to clear my sight, but the damage Julien had inflicted caught up with me. I had to get rid of the soul before it went back to his body or I took it in.

"Azrael," I whispered, hoping, for once, he would appear when I truly needed him.

Slowly, I sank down as everything went dark. I didn't feel the angel arrive, but I faintly saw him staring down at me. He took the soul from my fingers, relieving me of my burden. His wings were warm against my frozen body, comforting me while I moved into darkness.

32

CHAPTER THIRTY-TWO

My name is Miranda.

My Master had been destroyed, and now the Master's pet held me before I could avenge him. I growled low in my throat, struggling under the dog, but it was no use—he was stronger. At least the bitch was dying, just as Master wanted. In some way, she'd paid for what she'd done to him. It was glorious to see her sliding down the wall, her life candle extinguishing from the lack of air.

But as she hit the ground, a cold chill permeated the room, and a void opened. A man appeared, dark and pale. At first, I thought he was like me. His energy was slightly off, but still close enough that he could have been my kind. When he turned and caught my gaze, I knew he was Death.

He looked down at the bitch with sympathy. He motioned for the wolf to move. Slowly, I got up, trying not to anger Lord Death. He glared down at me, his eyes the bottomless sockets of decaying skulls. He said nothing, but rested his hand on my shoulder, sending a chill into the very atoms of my soul. I tried moving, but his grip was stronger than the wolf's.

His lips pressed against mine. Searing fire spread through my mind, catching me in its arms. It nipped at my feet, growing over my arms and legs until it engulfed me. I screamed, retreating into my mind, hoping his wrath would soon be over.

Blinking several times, I looked into the darkest eyes I'd ever seen. They were ominous, piercing the veil of my mind. The man they belonged to smiled warmly. I smiled back, not sure where I was or how I'd gotten there. The last thing I truly remembered was walking out of the Black Rose, hoping to give my life for Brenna's. There were just flashes of things after that, but they were fading as if they'd been part of a dream.

The man extended his hand. I took it, noticing pointed, glossy nails. His touch was light as air, but firm as he pulled me up. The room I was in held piles of rotten furniture strewn about, the dead body of Julien off to the side, and a very naked man bending over Brenna. I walked past the guy who'd helped me up and saw that Brenna was also half-naked.

You came after me anyway.

Her skin was tinged blue. There was no movement in her chest. The man who'd helped me up took off his cloak and wrapped Brenna in it, holding her close to his chest.

"Is she dead?" I asked.

"No," replied the naked man, "but she's close."

The dark stranger smiled and looked down at Brenna. "I do not think Death will take her today."

I stepped forward myself and wanted to comfort her, but he wouldn't let me. "Take hold of my coat," he said to me and to the naked dude in the corner. The coat was made from a silk material, but much finer and more finely woven. I scanned the room and suddenly, as if we were in a vacuum, everything changed.

The next thing I knew, we were back in Brenna's living room, which now had windows. I blinked, not knowing how I'd gotten there. The stranger wasn't a vampire. He was something else that I wanted to bow down and pay homage to. He placed Brenna on the sofa and replaced the cloak with the afghan on the back of the couch.

He looked over at me. "She needs rest. Both of you watch her, understand?"

Our savior sat down next to her for a second, barely resting his weight on the couch. His blank expression changed, wavering for a split second. Brenna turned in her sleep, moaning something and starting to thrash. He placed his hand on her fore-head and brushed away a stray hair. She quieted. A look of compassion crossed his features, or maybe it was even love. He traced the line of her cheek and kissed the top of her head. His eyes closed as he did, savoring the moment. Then, his expression returned to normal. As he looked up at me, the beast stirred, but the being hardened his stare, boring into my brain. My other silenced, running away like a fright-ened puppy. Then, he was just gone.

I blinked, wondering what the hell had hap-pened. Who was the naked guy in the living room? What had happened to Julien? So many questions crossed my mind, and the only one who could an-swer them was Brenna. As she lay on the couch, I realized she'd kept her promise and saved me. Now I had to watch her, but deep down, I got the sense that everything was going to be all right.

33

CHAPTER THIRTY-THREE

My name is Brenna.

The passage of time was evident as voices hovered on the periphery of my consciousness. One of them was Miranda. Her presence watched to see if I was okay. Then, Azrael's cold energy pressed on my thoughts as he spoke directly to my mind, sensing that was the only way I could understand him. He came while the others were gone, never saying anything of course, but giving me the most comfort, helping lead me through the darkness to find a way back to my body while my soul healed.

I wasn't dead, but I floated in between dimensions. It had taken much of my energy's resources to heal. Somehow, it was easier to drift around in the astral realm so I could be restored. It was peaceful there while my soul regained the energy I had lost. There wasn't much to see or hear. I was just a thing surviving in a space. My mind was free to go where the astral winds took me. My body was formless, but even though my connection to the flesh had been stretched thin, I was alive. I experienced a warm presence surrounding me on that side. It was familiar and loving. It was Veronica.

There was no verbal communication between us, just feelings. She showed me that she didn't want me to die. I could tell by her overwhelming sorrow when I brought up the subject of me joining her. I wanted ever so much to talk to her, as her soul hadn't fully crossed over into the other realms. It would take a full year to do that, and until then, this was what I had. At least that was what I had been taught as a psychic.

Edmund had always told me it took a year for a soul to journey to wherever it went after death. Veronica's spirit was a mass of energy that hovered, waiting to ascend to high planes. But just to know she drifted on the fringe, sending her love, made everything worthwhile. It put me at ease, for she no longer fought what she had been, and she'd found a peace in death she hadn't known in life. That didn't mean I didn't still have a beef with Azrael, and yes, he'd helped me, but now was not the time to fight with him. I didn't have the strength.

Edmund was in the astral realm as well. He came through stronger. I actually saw him while I drifted about. He'd moved further on in his transcendence, and I could talk to him. His energy was the same as ever, overwhelming, as he'd been in life. Now his aura was healthy and not sickly. In life, he'd been my old boss and the one I inherited the Tearoom from. He'd showed me how to read cards, and he'd assured me that I wasn't crazy when it came to talking to the dead. He'd also told Veronica it was my Fate to become a vampire, for I'd chosen my path before I incarnated into the life I led now. It made me wonder how much of my life I had decided with all the bumps I'd gone over. Even though I'd become a different type of vampire, who knew if it was Fate that decided my path?

Why does it seem I only run into you when you're on Death's door? Edmund laughed. His energy made me pick up a little.

Yeah, well, Azrael won't take me. So, I don't think this is it. It would be nice if it were, though.

You wanted to be with Veronica. It's understandable. I've known how much you loved her. But I still think you have a lot to do. I've been watching you. You've been doing well. Keeping the Tearoom up and all. I know life wasn't easy for you even when you were mortal, and you're still in for a rough ride. But remember, you have many to guide you, even if you push them away. I don't like the idea of you shutting your powers down. The consequences can only be bad. As for Azrael, you push his buttons. Have a few laughs when you can. One day, you'll join Veronica, but don't shut down your abilities just because you blame those that helped you. It's unlike you to be selfish. Remember that in the future. Don't turn your back on others. You might not like the results. If you do, things will only get worse, so accept your losses now rather than later.

What does that mean? I asked, remembering that, in life, he'd been like Azrael when it came to giving puzzling information.

You know what I mean. Think of all the advice you give your clients when they're grieving. Don't expect the universe to love you if you reject it and all those who live in it as well. We all have to deal with hurt. Don't blame the messenger for doing his job.

I sighed as Edmund's voice retreated into the darkness, and the cold wasteland withdrew as rapidly as it had come. I knew exactly what he was talking about, but I had no time to deal with it as I was thrown backwards, pulled along the stretched connection to my body. The experience was disorienting. I was aware of everything.

The first thing I heard was the drumming of my own heart. A long inhale filled my lungs, helping to orient me to my body more. My fingers moved slowly, extending and bending as I reminded myself I had a physical being. Then, I opened my eyes, surprised to see who was there. I looked up and saw naturally dark eyes staring down at me below short, spiked black hair. Zhen. She smiled. As quickly as I looked at her, I shut my eyes against the light. Never had it been this bright before, and it seared my flesh. She must have sensed this and covered the windows, throwing the room into near darkness. I was able to look at her.

"You look like shit." She smiled.

"Thanks," I muttered, but it came out as a cracked whisper. "What're you doing here?"

She laughed. I glanced around. Tarps and sheets blocked the light, but nothing held them up. Zhen must have held them up with her mind as she had in the club with me. It was interesting to see that she could move so many things with her mind. It made me wonder when I'd be able to do that.

"I stopped in to see how you were doing. And to congratulate you for getting rid of Julien. But I see he got a bit of you as well. How are you feeling?"

She wrapped a blanket around my shoulders; I realized I was shivering, quivering from being thrown back into my body. Somehow, I'd sat up, but I couldn't feel the bottom half of my body. I moved my toes, but my legs felt like dead weight. Even though my energy felt stronger, I was still weak.

"I feel like my soul has been sucked out of me. How the hell do you think I feel?"

She sighed. The front door closed, and soft footsteps came in. When I looked over, I saw Xavier standing in the doorway carrying several bags of groceries. He looked the same as he had before, but he was dressed in an old red sweatshirt and black jeans. He dropped the bags when he saw the vampire sitting next to me. His form bubbled and shifted, growing into his wolf. He growled and lunged, shifting in mid-spring, but he stopped in midair when I put my hand up.

"She's okay, Xavier. She's my friend." I looked at him and then at her and realized that I truly felt that way about her.

He said something under his breath that I couldn't hear. Since it sounded like everything was in control, he picked up the littered foodstuff and walked into the kitchen.

"You have Julien's werewolf. Impressive. You have to tell me how you did that."

"I don't have him. I didn't even know he was staying here. I've been out a while, remember? So what brings you here anyway?" I asked again.

Zhen ran her hand along my leg. I couldn't feel her butterfly caress, but I moved it away. This didn't anger her at all. "I came to check on you, as friends do. And to tell you your debt to me is paid. You owe me nothing. I fear I might owe you a thing or two, but maybe we can negotiate."

I chuckled. Xavier put things away in the kitchen, and I only imagined what it was Zhen owed me. So I just smiled, happy that she was here, showing concern, considering most vampires were not the type to befriend one another. It would be nice to have someone else to talk to, another who knew what I went through. I had Peter, but he was human and couldn't understand everything. Thinking of him, I wondered how the Tearoom fared, but I had a feeling it had survived just as I had.

"Brenna," Zhen called.

She got my attention, and I saw that she offered her neck. This was a shock. Her vein stood out against her skin, pulsating as she willed her heart to speed up for my eye to catch the movement. I watched it, feeling my fangs grow without me even willing them to.

I felt like a sagging bag of bones. Zhen said nothing at my reaction, but wrapped her hands around me, bringing me close as a mother cares for a child. I thought of nothing as I sank my fangs into her neck. Her blood hit the roof of my mouth, old and powerful. I couldn't describe the taste as it went down. Just by drinking it in, my body came back to life. I wasn't so cold, and the light seeping in through the cracks didn't bother me as much. My arms went around Zhen, and I felt like I was going to crush her since she was so little. I took more blood in, not wanting the fount to stop. Then, the front door opened again.

"Brenna?"

It was Miranda. I took one more swallow and let go of the vampire, thankful she'd helped me and wondering what Miranda thought of the display. She rushed into the room, transfixed at the sight. I pushed Zhen away, licking the remaining blood on my mouth as Miranda started crying, but not from my feasting. She'd thought I was never going to wake up.

"It's okay, Miranda. I'm all right," I told her, giving her a huge hug.

"I thought—" she sniffled.

"I know, but you don't have to worry. I'll be fine. I feel like shit, but I'll be fine."

"Yes, little one. She's strong. And she faced a very powerful vampire to get you back. Now I have to be going. Brenna, stop by sometime, and we'll get together for a dinner date." Zhen smiled and showed me her fangs. "By the way, I found this in the coat room. I think it belongs to you."

I turned back around, and Zhen held the jacket I'd left at the Rose ages ago. "Thanks."

She nodded and then vanished. When she did, the window coverings came crashing down. Night air rushed in—somehow, hours had passed since she'd first appeared. The air was cool, and the essence of rain caressed me and gave me strength. It made me realize how much of the world I'd missed when I lingered in a void of nothingness.

Even if I couldn't be with Veronica, then the little things would have to give me solace. I let go of Miranda and sensed Xavier in the room. They were my new family. I had protected them, and now they watched over me. I laughed internally. I may have lost Veronica, but in the end, I gained a werewolf and a half-vampire. It didn't matter, because they'd be there for me no matter what happened. Hopefully, I could find some degree of solace in their company to ease my broken heart.

EPILOGUE

My name is Brenna.

I leaned on the bridge overlooking the duck pond, holding the jar I'd placed Veronica's ashes in. The moon was going into its new phase, but for now, it was dark with only the stars to light the sky. Within the city, it was hard for even them to shine down through the lights.

As I searched the horizon, I knew Veronica was somewhere better, beyond the reaches of the world and the hungers she'd fought against for centuries. Slowly, I unscrewed the jar and sprinkled her ashes into the pond. They hit the surface of the dark water, not even causing a ripple, gradually slipping beneath the surface to rest on the bottom, where she would have no more troubles. A slight breeze caught some of them and my hair. I went to move it out of the way and felt a hand on my arm. I turned around, and there was Azrael.

"She is at peace." His voice was a mere whisper in the dark.

"I know."

I screwed the cover back on the jar and began to walk off the bridge. It was nice to know Veronica watched out for me, even if it was in death. I would be happy when the day came that I could see and speak with her spirit again. Hopefully, one day, after she'd crossed far enough into the afterworld, I could speak to her spirit and Death would let me join her.

There was still much left to the night, and I wanted to experience it. It seemed I'd found a new love of life in the past month, after my close brush with losing my soul.

The Angel of Death stayed close to my side. He was around more than he'd ever been, continually checking on me. However, I truly didn't want him there. He only reminded me of everything that had happened.

Only in the past week had I really felt like my old self again. It had taken me this long to completely heal, to regain full feeling in my toes and reclaim all my power. So I guess my soul did re-grow, but I still hadn't figured out how I'd gotten hold of Julien's soul. And the one who could tell me was Azrael.

"I took the old woman you mentioned. She didn't recognize me at first, but I told her you sent me, and she remembered you. I went through the rest of the home, but there was nothing. Even the rest of the nest had disappeared."

"They wouldn't stay after Julien died. Most probably went to find a new Master. I don't know who will take them, though. They're all mindless creatures."

"How is Miranda?"

I stopped and sat on one of the benches underneath a willow tree. The wind whipped through the branches with a sound like the echoing of the ghosts I'd shut out. As it did, the branches tickled my hair.

Miranda now lived with me, trying to adjust to a normal life. She'd returned to Crimson Liquids and was refurnishing it. The beast seemed to be staying at bay, but every once in a while, it peeked through. She always managed to contain it, but she knew she was going to suffer the hunger for the rest of her existence. Julien had given her too much blood to hide the vampire behind a wall. There was nothing I could do for her except be there when the beast surfaced. For now, things were okay. At least she didn't blame me for killing her Master, as Veronica's other half had done.

"She's adjusting, like everyone. Even Xavier is doing well. He's getting on at the Tearoom. I think Peter has taken a liking to him."

Azrael laughed. "You took the werewolf into the Tearoom. I never thought you would employ him after he tried…well, killed you. Does Miranda know he is a relative?"

"Yeah, they're working it out. It's funny, he keeps asking about her mother and what she looked like. Miranda keeps asking about what happened when Julien attacked Marie in the first place. It's kinda funny when they get around each other. They lock up on words and start stammering. If Miranda wasn't related to him, I think he'd try to date her."

Azrael chuckled and sat next to me, placing his hand on my knee. His nails scraped along the grooves in my jeans. The slight pressure of his fingers reminded me of the first time he'd touched me with his frigid powers. But he was no longer the cold being I'd met. He had feelings. In that instance, I fell under his spell as I wondered if I meant something to him, or if I was just another being he'd decided to take pity on.

"How are you doing?" he asked.

I smiled, gazing deep within his eyes and seeing galaxies swirling around. The further I looked, the more I saw. In that moment, I forgot my hatred and loss and let myself drown in him. I was drawn to him more than I'd ever been to Veronica, as if he was part of my soul, fitting a key piece I wasn't sure about.

I raised my hand and touched the side of his face, feeling the silky texture underneath. I was surprised when he let me pull him toward me. My lips touched his in a gentle kiss, a slight brushing of our mouths. We both kept our eyes open. His statuesque expression changed from shock to pure awe as he let me touch him.

Shivers ran through me, and they weren't from his power. Azrael stayed connected to me for an instant and then, keeping his hand on my knee, he pulled away. The air turned heavier, and the place where his hand rested turned to ice. This time, as his power seeped through me, it didn't hurt. He didn't know how to handle my display and his instinct to protect himself switched on, as mine had when I'd let out the blazing heat, a power which I now had some understanding of.

"I'm fine," I whispered, and trailed my fingers down his cheek as his power began to ignite mine, touching a core of me that was just beginning to take shape, like a newly forming star. I wanted to understand what the core was, and he could help me do that. He could unlock my questions and true identity. Part of me wanted to shake him, curse him, but another part was held in thrall.

"Azrael, what's happening to me?" I whispered.

The Angel of Death removed his hand from my knee and smiled. The same smile I was used to receiving when he wouldn't answer. I shook my head.

Without a word, he disappeared, just as he normally did whenever I asked him an important question. I sighed. The shivers remained from his lips, and the shadow of my unrealized emotions lingered as well, haunting me. Then, the spell was broken, and my anger returned.

I got up from the bench and gazed up into the night, sending my well wishes to Veronica, hoping she heard me. Things had just begun to put themselves back together and make sense, but with time, I'd figure out exactly what kind of being I was. For now, the night was keeping that hidden from me. Until Death would embrace me, the night was young, and I was free to discover the mysteries that awaited me.

ABOUT THE AUTHOR

Crymsyn Hart is a bestselling author of Erotic Romance. Her worlds are filled with luscious vampires, gorgeous gods, quirky witches, and everything else that goes bump in the night. Crymsyn worked as a psychic for many years in Boston while attending Emerson College. She graduated with a BFA in Writing, Literature, & Publishing. When she gets bored, she sneaks away to local cemeteries and coffee shops to find peace and quiet. Crymsyn shares her life with a small zoo, two playful puppies and her hubby Mark. If you come after dark, you're more than likely to find her snuggled up with a gory horror movie, or a bloody vampire movie. Crymsyn has a collection of Living Dead Dolls and five bookshelves overflowing with books. Of course there's always room for more.

Visit her on the web at:
www.RavynHart.com

PURPLE SWORD PUBLICATIONS
Romantic Speculative Fiction
www.purplesword.com